THE PILOTS OF
BOREALIS

THE PILOTS OF BOREALIS

DAVID NABHAN

New York

Talos Press books may be purchased in bulk at special discounts for sales promotion, corporate gifts, fund-raising, or educational purposes. Special editions can also be created to specifications. For details, contact the Special Sales Department, Talos Press, 307 West 36th Street, 11th Floor, New York, NY 10018 or info@skyhorsepublishing.com.

Talos Press® is a registered trademark of Skyhorse Publishing, Inc.®, a Delaware corporation.

Visit our website at www.skyhorsepublishing.com.

Cover design by Owen Corrigan
Cover image: ThinkStock

10 9 8 7 6 5 4 3 2 1

Library of Congress Control Number: 2015935672

ISBN: 978-1-940456-23-2
Ebook ISBN: 978-1-940456-28-7

Printed in the United States of America

*To my family,
and to my friends and colleagues on the West Coast*

Every gun that is made, every warship launched, every rocket fired signifies a theft from those who hunger and are not fed, from those who are cold and are not clothed. But not just money is spent for arms. The sweat of laborers, the genius of scientists, and the hopes of children are wasted too. This is not a way of life in any true sense. Under the cloud of war, it is humanity hanged on an iron cross.

Dwight D. Eisenhower, April 16, 1953

CHAPTER ONE

RUMORS OF WAR

NOT A WORD WAS uttered by any of the tense competitors crowded into the most exclusive locker room in the Solar System. The corps of superbly trained, titanium hard, invincible gladiators was surveyed by the grey-haired race master, an incomparable, ruthlessly aggressive flyer himself in his day, paying no attention to any timetable save an inner clock that sounded when he saw fit. With a quick nod he determined that the moment was at hand. "Good flying," he said in a solemn tone, and threw open the doors of the athletes' hypogeum, debouching the pilots onto the highest platform atop the most illustrious city ever built by human hands.

The shock was sufficient to quicken the pulse of even Clinton Rittener. He'd cruised over volcanic rings the size of Germany exploding on the Jovian moon Io, sending furious plumes of ejecta five hundred miles into space, and traversed frozen methane floes drifting in Titan's hydrocarbon seas. Nothing could prepare him or anyone else for this though. Into the dayglow reflecting off Borealis' translucent Dome he was thrust, simultaneously greeted with the throaty cheers of every citizen who could stand and shout. The low-frequency roars rumbled strongly enough to vibrate the Dome slightly and to resonate in his very thorax. It wasn't just the ears that had to struggle to maintain equilibrium. Rittener, even though his eyes were accustomed to the seven wonders of the universe, was a new arrival to Borealis and had no defense against the eighth. They promptly glazed over, focused on a vista that should have naturally been reserved for seraphim or demigods. No human being, even the most celebrated mercenary of the last five centuries, could view it for the first time without surrendering to its awesome power. The media, no stranger to such vulnerability, attacked—with gusto.

"Clinton, did you see the latest releases? The Terran Ring has put a five million credit price on your head," one reporter screamed at him. "How long do you think you'll be able to keep it attached with that kind of bounty out there?" The news anchor for *Orbit*, herself a first-rate headhunter, bristled at the remark, put her elbow into the offending colleague, and jostled her way to the front of the gauntlet line through which the pilots were being squeezed. She managed to put her arm on his shoulder and pulled herself closer to him, flashing the smile familiar to billions of her fans.

"Clinton Rittener, so many of my viewers are wondering: Why piloting? Why now? Does it somehow make the pain go away? Is that it?" Her smile and form were perfect, and frozen, waiting for a response in the way a mantis delays springing on its prey until it makes the killing lunge.

"Pain?" He only negotiated the one word when she took over again.

"Yes, the pain." She gave a dismissive nod to her provocative associate. "More people have been killed by the armies at your command than even Tamerlane's." She had done her homework. "They tabbed you just below Zandruss II." Her smile widened. "My point is that you're retired now, but surely with such a distinguished past, there must be some lingering pain." It was her signature journalistic bravado to switch lanes without signaling and she veered recklessly here too. "You must also realize, by the way, that you don't stand a chance to win this race?" She couldn't imagine her gall could engender it, so she mistook his silence for bewilderment. "You know who Tamerlane is? You know the name, right?"

He had heard of him. Pan-Turkic insurgents once had Rittener surrounded in the Fergana Valley near Samarkand, quite near to the tomb of the 14th century conqueror and scourge of Central Asia. Their pitiless warlord, Tevfik Bey, called a cease-fire for a last-minute parley, sharing some disheartening information, namely that his forces had commandeered a Fung Shang military class satellite which he now threatened to turn loose on Rittener's positions in the valley below. He advised surrender in blunt terms. "You haven't any way out," the chieftain told him, with much the same tone as the anchorwoman's, so Clinton repeated what he'd answered to the warrior. She was no Tevfik Bey, but Rittener thought she deserved a shot across her bow too.

"Aut viam inveniam aut faciam," Rittener replied. "That's Caesar or Hannibal, it could be either. It means 'I'll find a way, or else make one.'"

And with that, he was quickly pushed along the ramp leading to the starting gates before he could see her reaction. He did just make out her parting shot though. "Are you talking about Zandruss II or the race, Mr. Rittener?" she called after him. "Which one?" From her tone he could tell she wasn't smiling any more.

THE FEW CITIZENS OF Borealis not crowded out on every terrace looking up to the Epsilon Observation Deck were those in Sick Bay, and even a number of them had struggled to their feet to witness the event. The crowds and activity seemed to buoy up the old adage that Borealis never slept.

Most thought that was due to the case that night didn't exist here. It was a common misunderstanding since it was a select group of human beings, indeed, who'd ever seen the place with their own eyes. But the constant, lively bustle was more grounded in the fact that there had always been something to do since Settlement Times, and that industrious habit was instilled in every Borelian from childhood.

Few things could bring the city to a standstill, except maybe a good piloting match—Borelians were absolute fanatics for piloting. And this one was going to be a good one. The media thought so too. The match was being beamed out to the five billion people living on the Terran Ring and the quarter trillion people in every Alliance below on Earth. The pundits of the innumerable news services—*Orbit* and all the rest—had run like crazy with the lead-up to the race, dissecting for their audiences every byzantine twist to the story.

This was more than just a possible monument in human endurance and grace, they explained. Nerissa was flying for Borealis, and Borealis' cause, in front of her fellow citizens, under Borealis' Dome. Demetrius Sehene, her arch-rival from the Terran Ring, didn't come a quarter million miles to lose either. There was a dark horse too, and the commentators hadn't ignored this angle either. Quite a number of them were asking aloud what was to be made of Rittener in this contest. None of the analysts could seem to have imagined that the next time he'd surface would be in a *piloting* match.

It stunned everyone in the Inner Solar System that Clinton Rittener was actually showing his face in such a public way, and more shocking, so close to Earth and the Terran Ring. Neither was ever out of sight for anyone willing to exit the Dome and climb the escarpments that ringed the lunar city.

THE PILOTS OF BOREALIS

The view of the Terran Ring from the Moon, hanging around Earth like a metallic halo, was the most iconic image of the day. Everyone who saw it lost their breath.

The more sage critics explained that Borealis was the only place in which a man like Clinton Rittener *could* show his face. Certainly, he was a hero to billions of people on Earth, but it was doubted that anyone alive had also made as many enemies, the kind who'd find no expedient too nasty for them to eschew if it meant they could get their hands on him. Some were wondering aloud why the Council even allowed him to compete, so sure were they that an assassination attempt was at least being considered.

Nerissa, like everyone else on the Moon, was known only by her given name. Borelians had long since dispensed with the use of last names, a source of but one of many differences between themselves and the Terrans living in the stupendous, planet-girdling megalopolis orbiting Earth. Borelians considered their amazingly few—yet obviously elite—numbers small enough that surnames were superfluous. There weren't more than a quarter of a million people living on the Moon and any new arrival or newborn simply added or chose another name not already listed on the Citizen Roll.

Borelians didn't need to say out loud what that said about their opinions about themselves, nor was it required. Their arrogant pride and outrageous stubbornness were among the few things upon which the people of Earth and the Terran Ring could both agree. The Borelians got under everyone's skin. Yet tens of billions of pairs of eyes were nonetheless glued to the event, internally torn between having to betray their addiction to something so totally Borelian, and yet hoping that they might witness Nerissa and her haughty supporters going down in flames.

This might be the last great piloting event for a while, many exclaimed, leaving unsaid what that meant, and allowing the words to sink in as a plainly spoken threat to the overbearing Borelians. The pessimists had reason lately to mutter such bellicose warnings, as unnerving incidents had been taking place with worrisome regularity. Squadrons of ships from both sides had been brushing wingtips in the space between the Ring and the Moon, feint met with counter-feint.

Only weeks before, the entire population of Borealis had rushed into the safety of the Core, and done so with astounding quickness, sealing the locks with everyone inside but a few stragglers in amazing time. The authorities never explained the reason behind the lock down, and no one outside of Borealis even knew that such a drastic defensive move had taken place. Nor was the Council on Borealis willing to allow the news off the Moon; anyone who even spoke of it could be accused of sedition and risk extremely grave consequences. But there *were* nervous whispers exchanged in private between apprehensive citizens who quite naturally had to wonder if the system of impenetrable shields protecting the city was everything it was touted to be. Privately, even the mad scramble that had emptied their city within the cone of lunar regolith upon which the colony was built, even this astounding evacuation had many on the Council worried. Borealis might not have any time at all in the worst-case scenarios they were examining, but that was of a nature so classified that no level high enough existed as the proper repository for such secrets.

In any event, to the amazement of almost every soul in the Solar System, it had been decided that the piloting match would nonetheless be held. The pretense that normalcy prevailed fooled no one, when everyone knew that "normal" was the last thing one might say about where relations between the Terran Ring, Earth, and Borealis stood.

THE PILOTS OF BOREALIS

The recent scare had laid bare to the Borelians just how serious the State was to protect itself, and how far it would go. Even the staunchest Terran could appreciate how deeply and gravely the Borelians had moved to the idea that war was sooner or later inevitable. The only questions for the Council were how to delay the conflict until the opportune moment, and how to handle the "Earth Tories" in their midst when push came to shove. Earth, that unintelligible, incoherent, confused patchwork of ephemeral Alliances that came and went with the seasons, could be counted on to do just the opposite of acting in its own interests, never mind Borealis' benefit. And yet love of the mother planet was alive here still after so many centuries, albeit the kind of logic-defying affection that binds parent with child, even as one of them descends into the insane self-destruction in which Earth had dwelt for generations now. Every single word, every smile and frown, every unrestrained grimace or cheer during the coming contest was to be monitored and recorded, according to the rumors, and hopefully a complete catalogue of the citizens rooting for Rittener, Earth's antihero, would emerge. This, said those supposedly in the know, was the real motive for the Council's decision not to cancel the piloting match.

Everyone in the Inner Solar System, from as far out as the lawless mining outposts in the Asteroid Belt and the dusty Martian colonies, and back to Earth again, would be watching—and wondering about an impending war. The Borelian Council appeared willing to challenge the immense power of the Terran Ring, seemed determined to free itself from its influence, and inaugurate a *truly* independent Borealis. After years of debate it had come to that. When the Terrans made their next heavy-handed move, which the Council could certainly count on, Borealis might finally be ready to meet force with force. It seemed interested only in steering the final feints and thrusts in such a way that history should mark the Terrans as the aggressors. The events of the last week showed that the Terrans were much of the same mind. If millions or billions were to die in an impending struggle, each side wished the onus to be upon the other.

For Rittener, a newcomer to Borealis, politics and state-craft at the moment were as distant as the heliopause at the far edge of Sol's reign. Indeed, he was displaying the endemic condition of all neophytes to the city. He was "drifting." Even moments away from being thrust into a do or die crucible, no matter that every ounce of his determination should have been spent on preparing himself for the looming trial—he was drifting. The pilot next to him snapped a warning.

"You'd better get the stars out of your eyes, Clinton. This may look like Heaven, but these angels around us here, they're more like the kind that flew with Lucifer."

Adem Sulcus had crossed Rittener's path a few times and in a number of far-ranging places. They weren't friends but neither were they enemies, and that was the best to be hoped for in Rittener's profession.

"Not gentle like you, Adem?" Rittener replied.

It had been noted that people exhibited a tendency to wind up dying around Sulcus' footsteps. Clinton looked around the Field and wondered who might be the next casualty. Something akin to a smile streaked across Sulcus' face but was gone an instant later. It left him with a look Rittener judged almost pitiable; the same thought, about the same look, had crossed his mind before. He knew just enough about Adem Sulcus, probably more than most, since those who could be considered better informed quite often were also less alive. Sulcus was handsome to a fault, irresistibly head-turning, tall, dashing, and young—far too young to be such an accomplished assassin, but nonetheless his calling card was certainly genuine. He was a Terran, according to his birth certificate, but that carried little weight. His allegiances were transitory, ephemeral, liquid, and lethal.

Adem swept a hand across the impossibly beautiful vista and surprised Clinton by waxing poetic. "These five levels they say were crafted by God himself. He severed his own fingers to create it mindful that he wouldn't need his hand again, realizing he'd never outdo this." He gave a more mundane nod at their competitors. "Still, they're from the seventh level of a different locale."

Rittener was impressed. "I hadn't realized you enjoyed reading the classics."

Sulcus answered back quickly. "There's a lot you don't know about me.

Rittener shook his head in agreement. "And that's probably healthier for both of us."

Now a real smile appeared on the young torpedo's face, one so conspicuous due to its rarity, so incongruous with the warning that came with it. "Get the stars out of your eyes, and stay out of my way out there. That's a prescription you can trust."

Sulcus was counting Borealis' levels the careless way. The city stood at the middle of the Traskett Crater, a depression resembling an Assyrian shield—flat, round, and with a long, thick spike protruding from the center. It's strategic position so close to the lunar North Pole made for the most efficient and secure ingress and egress, and kept it *just* out of clear sight of the Sun, or Terra. The fields around Borealis had been suffused with the richest deposits of helium-3 on the Moon, or anywhere else. Billions of tons of the purest ice—pristine, untouched, lying frozen at the bottom of craters which hadn't seen the Sun since the Solar System was young—were at hand nearby. With all this, it was foreordained that a great city should rise here.

The "Core" was the hollowed out "spike" on the shield. It was the Old City, the original habitation from Settlement Times—a rock-hewn labyrinth now used for other purposes and stocked with food, oxygen, fuel, and every other vital necessity. It was enough to last Borealis, well, no one knew how long, save the Council itself. In the worst of circumstances, should Borealis' Dome be ruptured, the city could certainly hold out long enough to affect repairs. That had never happened but people naturally never seemed to tire talking about what would occur if it did.

Around the Core, ring by ring, level by level, Borealis rose from the ground, wrapped around the exterior of the jutting protuberance in the lunar crust. It spiraled up twenty-seven levels. Each of these was named but the city's five Districts were designated by the places where the Core tapered dramatically—Alpha to Epsilon. From the Observation Deck atop Epsilon, where Rittener and the other pilots were preparing to launch, the view was spectacular. It reminded him of ancient illustrations of the Tower of Babel, only this one was as real as the geysers of Enceladus orbiting Saturn. Awash in what had been a virtual sea of helium-3, Borealis was rich too—rich beyond description.

The wealthiest on Borealis, people were at first surprised to learn, were members of the Artists' Guild. A certified master could command a wage from Borealis' glitterati that even Croesus himself might have had trouble paying. Borelians were so rich though that there wasn't much else on which to spend their credits. Even after the mind-boggling flood of imports from all over the Solar System were paid for, the surplus wealth had no place else to go. The State started it all—decorating all the public buildings, every square foot of them, with stunning bas-reliefs carved into the exterior facades. Private citizens were quickly infected and now it was the rarest domicile that wasn't faced with the most breathtaking murals and facades. The most affluent residents fashioned theirs in pure gold, silver, copper, or platinum, and gave them color with bucket loads of green emeralds, red rubies, blue sapphires, orange topazes, white opals. The motifs were scenes from every terrestrial mythology, watershed events in history, reproductions of the marvels of the Solar System—and anything else one could imagine, or *couldn't* imagine. Each domicile fit cheek to jowl with the next, creating a series of spectacularly decorated toruses built into the Core, stacked one atop another, all the way up to Epsilon. It was a fantasy city gone mad with wealth and addicted to public beauty, around which the racing pilots were to circle in the air, with the idea that this paradise—in Adem Sulcus' words—required angels of its own.

WHEN NERISSA EMERGED ONTO the Observation Deck an immediate roar from tens of thousands of Borelians went up, a cry so loud and powerful that it reverberated off the Dome that encased the city. She was helped to strap on oversized and unwieldy wings, and then stepped onto the launch pad and gave the citizens her hallmark pose, with wings outstretched and her face fixed with the iconic, aloof look of Borelian superiority. No one in the Solar System could mistake her; she looked like no other flyer in history. Nerissa certainly seemed almost totally nude—barefoot and wearing nothing save the most diaphanous lycraplastique brief and top; it was said to weigh less than a lunar gram. Her hair was as thick and black as the image of the Roman goddess of the Moon, Diana, on Borealis' Great Seal. It was tightly twisted into an ebony braid that fell almost to the small of her back. As she stood on the podium displaying her wingspan, every contour of her impossibly muscled body strained for the audience of hundreds of billions. As stunning as she was—malachite green eyes, chiseled patrician face, taut muscles that rippled from her lower abdomen to her rib cage—even the most lascivious would be struck first with just a plain and unavoidable admiration for her classic beauty. Journalists had long since ceased to ask if she felt ashamed to fly so scantily clad.

"We have a different view of the human body," she had so often curtly answered in the past, "much different than the pornography-addicted degeneracy of the Terran Ring."

This was an historic insult meant to sting. One of the pistons that powered the development of the Terran Ring was the economics of sex tourism in its first century. The never-before-experienced allure of lovemaking in weightlessness was in fact just a footnote in history. Borelians, however, never allowed an opportunity to pass without reminding Terrans about it.

She could have been mistaken for a statue, standing so erect and motionless at the highest point above the city, her skin the same rich color of flawless beige alabaster, like smooth wheat porcelain. Such a complexion was common for residents of the lunar colony, for Borealis had been built almost precisely on the Moon's North Pole, quite near to the immense stores of ice which had lain frozen for eons at the bottom of deep craters, in perpetual shadow and cold. The city itself never saw the *direct* Sun, for it too had been built around a thick cone of lunar regolith, thrusting up from the floor of a perfectly situated crater and surrounded on all sides by natural sun shields. Reflected light though, incessant but mild, bathed the city unremittingly, and gave Borelians a beautiful skin texture and tone found only here. The "day-glow" gave life to everything on Borealis and suffused its residents with a healthy yet seductive beauty. That, and the feeble lunar gravity that permitted limbs much longer, more lithe and lissome than on weighty Earth, made Borelian athletes into tall, supple greyhounds. And Nerissa, the image of

Borelian beauty, didn't have a gram of weight in the wrong place. Visitors walking the streets of Borealis were taken aback by the fact that hardly a single overweight citizen was to be seen, the entire population having long since put food and carnal desires far down the list of their priorities. And, although it wasn't actually against the law to eat meat, no one could remember the last time anyone had done it. It was considered a thoroughly disgusting habit, a hallmark of the aboriginal culture that had been thankfully left behind for the "cannibal" hoi polloi on fetid Earth, or of the sensate "gluttons" on the Terran Ring.

Clinton Rittener was on the pad next to her, and he'd told himself this luck of the draw meant nothing and that he wasn't going to give her a first, much less second look. He simply couldn't restrain himself though. And with her being so close, the glances hadn't any hope but becoming stares. In a moment of weakness he turned to her and spoke.

"I'd like to wish you . . . "That's all he got out. She turned so quickly and fixed him with such a cold, deadly stare that the "good luck" caught in his throat. It stunned him, stealing his words and leaving him with just the look they were sharing, she also refusing to take her eyes off him. He could see now that her hair had raven tufts and faint streaks running through it; it wasn't as jet black as he had first thought.

She arched her eyebrows as she calmly spoke, a firm composure that stoically restrained what quite honestly could almost seem to be identified as a roiling hatred.

"You're Clinton . . . Rittener, aren't you?" She paused between names, letting him know in no uncertain terms what disdain she felt for a supposed Borelian who sported an Earth name. She shook her head slightly as if wondering to herself under what confused cloud this man must live. She didn't wait for a response.

"What are you doing here, anyway?" she blurted out. She nodded at the throngs who now stood silently watching the encounter. "You're not part of us. Why *are* you even here?" She sniffed her delicate nose up at him in a way that told him she smelled the grease of Earth on him and was revolted by it.

"So what sort of game are you playing?"

CLINTON RITTENER HAD BEEN accused of many things in his forty-two years, but playing games had never been one of the charges. In fact, in this new age of a quarter of a trillion humans crowding out most opportunity for individual accomplishment, he was considered far and wide to be perhaps one of humanity's last best chances for personal heroism. The list of men respected on Earth and admired also in Borealis was a very, very short one. The Borelians didn't hand out honorary citizenship to just anyone; in fact, the last time it had happened was more than a decade ago. There had been almost unanimous support for it, but that was before all the saber-rattling. And many, like Nerissa, would obviously be pleased to see it revoked. That wouldn't be easy though, for in all the Inner Solar System, there was just one Clinton Rittener.

"What *are* you playing at?" Nerissa rudely asked him again just before the match began.

"Verba competitorem verum non volant, facta sua manent," he told her. Rittener waited just the right amount of time. "That's Horace or Virgil, I'm not sure which. It means 'A master gamesman's words don't fly, but rather his deeds remain.' Good flying, Nerissa." That closed the conversation. Even she had to appreciate the quick cleverness of the double entendre; "good flying" was the standard polite salute to fellow pilots prior to a match.

Now, just moments before the contest would start, Rittener set to preparing himself, trying to concentrate on his breathing and stretching, but the panorama before him made that next to impossible. If a view of the Terran Ring was the iconic image of humanity, Borealis from the top of the Epsilon Level presented a good case for a very close second.

This was a fine day for flying too, Clinton thought absently, but then was reminded of the irony that, just like in Heaven, there existed nothing but fine days on Borealis and not even darkness in the city that put the image of the deity of the night on their seals, a place of perpetual springtime. Hundreds of stupendous mirrors ringed the Traskett Crater, beaming sunlight to the floor below. The mirrors' degree of curvature, placement, and height had been carefully calculated to both catch the maximum sunlight throughout the year and refract the concentrated rays into widened and weakened beams that bathed beneficent light over great swaths on the crater floor. It was well-named: the Goldilocks Array. It should naturally be a couple hundred degrees below zero on the Traskett floor, and a couple hundred degrees above zero Fahrenheit over the lip of the crater in the direct sunlight. Inside the Dome though, thanks to Goldilocks, everything was "just right." Not all the mirrors could be used all the time owing to Luna's dance with her celestial partners, Sun and Earth. But with gradual and automated re-focusing, thanks to the Moon's polar phenomenon of constant sunlight at least at some nearby horizon, there was never-ending dayglow in abundance, causing "night-hungry" Borelians to complain of it from time to time. Nighttime was required though for the lush cornucopia of plants in the Garden that ringed the periphery of the Dome, flourishing under a transparent lid infused with a photochromatic substrate that darkened every twelve hours.

Making his final preparations, taking an extended series of long, deep, rhythmic breaths, Rittener filled his lungs with the cast-off oxygen from both the tailings of crushed and vaporized lunar regolith and the exhalations of the millions of plants and trees in the Garden. It definitely didn't taste like air on Earth. But it was thick—dense enough to fly in, especially in one sixth the gravity of Earth.

Beyond that last green circumference, outside the Dome, lay the rest of the Moon—the "Field." It was the piston at the center of the engine that was Borealis. The tracts adjacent to the Traskett Crater had been exploited from the very first stage of primitive human colonization, pushing out prodigious quantities of helium-3. Nothing goes on forever though, and it was no secret that these fields, along with others even further out from Borealis, had long since approached the end of their productive life. Earth and Terra were much more anxious about this than the Borelians themselves who mined and exported it. There were other fields to be tapped, they'd answer calmly. Granted, the best potential sites were the equatorial fields some fifteen hundred miles away. Undaunted by the distance, Borealis was making preparations to plant her flag and her robotic regolith skimmers into this virgin territory and stubbornly maintained that the current pinch in supply need not precipitate a crisis in the future, as long as the correct steps were taken now. Terra and Earth were just as convinced that the opposite were true and that the helium-3 shortfall was more than just the current state of affairs, that it was the opening chapter of an endemic problem that everyone in the Solar System had been dreading, and from which too many eyes had looked away for too long.

Every voice in Borealis was shouting encouragement to the tense pilots. Rittener could hear a good number of brave ones screaming, "Good flying, Clinton Rittener!" These plucky citizens cheered him, regardless that the Alliances on Earth didn't support Borealis' contention that the new fields were being opened as quickly as possible. But then the politics of helium-3, the great question of the day, painted quite a few things in grey. And now there were a number of those areas that were threatening to turn blood red. Who *did* own the Moon, anyway? Certainly, no one refused to recognize Borealis' sovereignty and control of areas already developed and mined. But where was it written that she owned the *whole* Moon? She had soaked up incalculable wealth from all quadrants of the Solar System for centuries, but must such greed and self-interest extend forever?

RITTENER HAD THE CORNER of his eye on his Terran rival, two pads to his left. Demetrius Sehene was stretching and breathing too. But he wasn't directing a single furtive glance at the competition. He was the odds on favorite to win the match and one look at him told why. His Bulgarian father was the gold-medalist champion wrestler of the Inner Solar System Games XXXII. The seed hadn't fallen far. He was tall, superbly built, and as solid as spent uranium. This formidable clay was molded by the features he inherited from his Tutsi mother, along with also taking her family's name. Long-tendoned, quick-firing musculature had been fine tuned and tempered by intense training. His tawny skin and Abyssinian nose caused people to remark that he looked like the old Ethiopian emperor, Haile Selassie. Demetrius liked that and played it up. His fans referred to him just as "The Emperor"; the moniker fit perfectly.

World-class piloting required a body like Demitrius'. Every amateur who visited Borealis tried doing it though and anyone in decent health and shape could keep it up for a while. The beginners' platforms were fairly safe, although if one were clumsy enough to make a determined attempt it was possible to break one's neck, even at these tame heights. Piloting was basically a struggle against one's own body, a marathon work-out session that pushed the flyer to the point of complete exhaustion. While that point came at a different place for every pilot, the math however was the same for all. To effect flight on the Moon one had to continuously flap long, broad wings with the force equal to one tenth body weight as measured on Earth. A two-hundred-pound man, for example, doing "flys" in a gymnasium on Earth with twenty-pound dumbbells, could fly on the Moon. All he need do is put down the weights and strap on the wings to practice the "fair sport." Anyone could do it—children, women, men; the competition was fair because the bigger you were the harder you had to push to keep your weight aloft. Accomplished fliers though were easily recognized by the hallmark shared by all: admirably developed, V-shaped torsos topped by massive shoulders and arms.

It was inevitable that Terrans should come to overthrow the Borelians as the dominant force in the sport. They were stronger—how else to put it? The first match lost to them came as a shock to Borealis nonetheless. When it started to happen regularly the shock turned to dismay. Piloting was so characteristically Borelian, and here the Terrans had commandeered yet another piece of their culture. The Borelians were no push-overs, though. Watching a trained Borelian pilot was wondrous indeed. Their tall, lithe, lean form was made for the sport. What the light gravity took from their strength it reimbursed by permitting longer limbs that changed the calculus of leverage in their favor. Their other advantage was disputed by the Terrans, but it was fact: Borelians were better pilots. They grew up flying and were such agile, daring, practiced athletes that they gave Terra's best a hotly contested run for their money every time they met.

A COLOSSAL HOLOGRAPHIC TORUS switched on. It fit snugly into the upper reaches of the Dome, a concentric virtual racetrack, its imaginary center the spire atop the Epsilon Observation Deck. Each pilot wore ankle bands that remained within the volume of the virtual doughnut and a collar that likewise would immediately disqualify the wearer should he fly too high or too low. The wings were tipped with similar sensors—wings, one might point out, of the lightest material ever constructed. Most were fashioned with arcane genres of carbon fibers, but there were many trade secrets connected to the manufacture of the best wings.

The translucent aerodrome turned yellow; the pilots took their marks. The cries went up again, even stronger this time, final encouragement for the pilots. "Good flying, Clinton Rittener!" He always professed that he flew for himself alone, that he represented no one but himself. But his skin-tight, blue and red piloting leotard, the colors of the European Union, said otherwise. The old planet below might be in shambles but here was one son of Earth at least not quite ready to say die. The cheers made him glad that he'd decided to sport these colors; that was his last thought before the torus turned light green.

The pilots leaped into the air en masse and flew at top speed toward the gossamer ring. There was little room for maneuver at this point of the race; most pilots just clenched their teeth and literally beat their way through with their wings. There *were* some vague rules in piloting, but not at the start, not really. During the "scrum" no judge ever threw a flag. It was pure aerial combat and almost anything went. Some pounded a path through to the goal of the torus, others spiraled out either injured or with damaged wings, still others didn't make it within the confines of the holographic racetrack in time. Rittener didn't try anything tricky and flew straight at the closest sector of the floating halo. So did many other pilots. Converging vectors resulted in a number of "tangles" settled in the air as birds of prey would resolve them, with kicks and buffeting wings.

Nerissa wasn't among them. She opted for a daring stratagem, flying at a recklessly wide angle, trying to intersect the torus far down the course. While her competitors were making a straight bee-line for the track, Nerissa would have to traverse the much longer hypotenuse she'd chosen for her bearing—but in the same time. Demetrius had taken an angle too but nothing that audacious. Already the torus was blinking on and off at an alarming rate. By the time Nerissa's wing tips passed the virtual boundary it was flashing like a strobe light. Then it switched suddenly to a dark green. Any pilots' sensors outside the safe boundary instantly lit up red. They were out. Nerissa had made it with but a second or two to spare and her gambling short cut put her far ahead of the pack. Fearless confidence in her amazing speed was matched by graceful agility which had her hugging the extreme inside of the ethereal race course—"in the groove." But Demetrius was hard on her heels, coming up fast at a gentle angle of intersection, beating the air like a winged demon fleeing Hell. Just before the two vectors crossed, Nerissa banked out of the groove and heeled into Demetrius' path. It was a first-class impact. Surprised cries rippled through the crowd looking up breathlessly. Now a real "tangle" ensued, with each pilot trying to maintain speed while blocking the other, and desperately attempting to force their competitor to dip wings outside of the safe boundary. This was nasty flying.

Three circuits around the track were required before a pilot made his headlong "dive" to the finish line, a checkered holographic tape floating above Kepler's Arch. Nerissa and Demetrius confronted each other again and again over the three laps, frittering away both speed and distance in the lead in an astounding number of tangles, only diverting attention from each other when the pack caught up with them. The two best pilots in existence then broke away, gained a comfortable margin, and resumed another series of feints, blocks, pushes, and crashes.

Rittener was out of the race. Oh, he'd made it out of the scrum in time and was still alive, technically. But he was flying way out of his league. He had never really had a chance and was pleased that he'd been able to maintain a decent position in the middle of the pack that chased after the front runners. The spectacle Nerissa and Demetrius were putting on helped him in a way. Their aerial dogfights were enough to take Rittener's focus off the burning lactic acid building up in his arms and shoulders.

The two combatants reached the terminus of the third lap a fraction of a second apart. This was bad news for Demetrius; no pilot dived like Nerissa. As a matter of fact, not even Nerissa was supposed to be able to fly like Nerissa. Her hallmark dives were nothing less than superhuman. Both pilots skimmed the absolute virtual inside boundary of the race course at the third lap post. Both wheeled to dive and tangled wickedly, like two raptors locking talons in mid-air, whirling and falling. Demetrius broke away and effected a near-vertical swoop for the finish line. For Nerissa's fans, banking on her patented sprint, disaster struck. She wasn't sprinting, she wasn't diving, she wasn't even flying. She was gliding down in a gentle, defeated spiral, barely pumping her wings. She was quite obviously injured.

DEMETRIUS SEHENE FLEW THROUGH the finish line like a peregrine falcon, to the accompaniment of a furious cascade of booing that rose up from the city and reverberated off the Dome. A throng of Borelians crowded around the panel of judges, crying foul and gesticulating angrily. The referees were making a good show of ignoring them, leaning in together for consultation. They decided quickly. The holographic torus turned red again indicating that the race was over. There is no "second place" in piloting, or any other place, only winning. "Demetrius Sehene: WINNER!" was flashed across the race course now emptying of dozens of also-rans, in letters as high as terrestrial skyscrapers.

Rittener glided to solid ground at Alpha, so spent he could barely summon the energy to shake out the pools of sweat that flooded his eyes, blurring his vision. Giant, lethargic drops of perspiration—bloated by the lunar gravity and falling in slow motion—came flying off him in every direction as he shook out his sweat-soaked hair. When he could finally focus he saw the scene before him was almost pandemonium. Borelians, almost always reserved, *could* react very emotionally once pushed to their limits. The makings of a riot were all around him. Even the attendants were ranting and raving, oblivious to the fact that *someone* ought to have helped unbuckle Rittener's wings. He didn't really care, and just stood where he landed, panting, his arms quivering. Security officers were roughly pushing and threatening a path through the mob, half-dragging an exhausted Demetrius Sehene through the opening they created. Nerissa was herself surrounded by a cordon of security and medical staff. She was rubbing her left shoulder with one hand, but used the other to wave off the solicitous physicians who seemed determined to attend to her.

Suddenly they made eye contact. Their gazes locked for quite some time. It wasn't the face of dejection or defeat, nor did it radiate pain or anger. Clinton Rittener had saved millions of lives and had sent millions of others to their deaths by reading faces.

He was an expert at it—if anyone was. But Nerissa's left him at a loss.

CHAPTER TWO

IN THE SERVICE OF THE TERRAN RING

CLINTON RITTENER'S DANISH FATHER was the European Union's ambassador to the Asian Alliance, his mother an English heiress whose dowry came in money so old its provenance was difficult indeed to identify, but at least going back to the early 21st century. He might have grown up fat, spoiled, and lazy, but even as a child he seemed marked for greatness. His aptitude for mathematics and languages was both stunning and inexplicable, for it was said that he never spoke a word for the first three years of his life. He made up for that later with more than a dozen languages both Eastern and Western, and spoken with such fluency that he could play native in more than a few of them. He had mastered trigonometry by the age of ten, calculus by twelve, and had set the Earth's scientific academies on their heels when he published a proof of Galean's Eigenvector Conjecture—which ran in the peer-reviewed journal *Aegis* . . . on his twenty-first birthday! It took a battery of nanocomputers several weeks to find the errors in his proof, but the sword had been drawn from the scabbard nonetheless, and it was plain to see that the blade was sharp indeed.

NO ONE COULD HAVE guessed, though, what fate had in store for Clinton Rittener. The whole world was taken by surprise when the Fifth Planetary Depression let loose Armageddon. Ten million people were killed in Shanghai alone in the opening days, along with both his parents, when mobs stormed the embassy. He was dragged half-dead from his previously cosseted world into the hinterlands of China by a faction loyal to the European Union. There he spent the next six years of his life fighting in the horrific Great Eastern War, rising to the rank of *yuan shuai*, high marshal, over a coalition of fierce irregulars. He never spoke a single word of it—to anyone, ever—after the armistice. But it is certain that the pyramids of severed heads, the thousands of miles of crucified bodies that lined Asia's roads, and other unspeakable atrocities, changed him forever. The stories they tell about his cruelty and brutality are hard to verify and almost surely exaggerated. It is true, though, that he most certainly was as ruthless and cold-hearted as any of the soldiers in that planet-wide bloodbath. Both the Asian Alliance and the European Union offered him high military commissions when the war ended. He declined, took the remnants of his lost inheritance, and bought passage when the first maglev up the slopes of Kilimanjaro became operational again, into orbit and onto the Terran Ring, and then straight off for Mars. He never set foot on Earth again.

About the next years spent on Mars, with forays into the depths of the Outer Solar System, not much is known except for one thing: Rittener learned how to fly on Mars. And, as some whispered, he learned unutterable piloting talents on Titan. Mars still is a fairly wild place, and the perfect locale to lose oneself in the "underground," in every sense. Anything goes on Mars, and most of it is going on under the surface, including piloting. It's so much harder to fly on Mars that it's a good thing it's done within kilometer-long corridors that slope gradually down into the planet's interior. Pilots get pulled down by gravity a little more than twice as strong as Luna's, so it's just as well that Martian pilots fly inside and not from cliffs. Flyers on the Red Planet, though none too skilled in maneuver, are some of the most physically chiseled athletes in existence. In contests on the Moon, they could be serious contenders if only because of their stamina advantage.

Rittener joined a select corps of crack former soldiers at this strategic borderline between the Inner and Outer Solar System, many of them amateur pilots. These men—part tactician, stateless warlord, and émigré *condottieri*—formed an elite pool of mercenaries. A shadowy zeitgeist played out below ground on Mars, as assassins, spies, pirates, and agents attracted from everywhere, toward every purpose, were drawn to this free-wheeling, subterranean gloom land. It was here where Clinton Rittener was enlisted by the Terran Archonate itself when the miners on the Asteroid Belt revolted.

THE TERRAN RING HAD more or less sat out the recent planet-wide war, happy to see their economic and military rivals below annihilate themselves. Earth would, of course, never be the same again. Most historians were already marking this as the great turning point, the watershed when the Terran Ring in quick, successive stages became the cultural and political seat of humankind. Earth, having finally pushed her powers of recuperation past the reserve, degenerated into an insatiable market and a limitless labor pool lying beneath Terra, a supine, fallen colossus. A great renaissance was ushering in Terra's moment in the Sun and they were determined to take advantage of it, and, at present, just as adamant to put down the incipient insurrection dampening the hosannas being sung for the new age dawning.

Ethan Van Ulroy, aide-de-camp of the Chief Archon, the highest office on the Ring, was sent to negotiate with the defiant mining colonies. Mars was the half-way point between the Ring and the Belt, so it was the perfect place for the conference and Van Ulroy the ideal choice. He was the quintessential Terran—tall, well-built, pure business, utilitarian demeanor, and possessing a quality which most high-ranking functionaries on the Ring lacked: charm. The Terran Ring was an impossible feat of engineering, courage, brains, muscle, and determination; here was one of the men who had built it.

"You need not concern yourselves with your prior contracts with consortiums on Earth. As you well know, they're war-weary and undependable." Van Ulroy arched one eyebrow higher to chide the fact. "Earth needs some time to catch its breath. A fourth of the population is either dead or wishes they were. The kind of insanity that produced that result must be confined to the planet. We're here to sign an accord that will provide security, peace, and prosperity for all of us into the far future."

William Byrne, representing the hundreds of mini-states of the Asteroid Belt, thought that figure high. "One in four on Earth dead? That many?" Byrne's lilt told everyone he was Scottish. Everything else—his calloused hands, radiation-beaten complexion, enlarged joints—was proof of his profession: He was a miner.

Van Ulroy condoled. "We share profoundly in Earth's difficulty in this time of grieving." With the mother planet in a state of near-chaos and a sizeable fraction of its population swept away, the Terran Ring was enforcing a stewardship for

Earth. This was seen as a kindness, almost a filial duty—by the Terrans themselves, of course.

"The Ring is going to see to deliveries of all metals to Earth, or anywhere else in our 'sphere of influence,' as is deemed necessary." Byrne openly winced at the phrase "sphere of influence."

"The mineral exports of the Asteroid Belt to the Inner Solar System," the Archonate's envoy made clear, "should in future transit through the Terran Ring." The words were easy to say; difficult to comprehend. What it meant was that the staggering output of iron, nickel, copper, aluminum, magnesium, gold, silver, and all the rest—all of it—would be bought exclusively by Terra. All that the miners of the Belt needed to know was that the final destination for their goods was the Terran Ring.

Van Ulroy's insincere smile fell off and vanished immediately after speaking, his demeanor now much like Byrne's unblinking, sullen expression.

"How considerate it is of Terra to trouble itself to simplify our lives." Byrne thrust his jaw forward, getting straight to cases. "But do I understand correctly that Terra is proposing to pay roughly half the pre-war price?"

"Well, it's not half. It's something higher than that," Van Ulroy corrected. "But, it's fair, and it's an open-ended purchase order, into the far future."

"Into the far future, you say?" Byrne openly mocked his words. Now he pressed even closer into Van Ulroy's personal space, the heavy eyebrows lowered and threatening, the eyes florid and matching his cadmium red, faultlessly trimmed chin strap beard. "There are some back on the Belt who doubted that Terra would force a contract to bankrupt us and then have the temerity to extend the terms of indentured servitude into perpetuity. They sent me here to put those rumors to rest. But I do have one unanswered question."

"And that would be?" Van Ulroy asked, frowning.

"Have the powers that be on Terra lost their minds? I've never given any credence to slanderous fables about strains of Terran venereal diseases that play havoc with faculties, but this certainly won't help to dispel those rumors."

Ethan Van Ulroy's renowned charisma wasn't working with William Byrne. "I can tell by looking at you that you're a decent, reasonable man, Mr. Byrne, so I'm going to ignore that." Van Ulroy wasn't going to ignore it. He was already making up his mind to act on it.

"And I can see the kind of man you are as well." Byrne leaned back in his chair and in the calmest of tones gave the aide-de-camp a quiet, deadly serious warning. "But, if you're planning to make a meal of us you'll find that we don't break up into bite-sized chunks." He gave a faux-friendly nod and wink of the eye. "Of that, Mr. Van Ulroy, you can be sure."

AT FIRST THE MINERS just laughed, repeating Byrne's insult to Van Ulroy and adding others just as offensive. When they finally realized that the Terran Ring meant business, outrage set in. Depending on whose envoy was speaking and in which interplanetary forum, there was quite a divergence of opinion about what sort of control Terra legally had over the Asteroid Belt. Several more attempts at compromise broke down, and in the end the miners stubbornly just walked away, in Terra's eyes turning to open rebellion.

It would be a very nasty business to wage a war on the frontiers of the Solar System in the vacuum of space, against the sparse settlements that clung to city-sized blocks of metal and rock that meandered between Mars and Jupiter. It would no doubt be viewed as immoral and illegal by Terra's rivals.

Worse still, though, would be the severe withdrawal pain that Terra was desperate to avoid should the unending transports of ore cease to arrive. Dozens of settlements in the Belt were either threatening or had already enacted embargo. While neither side was going to find this pleasant in the least, Terra only focused on ending it. What the Ring was looking for was a quick *fait accompli* that could be presented to everyone, and one that gave them the option of plausible deniability if they needed it. Tactics were to be purposely left broadly and vaguely described. Those that wouldn't knuckle under "should be militarily convinced." Not many had any real idea what was happening half a billion miles from Earth out past Mars. If a few scruffy, unwashed misanthropes living on the edge of existence in the dead of space were to disappear, well, had they ever really even been there in the first place? Miners on the Asteroid Belt were as difficult to make out as shadows on Pluto. The Terran Ring had the right man for the job too. Clinton Rittener accepted a quasi-military commission, was given his privateering marque, duly signed and sealed by the highest body on Terra, the Archonate, and sent to put down an uprising that had echoed from the conflagration on Earth. He was told to bring them around, move them off, or wipe them out—whichever were easiest.

And here, even more than before, is where he made his name.

THE *PEERLESS* WAS WELL-NAMED. She was fast, reliable, and armed to the teeth. The ship was a hybrid-class destroyer, built to patrol the space between Earth and the Jovian System. No one knew what kind of swath she cut, but according to rumors that leaked in from listening posts at the far edges of the Solar System, her Quarrie superconducting ports sucked in so much of the solar wind that she cast a shadow as far out as the moons of Saturn. She was engineered to be constantly accelerating for the most part, and fast. But if her journey from Terran orbit out to the Asteroid Belt was to be a quick one, once there she kicked into another gear. Her fusion reactor, fed by helium-3 from Borealis, was capable of ingesting and spitting out absolutely anything. She fed on the detritus she was meant to patrol, ejecting stupendous quantities of ionized flotsam that had been broiled down to pure nucleonic matter. In theory, once within the confines of the Belt, there was no limit to her speed or her range. The same reactor powered her armament and defenses; both were terrifying. *Peerless* would be an incredibly hard gnat to swat, as she was impervious to laser and particle beam salvos, in the short-run anyway.

She could go anywhere she pleased, at speeds and ranges that were quite impressive, fairly immune from attack unless by multiple opponents, and with the offensive power to erase planetoids from existence. *Peerless* was armed with twin punches: a high-powered electron laser capable of melting through twelve inches of steel in less than a second, and a particle beam accelerator that emitted tremendous bursts of protons at just under the speed of light. The beam pulses could shred mountain-sized chunks of pure titanium. Little wonder that the Terran Ring sent only one ship, under one captain, to bring the miners on Valerian-3 to heel. It was not only all that was required—it was overkill.

THE *PEERLESS* SLIPPED OUT of Earth orbit riding the inertia of the half-kilometer-long steam piston that catapulted the ship from the Tycho Brahe Bay. The Moon was new, on the other side of Earth, so Borealis might literally have been in the dark concerning its departure. As far as Terra was concerned, *any* glimmer of light shed on this operation would be too much. The mission was under the highest secrecy protocols. Rittener, seated in the captain's swivel, noted the comforting green streaks across the virtual console of the *Peerless*.

"Valid indications across the board, First Officer," Rittener said in a monotone. Lieutenant Andrews responded in the same flat timbre.

"Valid indications, roger," he said.

The ship's fusion reactor was up and running.

"Engineering?" Rittener called out in shorthand.

"All in, Captain. Ready to initiate spars on your mark," Ensign Gutierrez answered.

Peerless' spars unfurled, splaying open like a giant umbrella around the axis of the ship itself. Within an hour the superconducting segments, kept frigid by the vacuum of space, had telescoped out to form kilometer-long spokes radiating out from *Peerless*. The enormous electric flux pumped through them from the ships reactor created a magnetic sail that extended much, much farther out, bouncing back a wide enough swath of the million-mile-an-hour flood of alpha particles in the solar wind to constantly accelerate the ship to close to half a g. Duty on the ceaselessly accelerating *Peerless* felt a lot like standing still on Mars. If the rare glitch were to have occurred, things would have gone awry by now, so Rittener confidently put the ship's system on autopilot.

"Helmsman, the course is to Valerian-3." It was one of the few, laconic phrases Rittener had uttered to anyone since the crew had come aboard. "Max speed."

Lieutenant Andrews had certainly noticed Rittener's reluctance to waste words and he responded with nothing more than requisite.

"Roger, Valerian-3, max speed."

The *Peerless* nimbly darted toward the black ink of space, her acceleration bringing the blessed feeling of artificial gravity. The crew could finally sink into their chairs and feel the comforting reassurance of their own, albeit Martian, weight. Rittener now addressed the ship's second officer as he rose and exited the bridge.

"Ensign Gutierrez, I'll have a word with the entire crew in the contingency galley, at the top of the hour. All hands."

"Aye, Captain. As ordered," she answered.

THERE WAS NOTHING PERFUNCTORY about Rittener's address to his assembled crew, it was all pure business.

"I'm going to dispense with the 'welcome aboard' speech. I'm sure every crewman has a pretty good idea of what this mission is about. There's not much more really I need add. We've been tasked with the mission to bring the mining settlements on the Asteroid Belt into compliance with an executive order of the Archonate itself, and that's exactly what we're going to do. They've suspended all shipments of vital materials and have given every indication that they haven't the slightest interest in further negotiation. It's going to be our job to change their minds and get those shipments flowing again."

Rittener paused a moment, surveying his crew.

"Our first destination is Valerian-3. It's not the biggest of the settlements but it exports quite respectable quantities of manganese and titanium."

Again he gave each crew member a hard look. He couldn't discern a flicker of anything coming back.

"Also, Valerian-3, according to reports, can be considered one of the ringleaders of this rebellion. With all of us pulling together and a bit of luck, this might be over in short order." Rittener slowly leaned back, propped with his fist under his jaw, and waited for comments. When he realized they weren't coming he asked.

"Questions?"

THE PILOTS OF BOREALIS

Ensign Araceli Gutierrez had one. "Well, sir, are we just showing the flag, or what?"

RITTENER THOUGHT GUTIERREZ BORE a striking resemblance to her amanuensis; he just wasn't sure if that were good or bad. One's amanuensis said a lot about the person—as much as clothes, hair style, jewelry, or anything else. The selection was as wide as the universe, from among every entity who ever lived, might have lived, or only existed in the mind. Some of the more popular choices were angels, elves, or leprechauns. Historical figures were just as popular though. Strolling through any of the Great Concourses on the Terran Ring, for example, one might see anyone from Aristotle to Zorthian II.

Gutierrez's amanuensis was a bandolero-wrapped "Adelita," a ranchera volunteer who rode with Pancho Villa during the Mexican Revolution. These one-foot-tall, all-knowing, three-dimensional marvels of cyber and holographic science were one's personal portal into the System. Plugged into every piece of information there ever was, and every nanosecond being apprised of all the data streaming in the present by the petabyte from every corner of the Solar System, they had the resources to resolve any question or problem ever conceived and became teacher, secretary, confidant, advisor. As *genii,* they stood almost as an alter-ego, recognizing facial expressions and voice timbres, allowing them to almost read human minds and moods, including most assuredly those of their host. For many, an amanuensis was a constant, indefatigable, infallible companion. Everyone recognized Gutierrez's current avatar.

Even the older models were miniaturized to such an extent that they were worn on wrist bands. Now it was rare to see a version other than those small enough to slip around a finger. Everywhere one went though—Earth, Terra, Borealis, or anywhere else under the umbrella of the System—billions of amanuenses were to be seen, and now with humanity thoroughly addicted to the synergy, often open with the avatar floating over the host's right shoulder in active mode.

RITTENER, OF COURSE, DIDN'T like the question. "Come again, Ensign?"

Gutierrez would have been one of the very last souls of the five billion on the Terran Ring to come away with an award for naivety. One look into her coal black eyes is all it usually took for people to realize what a strong personality dwelt behind them. She spoke plainly, like she was doing now, never parsing her words. Rittener had reviewed her file, what there was of it anyway. She'd joined the Service at the first opportunity, just a few days after her eighteenth birthday. Gutierrez hadn't opted for the officers' corps though. It hadn't taken long for her superiors to recognize that she possessed potential talent for operations of the nanocryptology at the heart of much of the ship's vital systems. She was given a commission in her mid-twenties, having spent her entire career so far on the Terran Ring itself.

"Explain what you mean about showing the flag, Ensign Gutierrez." "Permission to speak candidly, Sir?" That question never preceded anything good and Rittener would just have soon declined. He pretended that he was pleased by it nonetheless.

"Of course, Ensign. By all means, speak your mind."

"Well, we *must* be just showing the flag." She gestured with a self-explanatory and yet almost exasperated wave of her hand. "There are *twelve* of us. How are we supposed to enforce the orders of the Archonate? This is one hell of an occupation force for an entire Asteroid Belt. Do you think they sent too many of us, Captain?"

Berti Werth and Nicholas Yeshenko, both inseparable, both nearly indistinguishable, let out barely restrained snickers.

THE PILOTS OF BOREALIS

Werth and Yeshenko were two "Tartars" in the flesh, but who were yet born long after the time that the fad had started to fade. Their perfectly spherical and thick-boned skulls were shaven, save for tufts of straight, blonde hair left growing at the crown and braided to the nape of the neck. They had the Tartar mantra, "a thousand before I die," tattooed across the jugular in red and black Old Mongolian script. No self-respecting Borelian would have even breathed the same air in their vicinity, for they were walking, talking advertisements of everything that was loathed about Terrans and their Ring. Both were huge, strapping horses of men. Taking in the measure of these two, Rittener wondered how the Terran Ring had managed the sagacity to escape being dragged into the incalculable, planet-wide cataclysm that had ravaged Earth. There were tens of millions of Werths and Yeshenkos on the Ring.

"Seaman 2nd Class Yeshenko, tell me something," Rittener asked matter-of-factly. "You're obviously in pretty good shape. I guess what they say about the artificial gravity on the Ring is true after all, huh?"

It was a fact. You could definitely feel the difference on the Ring—1.08 g's. New arrivals from Earth took a little time to get used to it. Of course, the slight, nagging malaise that it produced in the native-born on Earth was a crushing weight for Borelians. They were accustomed to one sixth Earth's gravity. Lunar diplomats, businessmen, and other visitors had to be quartered in those "higher" sections of the Ring which mimicked perfectly the Moon's gravity and in which Terran pilots trained. Since the gravity on Terra was artificial, it weakened progressively the further "up" one ventured from the deck. As pilots' strength invariably gave out and as they sank lower to the "Ground" floors, the stronger the force of artificial gravity became. So Terran pilots could fly almost interminably in the loftiest concentric layers of the Ring, but the mettle of flyers was tested as pilots dared to fly lower and lower.

"It's simple physics, skipper," Yeshenko answered in perfect New English. "It's all inertia. Once you get something spinning, well, that's the hard part. After that it's all downhill and you can coast."

He smiled broadly now, happy to have shed some light on this aspect of Terran civilization for his foreign commander. Rittener could see his muscles flex, the rippling effect obvious under the military tunic that barely contained his formidable torso.

"But, you're right. You can't get ramjets like these any place other than Terra." He glanced down at his bulging biceps to make sure Rittener understood his slang.

Yeshenko's chortle was now followed by a slight smirk. The prior chuckle might have been spontaneous; this monkey grin was definitely purposeful. It widened the longer Rittener's icy stare was ignored.

"Well, about the gravity," Rittener continued, "I've also wondered if it doesn't also deprive the brain of the necessary blood required to form cogent thoughts?"

Yeshenko's expression changed instantly. He leaned forward, jutting out his square Slavic jaw as if challenging Rittener to swing at this menacing target. There were no grins or chuckles now. Whatever he was going to say though was now vetoed by Lieutenant Drake Andrews—Lieutenant, Junior Grade.

"Belay that, Yeshenko." It didn't take a mind-reader to guess that Yeshenko's retort would be better off unsaid. Andrews was always quick with a smile and even after the reprimand managed to purse his thin lips into something that looked like one.

"Captain, I think what is on everyone's mind . . . " Andrews began.

"I'm not a captain, Lieutenant Andrews," Rittener cut him off. "In fact, I have no commission whatsoever in the Terran Service."

Andrews was shaking his head. He understood this, of course. "Point well taken. How should we address you?"

Rittener looked again at Yeshenko, and then used his word. "Skipper."

"Skipper it is then." Now Andrews' lips went flat. C-class freighters, smugglers, and pirates had "skippers."

"The point Ensign Gutierrez is making, though, is a valid one. From what I understand, we're not going to be joined by any other force at some point prior to the Asteroid Belt? We're it?"

Rittener's words came out slowly, in a monotone, with as much emotion as someone instructing the mess monitor about the mid-watch meal selections. "There is to be no rendezvous in transit. Our destination is Valerian-3. I just said as much."

Andrews reminded him of his tensor calculus teacher in Shanghai. He was a professor at the Loo Keng-Hua Institute. The European Union picked up quite a hefty stipend to have had such a renowned mathematician tutor the ambassador's son. Andrews opened his eyes wide like Ch'in Tsu. "So it's just us, then?"

Rittener was tiring of this. He didn't like being cornered into discussing classified orders with a crew member.

"Our actions will be determined by exigencies in the Field, Lieutenant. I'm not going to go into anything more specific at this time. I can assure you though that you'll be apprised of everything you need to know, as you need to know it. Until I advise the crew otherwise, what I'm now repeating for the third time is that Valerian-3 is our destination, and our mission is to convince that settlement and the rest on the Belt that it's in their interest to abide by the executive order of the Archonate that we're enforcing. You may consider those your orders."

Each man was sizing the other up. Rittener noticed the five stars embroidered above Andrews' name on his tunic—one for each of the five-year tours of duty under his belt. Yet there wasn't another single badge or ribbon pinned or sewed anywhere. A fifty-two-year-old lieutenant—*junior* grade? Could such a thing actually be possible—and if so, were there any others in existence? Rittener's amazement was well-founded; there were only two others in the Service—if the one currently posted to the Virgo Brig awaiting court-martial were counted. Somehow, such a competent imaging specialist such as Andrews had managed a lifetime in the Service and had accrued just a single lousy promotion to show for it.

Andrews pushed on.

"Not to put too fine a point on it then, Skipper . . . " Andrews stopped himself, opened his eyes wide again and asked, "Are we still speaking candidly?"

Rittener nodded affirmatively.

"Well, this ship is hardly anything more than a floating electron laser platform. If we're going into combat, where, may I ask, are prisoners going to be held?"

Now Yeshenko jumped in with both feet.

"Prisoners?" The laugh that followed was too loud and abrasive to be smoothed over by Lieutenant Andrews, who just stared at Yeshenko with blank eyes. "Come on, Lieutenant. Even slow-witted, blood-deprived Terrans like us can figure that one out. You know how Earthers fight. Dirt crawlers don't take prisoners."

He turned to Rittener, and in the same tone he used with a drinking buddy called on to settle a boozy debate, invited him to chime in. "You've been in a hundred battles—hell, maybe even a thousand—against dirt crawlers. They ever take one of your guys prisoner?"

Rittener, born and raised on Earth, was himself, of course, a "dirt crawler" too. He had heard the pejorative so many times that its power to sting had long since faded into insignificance. Being labeled one, however, in front of every single crewman on board made it easy for Rittener to choose how he'd couch his next comments.

Rittener withdrew from his waistcoat pocket an impressive-looking document. It was bound in a leather sheath—*real* leather—and was embossed with the seal of the Terran Archonate, the image inlaid with gold. There were still a few records kept on paper, but it took the crew a moment to recognize what the credentials actually were. Now Rittener was speaking to no one—not Yeshenko nor Andrews nor anyone else really. He was just speaking the words, by law required to be said out loud. He'd planned on making this speech in a perfunctory way, as gentle as possible. He now decided on a different course. He started speaking as he passed the document to Lieutenant Andrews to verify.

"As per the War Act, section nine, codicil five, and in accordance with the Interplanetary Conventions articles twenty six and twenty seven, I am hereby formally advising all officers and crew of the following. This letter of marque gives absolute and complete authority over the ship *Peerless* to the holder of this marque. Any and all orders given by the holder of this letter shall be lawfully and strictly obeyed by any and all Terran crew and/or passengers aboard the *Peerless*."

He paused. "You'll sign that please, Mr. Andrews, and then pass it to Ensign Gutierrez." Noticing that the lieutenant was at sea regarding how this old-fashioned paper and pen stuff went, he slid a handsome stylograph which even worked in zero gravity across the desk to him. "Your signature, at the bottom, by your name." He then went on.

"The holder of this marque is granted the authority to pursue the legitimate interests of the Terran Archonate in dealings with its enemies in whatever manner the holder deems necessary, prudent, and efficient, subject to the above mentioned interplanetary conventions."

While Ensign Gutierrez was reading and signing the letter, Seaman Werth came to an overjoyed epiphany.

"*Gott im himmel*! I'm on a pirate ship!" He slapped his friend's muscled back. "We're damned pirates now, Yeshenko—and with double pay and a promotion waiting for us when we get back to the Ring! Ah . . . and I was the German donkey too stupid to know that no one with a whit of sense volunteered for anything, no? What do you say now?"

Rittener gave him a real smile, showing a perfect set of teeth. Of course no teeth could be *that* perfect, but nineteen of them were actually real; the rest were lost in countless battles. His eyes lit up listening to Werth's blunt translation of the letter of marque. Well, the green one lit up anyway, not the blue one. There were so many parts of Rittener's body that were biosynthetic that he himself had long forgotten what it felt like to have been at one time in one single piece. The biosynthetic eye had over the years changed from the original green to aqua blue. This was not unusual and there were remedies for it. Rittener just opted to leave it as it was.

Gutierrez made to hand the document back to Rittener, but he waved her off. "Seaman Werth, you're absolutely correct. This isn't a Terran ship; this is my ship." And with that he dropped the other shoe. "Ensign Gutierrez, please count the number of 'up to and including the penalty of death' admonitions in that document. The number escapes me now."

Rittener wasn't smiling now. He looked like a Celtic warrior—after a long, hard, lost battle. Or perhaps a closer approximation, especially with the long, swooping, ochre mustache, would be a tough trooper of the US 7th Cavalry from the time of the Little Big Horn. His blonde hair was parted in the middle and fell to his collar. It was straight and very fine and hadn't receded in the least. That feature was boyish still, unlike very much else about him. Having called various purgatories his home since his youth, and surrounded by the denizens of these cruel precincts, he had allowed himself to be influenced by them. His face was long, narrowing to a blunt jaw and accentuated with a meandering, deep scar that ran from his left cheek bone to the cleft in his chin. In Rittener's profession, as with 19th century students in duel-crazed Prussia, scars were almost prized and it was far from rare to forego having them cosmetically erased. The eyes though, in Rittener's case, were almost hypnotic. The green one, the real one, still reflected a virtuous humanity, an eye that seemed to want to shed tears for what it had seen. The blue one warned of another side, a dead side, one that had seen very little other than ruin and destruction.

The only sound in the room was that of Gutierrez nervously flipping through the paperwork, her agitated hands rustling the document. After what seemed an interminable duration, she answered bluntly. "Six, Sir."

Rittener moved his eyes slowly from crewman to crewman as he spoke. His reputation had preceded him, as he well knew, and he now brought that weapon to bear. "This isn't a Terran ship; this is *my* ship. I will personally execute every single crewman, if I have to, and send the *Peerless* spiraling into the Sun before I'll see a single one of my orders disobeyed." It wasn't anxiety or fear or outrage or any other emotion he saw reflected back in their eyes; it was utter shock. As if what he'd just said to the crew was nothing out of the ordinary, as if he'd made a bland comment about the weather or some other mundane topic, he simply moved on to close the meeting. "I'll summon each of you individually to discuss the particulars of your specialties and how I want things run in short order. Unless there are any other questions, you are all dismissed."

The whole crew sat frozen, no one knowing just exactly what to make of what had just happened. Rittener seemed slightly irritated with their discomfiture and broke the spell by waving his hand and repeating "dismissed." As the crew silently started to respond, he overruled himself, as if suddenly remembering an afterthought.

"Oh, one more thing. Mr. Kendrick, place Seaman 2nd Class Yeshenko under arrest and escort him to the brig."

With that one off-handed remark Rittener turned his entire crew to stone just as surely and quickly as if he'd shown them all the head of Medusa. Now a *truly* interminable and deathly silence descended. Rittener was looking down at his letter of marque, checking to see that all was in order, so he wasn't taking in the looks of astonishment on the faces of his flabbergasted crew. Owen Kendrick, though, reacted automatically. He pulled himself up, put his meat hook hands on his hips, and gave Yeshenko a gruff order.

"On your feet, Seaman."

The Tartar Yeshenko slowly obeyed, but while fixing Rittener with a deadly stare and slowly nodding his head as if affirming a stream of unspoken yet toxic thoughts within. Chief Warrant Officer Kendrick was the security officer—a barrel-chested sailor who resembled a bear as much as a man. Yeshenko was sane enough to obey but was tarrying, still playing at sending visual daggers in Rittener's direction.

"Let's go, Yeshenko. You heard the skipper." He motioned to the hatch with one of his bear claws.

As they were exiting Rittener gave a final order. "He's to be held 'hard,' Chief. Seventy-two hours. The charge is 'overt contempt.' Log it."

Held 'hard' was simplicity itself. The offender was just stuffed into a stainless steel compartment the size of a closet and forgotten for a while. The only amenities were a miniature commode and a quarter-inch tube that gave out a weak stream of drinking water when pressure was applied. That was it though. No food, feeble light, not a sound worth listening to, no nothing; it was meant to be three days of Hell.

All in all, Rittener thought to himself as the crew exited in silence, the voyage could have gotten off to a better start. But, then again, he reminded himself, it could have been worse.

CHAPTER THREE

ACROSS THE RIVER STYX

THE FESTIVAL OF *SYZYGY*, a celestial alignment drawn from the lunar almanacs of the thousands-year-old *saros* of Babylonia, took place shortly after Clinton Rittener's arrival and inaugural race on Borealis. He was en route to celebrate it with almost every other pilot, at a most unique locale, this one several hundred kilometers south of Borealis. Lunar lava tubes provided many of the things Borealis needed and some were huge and deep, like Tartarus. To reach this ageless pipe, formed during the Moon's childhood, Rittener and a group of Borelian pilots shuttled across the Field—the lunar surface outside the Dome. Passengers on this track never concerned themselves with the weather because there was none. Air was a prerequisite for climate and there was none of that either. The vacuum, impervious to change, bore down all the way to the lunar surface, rendering it more part of space itself than the realm of humanity.

"Old hands in the Field call it 'clean.'" That's what the young man sitting across from Rittener said to him. "I know because my grandfather is one." He gave an ill-behaved grin in the direction of the elderly gentleman seated next to him. A soundless landscape of sun-broiled crater floors and steep rifts of low, sharp mountains rushed by, exuding eternity. Not so much as a grain of sand had moved here for eons, and even the superbly engineered steel and magnesium arrow that cut through it, sliding on frictionless, magnetic, insubstantial wheels, didn't—couldn't—as much as make a swoosh in it.

Rittener had never seen the Field before. Naturally everyone in the car knew that, since his identity was hardly indistinguishable. The young man stretched out his hand. "Hello, Clinton Rittener; I'm Jaager." He'd ridden this line before and pointed out the starboard view ports. "Watch in a few seconds, as we pass through the next tunnel. Get ready." The shuttle broke through the next subway, debouching into a stunning Japanese rock garden of stupendous proportions, the precisely raked rows of combed regolith stretching to the horizon. Something had moved these grains, having wrung from them every precious mote of helium-3, and not long ago.

The Field was where helium-3 had been delivered to the Moon via the solar wind, blasted into the airless, defenseless lunar surface amid an angry stream of alpha particles hurled at the Moon over four billion years. Earth's magnetic shield prevented this gift of the Sun from being deposited on the home planet and it couldn't be obtained anywhere else. For the benefit of sticklers, there might be stores on Jupiter, Neptune, and Uranus, but few considered the kind of Herculean efforts that would be required to get at *that* supply, especially when the Moon was such a close and relatively friendly and benign place.

It was mined so simply and easily too on the Moon: it was just scooped up by robotic regolith skimmers. The top few inches of the lunar surface was scraped off, vaporized by solar collectors, and the liberated gas obtained. Exporting it to Terra and Earth was even easier. Canisters of pressurized helium-3 were loaded like ammunition in the breeches of Materials Export Cannons with 800-meter-long barrels. These "pea shooters" couldn't have been erected on Earth, and along with the Goldilocks Array, would have collapsed under their own colossal weight. But as Borelians reminded everyone, "Nothing is impossible on the Moon." These behemoths fired projectiles at escape velocity—only around a kilometer per second on Luna—fast enough to overcome the Moon's gentle gravity and non-existent air drag, and sent the cargo on to parabolic orbits meant to intersect eager customers throughout the Solar System. Fusion reactors, by the hundreds of thousands, powered mankind's universe and helium-3 was the fuel that fed those reactors. No more simple equation existed.

"Look there," Jaager had caught sight of one of the pea shooters discharging its precious freight. "That could be headed anywhere." He sounded genuinely pleased to be acting as guide for the distinguished fellow passenger.

Jaager's grandfather had settled on an opening remark. Borelians weren't known for their subtlety. Rufinus, like a lot of miners with decades of experience in the Field, had the tact of a blacksmith pounding the impurities out of an ingot. "On Earth and on the Ring they call this 'terra incognita.' It's amazingly developed, wouldn't you say, for territory supposedly lying fallow?"

Those were almost fighting words, probably to wind up being used in the next great rallying cry. At the heart of the problem was a hard reality that couldn't be ignored: the helium-3 was running out. That was the plain fact. For many in the know both in the Inner and the Outer, it was an obvious reality that wasn't up for debate. The only question was if this new energy crisis would spawn horrific wars like the last one. Earth and Terra both considered the Field "terra incognita" and saw no reason why their considerable muscle shouldn't be brought to bear to increase the supply of helium-3. Having her customers help themselves to Luna's reservoir on their own though was an idea that held few Borelian adherents.

Terra had lately increased the pressure, exponentially. Dante Michelson, the fire-breathing Chief Archon of Terra, was well-known to the Borelians, thanks to his prior office as Terra's ambassador to the city. Michelson was a hard-liner and had his reasons for the extreme opinions. Like most "ambassadors" he had been first and foremost a spy, and through his network of contacts was in a position to see and hear things like few others.

In short, he believed the Borelians were lying—plain and simple. He thought they'd been lying for years about the equatorial fields. He suspected that their potential yield had been purposefully exaggerated and that the speedy timetable which would infuse the market with additional supplies was hardly more than fantasy. Finally, he knew what this all meant, thinking four or five steps ahead as always. It was ironic that it was his signature on the accord that put the tough questions off a few more years. The Field was legally neither Borealis' nor was it terra incognita, which would have left it open to anyone. By interplanetary law it currently lurked in the limbo of "disputed territory." But he'd signed that as the ambassador of a previous regime. He was no ambassador now. As Chief Archon of the Terran Ring he was the most powerful man in the Solar System, and in his mind it *was* terra incognita.

"I'd only hope that history doesn't repeat itself." Rittener tried to say it softly but everyone in the car heard it.

Rufinus wasn't sure he liked it. "What's that?"

"Well, the four Petroleum Wars," Rittener replied.

These conflagrations of the Old Modern made the World Wars of the 20th century seem like polite skirmishes. The comparison came from the mouth of the only person on the train who'd directed campaigns that cut down great swathes of humanity, so it should have held some weight.

"Supply and demand can't be disobeyed; they're as uncompromising as the laws of motion. Demand for helium-3 increases relentlessly, and as for the supply, well, as with petroleum, it has long since ceased being created." Rittener put it as simple as that, even though it was a little more complicated.

The shuttle was designed for comfort and amicability, not moving great numbers, like so many contrivances on the Moon. A padded island ran down the center of the car between long cushions along the wall. Many of the pilots sidled closer now, filling the spaces around Rittener, drawn to the conversation. Borelians didn't hide their curiosity like others and were strangely overt when it came to showing interest. A knot of pilots and others had already formed when the middle-aged man took a seat on the island cushion directly in front of Rittener. Clinton didn't need to scan him to know who he was. Borelian scientists were as easily recognized as approaching dust storms on the Red Planet. He acted like one too.

"Gresling, here," he said his name with an ear-to-ear smile, offering his hand affably. "I'm a PI at the Geologic Survey and overheard your discussion." He looked like a Borelian principal investigator. Their uniform appearance began with the hair, clipped so short that it lingered in the nether realm between baldness and crew cut. It was the rare man of science though on Borealis without whiskers—but just pencil-thin embellishments. Gresling's were a horizontal line above the lips and a vertical stripe below them to the cleft. Squeezed under the chin, his overly starched collar was so high and stiff it didn't seem even part of the tunic. It kept the head on a swivel, alert and observant.

"Things aren't so clear-cut in the Field and many can be easily misled about helium-3." He swiveled his head toward the moonscape sweeping past. "It's not out there, every-where, just to be picked up and exported." It was clear he thought anyone who believed that was as simple-minded as the statement.

"Elementary physics says that the Moon's equator, for instance, should be loaded with helium-3," Gresling explained. "That's a good example. Certainly, sunlight striking the Lunar Equator has always been ferocious and packed with helium-3 ions stripped of electrons. If mother lodes of the stuff should be found around the Lunar North Pole where the light struck so much more obliquely, common wisdom intimates that there should be astounding quantities yet to be mined in the equatorial regions."

The scientist consented that much, but more complex physics gave some answers as to why the simple view was flawed. "Sadly, that's not the case," he lamented. "Opinions are changing about the relative weakness and duration of the Moon's ancient magnetic field. There are many respected scholars who have very plausible evidence that it had been a real force in the ancient past—deflecting the solar wind and depriving Luna's equator and temperate zones of helium-3 while at the same time funneling the concentrated stream straight to the place where great quantities had already been found—the Lunar North Pole."

Rufinus was shaking his head in agreement. "Don't forget the South Pole. Don't leave that out."

The scientist's collar was so tight and stiff he could hardly shake his head affirmatively.

"And certainly as you might imagine, Clinton Rittener, the alpha particles weren't just deposited on the Moon like rain falling on the surface of Earth's continental prairies to be soaked up by the sod." He had a look of satisfaction that he'd been able to reference the old planet so elegantly for the newcomer. "The mineral composition of each site played a very significant role in the calculus of absorption and retention. Depending on the chemistry and geology involved, the precious motes could penetrate too deeply, too erratically, fail to be captured, or even if suffused originally might not be held for billions of years awaiting the robotic scoops of our mining operations."

Rittener decided to take the scientist skating onto thinner ice, just for fun. "That all sounds very complicated and thorny. It's amazing you've been able to find any at all. So how much do you reckon there is left, and where's the best place to look?"

What those mineral and geologic hallmarks were for potential h-3 deposits was the most highly guarded secret of the Council. There *were* fields yet to be mined, but they were scattered all over Luna. And even though Borealis wasn't speaking plainly about it anymore, from the reserved communiqués issued about the matter from time to time it was fairly obvious that the good old days of h-3 flowing in abundance from the Moon were quickly coming to an end.

"The popular conception that there are oodles of the stuff at the equatorial regions," he chose his words carefully, "might not necessarily be true."

Rufinus frowned derisively at the word mincing and answered Rittener's question with exactitude.

"I can tell you where there *isn't* any h-3. Don't go looking for any at the Lunar *South* Pole," Rufinus advised strenuously.

"If conspiracy theorists wish to peddle their rumors about vast stores, secret mining ventures, and all the rest, we Borelians shouldn't be bothered with it. I've been on teams that surveyed every dry hole in every sector around Australis. There isn't any h-3 there."

The Aitken Basin straddles the Lunar South Pole, one of the largest craters in the entire Solar System—2,500 kilometers across. Much of what was thought to be known about the region changed after a number of conflicting Borelian surveys were read correctly. The bombshell was that prior astrophysical assumptions about the basin were just simply in error, the reports made clear. Scientists had always guessed at the age of around 3.8 billion years for the crater.

Borealis now had proof that the guess had been off—way off. Radiometric age-dating techniques were a sure way to tell the last time the surface of the basin had been molten. The surveyors had no doubt after checking when those geologic clocks within the lunar regolith had been melted and reset. The Aitken Crater wasn't age-old, it was actually quite young. They determined that the object that struck came in at a low angle—around thirty degrees—striking a glancing blow that didn't dig in so much as scrape away. This object still packed quite a punch—blasting into space the top layer of the Lunar South Pole to a depth of 13 kilometers. The event occurred not 3.8 billion years ago but rather at some time within the last half billion years. This accounted for the dearth of helium-3.

"I've been down there, turned over stones, even looked under the ice in the pot holes that litter the place. There isn't enough h-3 there to boil a cup of tea. Whatever walloped the Moon hit it in the chin hard enough to knock its beard off. The crater goes on forever." Rufinus made a fist and punched his hand to emphasize.

If the Lunar South Pole had been soaking up helium-3 since the dawn of the Solar System, that treasure was lost forever, having been jettisoned into space along with everything else within the erstwhile surface of the Lunar South Pole.

"Australis is the scene of the greatest theft in the history of mankind," Gresling philosophized. "There's no broken glass or splintered door, but the h-3 is missing and the only thing left is that enormous hole."

Jaager had been minding his manners, seen, listening, but unheard. He took a chance here since he had what he considered a good point. "One asteroid snuffs out the dinosaurs and opens the door for our existence; another robs us of what possibly could have been half of our helium-3 supply." He shrugged his shoulders over the "spilled milk" that he called it. "I'd say our batting average isn't that bad."

"Spilled milk? That's your analogy?" His grandfather's snorting reproach made him wish he'd kept his mouth shut. "I've heard it estimated that if the reserves lost were anything like those of the Lunar North Pole, it represented an amount of credits sufficient to buy quite a sizeable homestead: North America."

Whether or not Rufinus had his astronomical figures correct, the ridiculous price of helium-3 had risen to undreamed-of prices and as such was the standard complaint of everyone, from barbers on Terra to chicken farmers on Earth. It was playing havoc with the economy of the entire Solar System. The party line on Borealis was that there was no need to panic and that steps were underway to put everything right. Dante Michelson on Terra knew otherwise, and so did Clinton Rittener. As one of the most famed *condottieri* of Earth, he was several steps up from just an average mercenary. He had a few contacts of his own.

The conversation about Australis petered out and a short silence ensued. Gresling intelligently now decided to change the subject.

"I've read some of your papers. I wish we had time to talk about your ideas."

That was a lifetime ago, Rittener thought, and he said so.

"I was hardly more than a teenager when I wrote those. They were sloppy—and worse—wrong."

From the far end of the car there came either a cough or an ill-disguised rebuke. It became apparent which when Clinton saw it was Nerissa who had chosen just this moment to clear her throat. She and Clinton had scrupulously avoided making eye contact during the entire journey. The glance they now exchanged was brief but decidedly unfriendly.

A smirk crossed the thin lips of the scientist, proof that very little escaped his rigorous attention, and certainly not this obvious and frosty snub. Gresling couldn't agree though, and stuck to his guns. "That's nonsense. Many great things are only accomplished in youth. Jaager here is an excellent example. You know about Jaager, of course?"

Jaager had made a mark of his own already: he was the youngest pilot on Borealis and was clearly very happy to set this straight.

"I'm a genuine pilot, officially inscribed. I'm young but experienced; I've been flying since I was three." Rittener hadn't even uttered his first word by his third birthday, but declined to make the comparison.

A young woman had come from the far end of the shuttle car to join the conversation. "I'm the late starter," she said. She looked very much like Jaager—same sandy blonde hair, both sharing big, prominent eyes. His were blue and intelligent-looking, spaced slightly wider, hers a delicate shade of light green, the color surrounded by a sea of pearl white. Jaager made the introduction.

"This is my sister, Darda. Her first flight was at six; that's what she means."

She was holding a plate of steaming, blue-green mush. The ghastly reek came in front of it like clouds of tear gas announcing truncheon-swinging riot police.

"If my family is going to indoctrinate you," she granted, "at least we can see you're fed properly."

This was infamous Borelian "flux." She offered the ill-smelling pottage to Clinton with some pomp. "Blue-green flux is my favorite. Have you ever had it?" Her big eyes pretended to say that she hoped he hadn't. She didn't wait, though, knowing Rittener couldn't have ever tasted flux. No one but a Borelian could have. Her grandfather's disquieting grimace cued Rittener that if Darda were a late-starter she might be making up for it now like most Borelian balls of fire who had earned wings.

"Don't believe them, by the way, when they tell you the first pioneers existed on it. That's pure fiction." She leaned in closer as if she and Rittener were sharing a secret. "Even in Settlement Times they grew crops using pathetic forerunners of Goldilocks. No one ate well in those primitive days but they sure didn't dine on flux exclusively either." She shrugged her shoulders to accentuate the apocryphal. "Yet even the Old City Museum is happy to play along. The restaurant there serves thirty-three varieties. Can you believe it?"

Rufinus was squirming on his cushion.

Before Rittener could critique it she had to make sure of something else. "That's not from the canteen. That's homemade; that's real flux." She actually winked at Clinton. "Go on, take a bite."

If the Goldilocks Array was built to heat and light Borealis, there was another tremendous benefit. It also converted the regolith out from the Dome to the Shadow Line boundary near the edges of the crater walls into a verdant Eden. To go past the Shadow Line was the same as to go over the lip into the direct sunlight, certain death if unprotected. But, from the circumference of the Shadow Line to the periphery of the Dome, a circular, transparent dextrite lid was erected, suspended on steel struts. This let the ceaseless and tempered reflected sunlight through, kept out the vacuum of space, and held in the carbon dioxide–rich micro-atmosphere. Fruits, vegetables, grains, herbs, spices, and other flora of every conceivable type thrived below in a fantastic version of the Late Carboniferous period of Old Earth, the carbon dioxide levels only restrained by what the bees could tolerate. The bounty this green carpet gave forth was more than sufficient for Borealis, along with blessing the city with tons of clean oxygen and soaking up the exhaled breaths of thousands to convert to sugars.

The "Garden" was also exemplary of yet another wedge driven between the peoples of the Inner. The culture of death was on Earth and Terra, not here in peaceful, vivacious Borealis. No animal had been butchered legally on the Moon since Settlement Times and they meant to keep it that way. It was a tangible and sanguine proof that they—and not the other cultures of the Inner—that *they* were the enlightened entities into which humanity had been meant to evolve. Borelian cuisine was actually then quite delicious and particularly healthy, excepting flux. That was an acquired taste.

Rufinus fidgeted and groused, muttering something about the South Pole. "Oh, enough of that, Grandfather. Clinton Rittener isn't going to Australis. Let him enjoy his flux in peace."

There was silence all around. Everyone's eyes watched Clinton Rittener take his first heaping spoonful of the fibrous, gelatinous pap. It was Borealis' comfort food and he managed to get it down.

"Well?" Darda asked, big eyes wide open. "The taste?" She gave him a knowing smile. "Awful, isn't it?"

The young pilot let Rittener off the hook, boldly taking her seat right next to him, wiping away the remnants of the horrid paste from his lips with a crisp linen serviette.

"Flux wasn't born of necessity, Clinton Rittener, but rather of other purely human attributes: boredom, curiosity, the need for diversion. That tells much about us. Settlers had asked themselves if it were possible to produce 'indigenous' lunar food, something that could be grown nowhere else but on the Moon—creating the hardiest, genetically engineered plant mutants, putting the monster hybrids into the face of the scorching Sun."

She folded the napkin and put it in her lap.

"They never imagined for a minute that it couldn't be done, Clinton Rittener. And that's been the history of Borealis ever since. So I'll answer for you. Flux tastes like perseverance. It's the flavor of resolution."

She said the next as if intimating that not all of Rittener's teachers on Borealis should be of her grandfather's generation.

"I don't know how much helium-3 is on the South Pole," she said, "but we all know you're provisional and no one should have to pass through citizenship initiation without some support. I'll be happy to help if there's anything you want to ask or need explained." Darda stood and with a final flourish curtseyed and made an end, "Said the mouse to the lion." Rufinus cleared his throat, and not surreptitiously, so loudly the viewing panel almost vibrated.

It was such a candid and guileless offer, and it made a real impression on Rittener. Jaager was a little uncomfortable about the suggestion and tried to smooth it over. "Clinton Rittener has probably been briefed by highly capable cultural attachés where he comes from, Darda. While you're teaching him something I'll be showing Grandfather where to find h-3 on Australis."

Before anyone could laugh it off or defend, it a voice, again from the far end of the car, interrupted and changed the conversation altogether.

"And where is that? Where does Clinton Rittener come from?" It was Nerissa's. "Earth? Is that where you're from?" There were a score of pilots and their relations and friends in the car with connections beyond the Moon. By the time she finished the last of her words they were delivered in crystal clear silence, as if the vacuum outside had slipped in and quashed every other conversation.

He set down the plate of flux. "I am from Earth."

"I see. From the Asian Alliance or the European Union?"

"I held dual citizenship."

"How unusual," she said thoughtfully. "But I thought Mars claimed you?" she followed up hard and fast.

"I learned to fly on Mars."

"Really?" A look of puzzlement came over her face. "But I thought you flew on Titan?"

"There, too," Rittener answered.

"Oh, that makes it clear." She smiled and put the sweetest nectar on the derision. "Of course there aren't too many first-class pilots on the Asteroid Belt, but your name is not unknown there either, is it?" Before he could answer she added another "but I thought," like a mantra. "But I thought you were the commander of a Terran warship sent to terrorize the people out there?"

"The Borelian authorities have asked me to refrain from making any comments about the Terran Ring," he parried. "I'm trying to accede to their wishes."

"The Asian Alliance, European Union, Mars, Titan, and yes, let's not exclude the Terran Ring," she ran off the names counting with fingers as visual aids for the listeners. There was no need to say out loud her implication.

"And now it's our turn. You arrive here at a moment of great decision too. How fortunate for Borealis."

A seemingly interminable silence reigned until Darda broke the spell. Maybe Rittener could use her help after all with Borelian customs. "That's sarcasm. We Borelians are said to be very skilled at its use."

She was being a little sarcastic herself, so said her rascal's smile.

TARTARUS HAD BEEN CAPPED decades ago, sealed with a slab of the strongest concrete anywhere, stronger even than the dome of the Pantheon that had been hardening for millennia. A seam holding a vein of excellent pyroclastic ashes and silica had been pulled from the tube itself to create the lid. The interior was then flooded with a mixture of nitrogen and oxygen, in the same proportions as under the Dome or on Earth, drawn from the regolith scraped from the sides and processed. The Moon is almost half oxygen by weight, so that and quite a number of gases and volatiles were obtained from Tartarus. The scrapes and gouges in its sides were converted to habitats. They spiraled down the walls of the lava cylinder. Numerous side tubes branched off from main, ready-made tendrils to other resources, not a few of them filled to the brim with great amounts of carbon dioxide, ready to be pumped to the surface when lunar night fell. The bone-shattering chill was used to convert the CO_2 to dry ice; cubes of frozen carbon dioxide were shipped all over the Moon from Tartarus.

The pilots came to Tartarus at *Syzygy* for something else though. The festival was one of the spokes in the wheel that carted piloting culture forward on Borealis. At the bottom of Tartarus lay the greatest of all lunar treasures: water. It was in liquid form, having long since melted due to the ambient temperatures humans brought with them. A section of it had been portioned and converted into a monumental sauna, named Styx, harkening to the mythical underworld river. It was fantasized that some natural yet inexplicable radioactivity deep at the bottom of this lunar pit was heating the spa. That was complete invention, of course, since heat from fusion reactors in abundance was the source. But this was an exotic pool and it required a hidden caché.

The sauna was reserved for pilots and pilots only. Their guild had long ago disbursed an enormous sum to the state for the right to develop it and annually paid an obscene stipend for its continued use. The race down the throat of Tartarus ended here, at Styx, and what transpired then no one knew— save the pilots themselves.

THERE WERE FEW EASIER ways to kill oneself. None of the flyers seemed to give that a second thought as waves of pilots spiraled into the mouth of Tartarus. Immediately the shaft took a ninety-degree turn, straight down. The torrent turned and followed that vertical path like bats headed into a cavern. Clinton had flown like this before and used the thought to give him confidence before the race. On Mars this was the only way to fly. But Martian corridors, cut by engineers and as straight as lasers, unfortunately didn't prepare him for this. The rock sides of the tube came at the pilots with extreme and killing speed as they followed its twisting and turning course into the Moon's depths. It was no surprise when the accident occurred.

Darda's wing brushed the wall, seemingly barely glancing. But her speed and momentum were deceptive. Her body was twirled like a splinter cast off from a saw mill. She slammed into the other side of the tube and was knocked cold. Rittener was behind her and saw it happen. His first thought was to wonder if she'd been killed. His second was to realize that she was in the worst of straits. Bouncing off the sides, her lifeless form caromed into an ancillary tube that channeled off. This one had been worked and was plumb, falling straight down into a dark abyss. At its bottom, tons of carbon dioxide were being liberated by an oversize regolith converter. The heavy gas piled up on itself, pushing all the air out of the void until it reached the main tube. Darda was falling to her death, being suffocated in a cylindrical reservoir of millions of cubic feet of pure carbon dioxide.

Her brother didn't vacillate for an instant, veering off wildly and following her into the tunnel, almost killing himself also but missing the rock, only grazing his wingtips as he entered the carbon trap. Jaager soon found himself at a terrible place. He couldn't hold his breath for another instant, and yet was still far above his sister. He'd have to either watch her die as he gave up and turned back or continue on to perish with her. His agony was brief though. Borealis' newest citizen—provisional—the one he'd only just shook hands with hours ago, sped past him. He was not in extremis. In fact, the look on his face was an expression Jaager would live his entire life without seeing again. It was a pilot flying in full and complete *yanta*. Rittener spent only a microsecond to throw his head back, signaling to Jaager to turn around and that he'd answer for his sister. He couldn't verbalize it because Rittener wasn't breathing. Nor was his heart beating like any normal human, nor was his adrenaline, serotonin, or other hormones at any level within standard ranges. Most importantly, Rittener wasn't thinking like any other human either, save those very, very few, those unapproachable masters in the Great Outer beyond Titan, from whom he'd learned this death-defying skill. That's what made him the very uniquely dangerous man that he was. "Dying this way, if you ever should fail, is thought to be most pleasant," they impressed upon him. "Have no fear of it."

His mind kicked into an unknown, untested, final gear. There was no way to describe how Titanian pilots did it, but he was more or less in the throes of multiple and intense conversations—with himself—crowding out the normal terrors and substituting with outrageous demands for both mind and body. One dialogue was with the mathematician in him, and it was gauging the slight difference in flying in the thicker carbon dioxide, comparing the calculus of Darda's slowed descent with the resistance it gave to his approach to her. His mind ran through the equations faster than a quantum computer because they weren't solved, they were felt. The final sum looked impossible; it looked like death. This was an old and powerful acquaintance of Rittener's though. He'd greeted it many times and fully welcomed it now as an old comrade who'd always relented in the end. All the inner conversations and organ manipulations came together, with the flood of reflection and will coalescing into a single mega-thought, as if a great and hitherto unseen escape were now at hand. He simply wouldn't breathe and yet live. He'd breathe when he got back to the top. He pumped his wings and went deeper into the now darkening cavern, past the point of no return, no matter that he willed that he would.

THAT EVENING, BATHING IN the waters of Styx, every single pilot of Borealis, one after the other, friend or foe, supporter or detractor, came to think of him differently.

Including Nerissa. Her words about terrorizing civilians at Valerian-3 had cut deeply and he had to put that right. What they said to each other though, their exact words, were known only to them, exchanged in one of the last veiled places in the universe, in the stygian depths of Earth's now powerful satellite, excluded even from the eyes and ears of the System itself.

CHAPTER FOUR

WOE TO THE VANQUISHED

PEERLESS' TRANSIT FROM THE Terran Ring to the Asteroid Belt was an uneventful but tense journey. Rittener had set the deadly serious tone. Yeshenko's venomous complaints, after his release from the brig, fell on deaf ears. No crewman wanted any part of it and quickly found another duty station that immediately required attention. *Peerless* hurtled past the orbit of Mars in radio silence, ignoring hails from the few stray ships they crossed in this lonely quadrant of space. There was some sense in the trajectory the Archonate chose which gave the spy net on Mars a wide berth, foregoing to avail the ship of the gravity boost the planet might have provided. Rittener had to assume ears in the Asteroid Belt would have heard he was coming though. If he should somehow arrive unexpectedly that would be so much the better. As the first few chunks of debris swept past the *Peerless* when she entered the fringes of the Belt, Rittener ordered the crew into combat status. Only three slept at a time, six hours off, eighteen hours on. G-suits were worn all twenty-four hours, even to bed. The ship's fusion reactor was on and hot, braking the *Peerless*, sending out a furious plume of effluvium in front of her, composed of the disintegrated remains of appropriate-sized chunks of flotsam she had picked up along the way.

At morning second bell Rittener wolfed down two protein squares in the galley and made for the bridge. The *Peerless* would be entering the approach to Valerian-3 shortly. In his left hand he had some spare protein squares, in his right he carried a sleep casquette. The helmet blocked sound and light to the point of sensory deprivation, depending on the setting. With all the exigencies which soon were to present themselves, he'd be catching his few winks at the captain's swivel from here on in. Catching sight of himself in one of the monitors as he trudged down the corridor, favoring his right biosynthetic foot a little, which acted up from time to time depending on the gravity, he looked tired. "You look like Hell," he said to himself.

Peerless was already decelerating and had been doing so for a while now, having long since passed the half-way point between Terra and Valerian-3. Slight adjustments now would guide the ship's elliptical path around the Sun into a cotangential orbit with the asteroid. Rittener buckled himself into the captain's swivel on the bridge, gauging the angles closing between the two orbits. A glance at the Near Bow Console—showing everything in front of the ship out to 1,000 kilometers—indicated almost nothing. The Intermediate Console was starting to show some debris. The Far Console though, which scanned out from 50,000 to 500,000 kilometers, made it clear that the ship was definitely advancing into the environs of the Belt.

Rittener sat mostly silently watching space hurtle past on the screens for close to half an hour, only querying the ship's amanuensis to decide how much velocity to squander, and how subtle maneuvers would affect the direction from which *Peerless* should make her final approaches to Valerian-3.

"Lieutenant Andrews, make your speed . . . " Rittener never finished giving the order.

A HORRIFYING ALARM SOUNDED in every quarter of the ship. It was accompanied with the simultaneous locking of every hatch on board. No crewman had ever heard this alarm before; few crews ever heard it twice. Rittener reacted instantly, screaming a pre-programmed protocol at the ship's amanuensis, "Evasive critical!"

Peerless' amanuensis hadn't waited for the captain's voice command. It had already judged the situation hyper-critical; Rittener had only called out the words in a moment of understandable human nervousness. A nanosecond later the ship's fusion reactor exploded into action. The autopilot used that power to throw the ship into an unbearable, hairpin, corkscrew course that slammed any crewman standing to the deck. They had a brief second or two to frantically attempt to connect their safety belts to something before everyone on board passed out. The best g-suits in existence were automatically deployed on each crewman or else death would most certainly have quickly ensued. As it was, though, even under the best circumstances, the crew wouldn't escape unscathed. Those crewmen unsecured, pinned unconscious to the deck by crushing g forces, now a half second later were squeezed against the starboard hull, subsequently slapped flattened against the deck above, then dragged along that surface toward the port hull by forces that shifted too quickly and too powerfully for human endurance. The *Peerless* though was less concerned for her human passengers; she was saving herself.

THERE WERE STILL WAYS to bring down a man of war. The never-ending *pas de deux* between offense and defense bizarrely left only the more primitive stratagems—methods used more or less by slingers in the first armies ever fielded in the Fertile Crescent in the third millennium BC, or the cold-blooded, cock-sure fighter pilots of the 20th century's World Wars. Every warship was clad in a thin outer sheet of moly-serilium. It was tough, durable, and reflected laser beams better than mirrors on communications and navigation satellites. Turning a laser on *Peerless* would be an incomprehensible waste of power.

Particle bursts would be just as fruitless. All ships, warships or otherwise, flew with a tightly woven magnetic shield around the hull—proof against solar storms. Military class shields were certainly capable of handling focused bursts exponentially more powerful. One could still punch *Peerless* though, physically. Nothing prevented that. One way would be to send a scattering, buckshot blast of high-velocity projectiles into her path. Another would be to detonate a tactical nuke in her vicinity. The defenders of Valerian-3 had opted for both. They'd weaponized a commercial ore cargo cannon on one of the nearby asteroids *Peerless* was passing on her starboard side. It was designed to hurl shipments of metal to the Earth system, and now had been adapted to fire thousands of chunks of titanium, just like a planetesimal-sized shotgun would.

Peerless' amanuensis could have targeted some of the largest projectiles and blasted them with her particle beam and laser. All that would have accomplished would be to turn the deadly swarm of thousands of killer projectiles into hundreds of thousands of molten globs that would have burned through her hull anyway when they struck. Instead the amanuensis obeyed Rittener's prescribed orders and directed the autopilot to take the random corkscrew path programmed—even though it calculated that this trajectory assured moderate damage. A stream of football-sized projectiles tore into the port side shuttle pod bay, thankfully at a very oblique angle. A few seconds later, stressed beyond tolerances, a section of the hull simply gave way and was flung by the centrifugal force into space. Everything in the shuttle bay bled into the vacuum; that included all the oxygen and nitrogen, the broken and loose implements within, and the bodies of Seaman Berti Werth and Chief Warrant Officer Kendrick.

Two seconds later the tactical nuke went off. It was nestled deep within another seemingly nondescript piece of space debris on *Peerless'* port side, a chunk riddled with uranium to disguise the bomb's presence. Peerless should have been making toward this trap should she have taken the most appropriate evasive action. Fortunately, her random zigzag flight was taking her away from the epicenter of the blast when it exploded. The ship was protected by her radiation shield from the blistering electromagnetic fury of the blast, but a bit closer and her molyserilium coat at least would have been melted. By sheer luck she careened past the ambush in one piece—but wounded, trailing gas and jetsam from the gash in her hull.

A FEW HOURS LATER, this angry, bloodied bird of prey wheeled into cotangential orbit around the Sun, a safe distance behind Valerian-3. Her port side shuttle bay had been jettisoned. Like all warships, *Peerless* was compartmentalized, and a fresh exterior hull now presented itself where the shuttle bay had been, a second, previously interior, gleaming molyserilium laser barrier taking the place of the one blown into space. She was built to take blows like she'd received without diminishing in the least her power to continue on. The only sign of what she'd been through was the fact that she flew now with only one asymmetric shuttle bay, the one on her starboard side. The enemy had no idea what the human damage had been, but there were serious casualties. Aside from Kendrick and Werth, another crewman had been killed and two others, including the ship's physician, seriously injured in the evasive action.

The image on *Peerless'* communication board was more or less expected. Even so, the bald, grizzled aspect of the man, with an absurdly wild and unkempt red beard, dressed in 15th century Scottish attire, and wearing the most bellicose expression, was enough to cause Yeshenko to mutter under his breath.

"Oh, man, what a sight!"

With only seven crewmen fit for active duty left, all able hands were strapped in on the bridge in the interior of the ship. Yeshenko was understandably furious at the death of his friend, and spoke loud enough for everyone—including the Valerian—to hear. Rittener flashed him a look that said that Yeshenko's failure still to govern his tongue might cost him more than the three days of Hell he'd recently endured. When Rittener turned back to face the screen his expression was quite different. He addressed the man in purely diplomatic tones, without mentioning a word about the attack and his losses.

"This is Clinton Rittener speaking, commander of the man of war, *Peerless.*"

The ship's amanuensis had facially recognized the Valerian on the screen. It wasn't the outpost's chief, William Byrne, it was another clansman, one Patrick McTaggart. His bio and vitals were being scrolled next to his image.

"Mr. McTaggart, whatever business the chief is attending to, I can assure you, this matter takes precedence. Where is William Byrne?" Rittener demanded to know.

"He's dead," McTaggart answered in a thick brogue. "You'll be parleying with me," he said bluntly.

Rittener responded bluntly too. "I didn't come halfway across the Solar System for a parley, McTaggart." Rittener cared very little about the obviously recent demise of the previous chief. If Byrne was dead, so were three of his own crew.

"I hold a valid privateering marque from the Terran Archonate, and am here to enforce the terms of the Pallas Commercial Agreement. The boycott in which Valerian-3 is taking part has been declared illegal, and due to the strategic nature of the goods embargoed, a casus belli. Regular shipments are to resume—immediately." He paused for emphasis. "Be advised, *Peerless will* use whatever force is required to effect those orders."

The Valerians were a strange bunch, yet every mining outpost had its particularly peculiar culture. Living on the fringes of civilization, settlements had always attracted the defeated, the footloose, the non-conformists of society. This wasn't Terra or Borealis or even Mars. This was the frontier, the next place where humanity was remaking itself, in serene and morose darkness, far from the heat and light of the Sun. The intrepid traveler could come upon anything in the Asteroid Belt—from purely female Amazonian settlements, to outposts run by every and any of the bizarre cults in existence, governed as democracies, fiefdoms, theocracies, and anything else. Valerian-3 had been founded by Scottish refugees. They had gone back to the old ways, or rather, the "auld" ways. They themselves preferred "clansman."

Valerian's auldies had carved a home for themselves—literally. The founders had bored into the core of the asteroid and set it spinning on a proper axis for artificial gravity. Year by year, as the population grew and mined, so did the void inside Valerian, the "floor" inching ever closer to the exterior of the asteroid. Someday, and rather soon actually, the miners' industriousness would seal the fate of their home. It was being taken apart, piece by piece, and shipped to all ports-of-calls in the Solar System.

Three thousand miners hunkered within the hole they'd made in the heart of Valerian, protected from the pitiless, sunless vacuum outside by the titanium exterior shells they'd yet to have bitten into, and carefully blowing on the embers of life they'd managed to keep burning within through fusion reactors fed by helium-3. Captured icebergs and frozen volatiles which glided past from time to time provided the clansmen with the rest of their needs. Valerian was impressive as a living museum of what humans could accomplish, even at these astounding distances from Sol. Every erg of energy though had gone toward establishing a bare, hard-scrabble existence. Valerian's only shield was the thinned walls of the asteroid itself, a barrier hardly suffi-cient to defy *Peerless'* weaponry.

McTaggart ignored the ultimatum. "If ye have come that far, a thought or two along the way must have been given to the fact that more than half the population here is women and bairns. Do you intend to open fire like a villainous demon, or are we to exchange a few words first?"

Rittener let out a half-exasperated sigh. "Say your piece, McTaggart."

The clansman explained Valerian's plight succinctly, even though at times difficult to follow owing to his use of terms from Earth's Middle Ages. Terra was putting Valerian between "the devil himself and the deep blue sea." She could barely afford the requisite helium-3 to keep the place running, much less churn out titanium for export. Cutting the price for Valerian's exports in half spelled the end—plain and simple.

"How would piling on such burdens to crush Valerian serve Terra's interests? Would the Archonate cut off its own nose to spite its face?"

Rittener listened politely. It all was true, and yet irrelevant.

"I'm not a plenipotentiary. I have no power whatsoever to conclude new treaties nor amend old ones, so I'm afraid that path is closed. Your future problems will have to take care of themselves. Right now I need to see shipments to Terra resumed—immediately." Then Rittener added in a graver tone, "And, just as importantly, I'm sure the Archonate is going to require some assurance that your embargo won't take up again as we move out of your orbit. You're going to have to satisfy me of that, McTaggart."

The Scotsman stared blankly from the screen, then in a bitter tone answered.

"We do nae want conflict with Terra nor anyone else. We simply wish to be left alone. It's peace we want, not war, nor anything else."

If Valerian-3 had wanted peace, Rittener thought, it should have prepared for war. That's what he told McTaggart and repeated it in the Latin it came in: "Si vis pacem, para bellum." This belated, pedantic advice got the highlander's blood up.

"Solitudinem faciunt, pacem appellant," the Scotsman retorted quite unexpectedly, saying the words as one would utter a curse. His lingo obviously went a bit further back than the 15th century. "That's what my ancestors told the Romans when they came bearing the same fiats you've just issued. You'd make an empty desert of Valerian, and then call it peace. Your peace is slavery to Terra, a peace found in graveyards, nothing more. That sort of peace can't last, and never has."

Clinton Rittener only responded with a clear warning. "You have six hours."

McTaggart had an undisguised mixture of hatred, dejection, defeat, and—most importantly—stoic acceptance on his face. Rittener could see it clearly. Valerian-3 had no choice; it had never had any real option other than submission.

"You'll have my answer shortly," McTaggart said nonetheless, as if any council on Valerian could change the obvious facts.

"Six hours," Rittener repeated grimly.

BY THE EVENING WATCH'S third bell a shipment from Valerian-3 had been fired into space. It scanned good, almost pure titanium, and on a trajectory to intersect Earth and the Terran Ring. A weight lifted from Rittener's shoulders and he now saw to a number of things that the prior emergency precluded. Near the top of the list was Seaman 3rd Class Ibrahim Hadad's body. Muslim tradition required burial within twenty-four hours. With the crew thinned by casualties, and in such close proximity to a hostile target, no other crewmen could be spared for the ceremony. Rittener saw to it himself, enshrouding the body, saying the Arabic janazah for no one but Hadad, and crisply saluting in front of nobody, as he jettisoned the seaman into space. He'd almost memorized the prayer, having recited it for so many fallen cohorts from Jakarta to the Gulf of Aqaba. It might have been a most trifling funeral, but it was all the more dignified, for Rittener upheld to the letter everything to which his dead comrade in arms was entitled, with not a soul to witness the event one way or the other.

A few hours later a second cargo capsule was jettisoned to Terra. A simple, terse message was simultaneously beamed to the *Peerless* from Valerian-3. It was just a few seconds of audio. "Valerian-3 will abide fully with all the provisions of the Pallas Commercial Agreement. Our embargo against the Terran Ring is lifted, and will not be renewed. Valerian-3 deeply regrets any prior hostilities, and will take no further part, with any other party, in any conflict against the Terran Ring." This was heartening, really the best to be hoped for. Rittener was on empty and needed sleep. He would have liked nothing more than to drag himself to his quarters and buckle himself into his bunk. As it was he gave orders to open fire immediately on anything that moved that wasn't titanium fired toward Earth and then simply donned the sleep casquette. He was out like a light, and after sleeping for a couple of blissful hours, was awakened. Ensign Gutierrez was shaking him.

"I'm really sorry, sir," she said. "But there's a level one missive from Terra for you. You'll have to take it in your quarters." *Peerless'* amanuensis couldn't deliver these encrypted messages anywhere else but in the captain's private station.

"You've been asleep two hours and ten minutes," she told him. "There's nothing to report except the transmission."

Rittener threw off the grogginess as quickly as he could, rubbing his real eye and doing the math in his head. There was a light lag of half an hour between the Ring and here. So Terra hadn't ruminated very long on the latest information streaming automatically back to her, that of the surrender of Valerian-3. As he closed the hatch which sealed him in his quarters and asked the amanuensis for his orders, he was still pondering what the swiftness meant.

"This is 'word of mouth,'" the amanuensis, who ironically had no mouth, cautioned him. That was the Terran Ring's highest secrecy protocol. The record was being scrubbed and erased even as they spoke. The amanuensis went through the standard warning routine, with Rittener responding a brusque "acknowledged" at each of the requisite junctures. Then it gave Rittener his orders.

"*Peerless* is to aerate Valerian-3. Care is to be taken, though, to leave the outpost intact. Destruction to the infrastructure is to be avoided as best as possible. Valerian-3 though should be rendered inhabitable. Hostile intentions on the part of Valerian-3 still present a clear and present danger to the interests of the Terran Ring, and her population is declared traitors and mutineers."

The unfeeling, inhuman, electronic messenger attempted nonetheless to assuage these bitterest of orders with a supposed empathy it couldn't begin to fathom. "The Archonate sincerely regrets such stern actions, but owing to circumstances of which *Peerless* is unaware, and in keeping the ship's safety and the completion of her mission as the two utmost important factors, such severe directives as those ordered are most definitely required."

Clinton Rittener didn't flinch or blink an eye, real or biosynthetic. "Acknowledged," he said, and not another word. When the amanuensis asked if he'd like the orders repeated he declined.

"Negative." He paused for the briefest of moments and then gave the amanuensis a terse order. "Have Seaman Yeshenko report to my quarters immediately."

WAITING FOR YESHENKO TO arrive, Rittener's thoughts turned over a great number of weighty matters, things he'd been thinking about for some time now. He set his jaw and grit his teeth, chewing the fact that three thousand Valerians had no say whatsoever in whether they were to take their next breath or not. This was not the first time he'd be required to send whole populations to their deaths. As daunting and terrible as the task in front of him was, he made up his mind very quickly in the end. It turned out to be much easier than he had ever imagined.

FOUR AND A HALF seconds after entering Rittener's quarters, Yeshenko was dead, the life ripped from him even before the body hit the deck. Rittener's hands weren't up to the task of tackling *Peerless'* amanuensis, but the shoulder-fired laser he strapped on from his security cabinet was. He made straight for the bridge and melted it in three successive blasts that sent the stunned and horrified crew ducking for cover against the molten slag into which it was converted. When everything shut down save vital functions and a cool green light bathed the now vacant space where virtual consoles had been, Rittener was sure *Peerless'* amanuensis had joined Yeshenko as the second victim in this mutiny. He addressed his shocked and huddled crew quite diplomatically.

"Engage emergency back-up control for all systems—all systems that can still respond anyway."

Just to let the crew know that he was still sane and had no intention of killing them most likely, he now grinned most incongruously, quite amicably even.

"We'll be flying bare-back from here on out," he said.

CHAPTER FIVE

HALO OF STEEL

SHORTLY BEFORE THE REVOLT on the Asteroid Belt broke out, Sadhana Ramanujan wasn't exactly *persona non grata* with the Terran Archonate, but neither was she invited to many of their holiday celebrations. Her views were too liberal and her mouth a little too open. But she was a descendant of *that* Ramanujan, which her father had never let her forget. And she *had* lived up to her illustrious Indian ancestor—Srinivasa Ramanujan, one of the great mathematical savants of the 20th century. Her ancestor was a genius who not only mastered higher mathematics as a child, but who was discovering new trigonometric theorems—by the age of twelve. Sadhana meant "long practiced." With her father pushing relentlessly from a young age and the string of important postulates she'd discovered herself, she couldn't have been more aptly named. Her breakthrough innovation of increasing the nanoscale cooling effect in graphene chips (only one atom thick!) catapulted nanocomputing into the next level and beyond. Heat had been the biggest obstacle in performance, a barrier which she hurdled in front of the astounded and grateful hundreds of billions from Earth to Titan. Sadhana Ramanujan had doubled the speed of the

System at a stroke, changing history. It would be difficult to say then whether the Terran Archonate or Sadhana Ramanujan were honored more by the request the Archonate sent her, or by Ramanujan's decision to drop everything and comply.

She'd been here before, of course. Standing in the foyer in front of the Archonate's massive portal, the same feeling as before came over her. It was meant to impress anyone with a pair of eyes and it rarely disappointed. Sadhana saw something else though in the outlandishly oversize set of solid steel doors. They reminded her of the images of the Second World War she'd seen, of the massive 20-foot-high mahogany and marble doors to the Fuhrer's private office. There was little subtlety in Terran architecture. Beyond this threshold lay the greatest single power in the known universe.

She was met by the highest ranking staffer of the Archonate, none other than Ethan Van Ulroy, and two security officers, all smiling and exchanging greetings, while forming a protective cocoon around her and whisking her through a beehive of activity. The Archonate was cavernous—the biggest single office space on the Ring. It went from Ground all the way up to the Exterior Decks, occupying an arc that stretched for miles. Her party commandeered an entire shuttle and was gently whisked toward the epicenter of the thousands of offices that kept the Terran Ring spinning. Every aspect on Terra—food, water, health, safety, security, economy, education, justice, diplomacy—everything was decided here. Keeping a metal ring that weighed as much as a decent fraction of the Moon in orbit around the Earth, while its massive sections themselves spun transversely for artificial gravity, with five billion passengers aboard, required a bit of maintenance from time to time. The Archonate did nothing else.

Sadhana was in her early sixties, a very pleasant-looking woman with long dark hair streaked with grey. She wore it in a bun, under a silk sari used as a veil and then tucked around as a shoulder scarf. Here was a grand dame that nonetheless wore such an earthy and convivial face that its authenticity had to be genuine. She took a close look at the young man in charge of escorting her. They'd met before and although she disagreed with his politics, she, like almost everyone else on Terra, couldn't help but like him.

Ethan Van Ulroy, only in his mid-thirties, his name soon to be infamously linked to the Belt's uprising, was the aide-de-camp of the Chief Archon himself, Dante Michelson. No matter how harshly the miners were to judge him, he possessed a sharp mind, a quick wit, and offered sage advice unusual for a man his age. His high position was enough to mark him as the most eligible bachelor on Terra. Sadhana half smiled pensively, contemplating the irony of two people so unlike in so many ways and yet both of them meeting at the request of the most powerful man alive. While she was short, a bit rotund, and far past her prime, he was tall, as lean and hard as dried jerky, and just entering the peak of his powers. His thick auburn hair was combed to the side and was flawlessly coiffed. He wore a thicker leotard, one that modestly diverted attention from his admirable physique and emblazoned with just the proper amount of distinctive marks of his rank without being brassy. The real difference between them though, was that Van Ulroy, aide to the militantly hawkish Archon, was playing host to the leader of Terran's doves.

THE TECHNOLOGY OF ATTACK and defense between Terra and Borealis over the centuries had closely reflected each cutting-edge breakthrough in science. The two states had never come to blows, but tension between them was the never-ending impetus for developing attacks against which there could be no defense, and barriers which would render any assault powerless. In the early days Terra worried that Luna had the "high ground," just as Earth said about Terra. What if Borealis were to send a chunk of the Moon crashing down on the Ring? This, of course, was nonsense, as all military analysts pointed out. Even Terra's archaic lasers in Settlement Times would have made short work of such primitive tactics, and now even if Borealis were to catapult the Sea of Tranquility at Terra, it would never make it over the walls.

Thankfully the reverse held for Borealis. Terra's ferocious lasers couldn't actually touch Borealis, the city tucked below the lunar horizon at the North Pole, situated at a blessed angle outside the range of Terra's photonic guns. Warships though could, and did, patrol vast sectors of the Solar System and it would be a simple matter for a Terran man of war to take a position with a clear shot at the city. One blast at Borealis' Dome would be devastating, ending any potential war in a millisecond. Borealis worked feverishly, and with supreme secrecy, to counter this peril, and the result changed the military calculus between the two sides: defense now reigned supreme.

BOREALIS' GRAVITONIC FORCE SHIELD bent the fabric of space, forming a cupola of discontinuities in space-time. It was best visualized by imagining space itself as water on the surface of a tranquil pond, with the force field as a ripple around Borealis that held at a steady distance. Matter passing through this barrier would be so violently scrambled at the subatomic level as to cause instant disintegration. Electromagnetic waves themselves—lasers or even benign radio—would also be diffused and scattered to the extent that beamed weapons were rendered useless and radio communication impossible. Sunlight too was scattered, and that was the reason Borealis gave out publicly for the creation of the Shield. It was touted as the next great step forward in Borealis' never-ending battle to tame the Sun, even though the truth was that it neither helped nor hindered the final efficiency of the Goldilocks Array.

As for the higher-energy ranges of light—from X-ray to gamma—they were absorbed into the shield itself, so a thermonuclear device detonated above it would only serve to help power it. Corridors in the shield were temporarily created as it was deftly turned on and off at selected localized coordinates so that shipments of helium-3 could be exported, and to allow in shuttles that had been scanned and deemed free of any potential threat to Borealis. Even communications had to be funneled through ever-changing millisecond-long apertures in the shield, after being relayed from Gatekeeper satellites that orbited the Moon. Terra, of course, immediately realized the shield's true purpose; they'd been working on the same technology themselves.

THE TERRAN RING ALSO had a gravitonic shield, but it needed to warp the astounding volume of space around the massive Ring and an incredible amount of energy was needed to accomplish that. An area on the Ring the size of Manhattan Island was devoted to creating and maintaining the Terran shield. It was never deployed though—as the peace party on Terra never stopped pointing out. This white elephant was the focus of a great political debate raging on Terra. First, how could such a monstrosity as this ever have been built when it sucked up more helium-3 then the Terrans could afford to feed it, especially *now* that the reserves were running very, very short? Secondly, was this not the best proof that the never-ending saber-rattling would end badly—for Terra and everyone in the Solar System? When would the simple, sane, mutually beneficial expedient of peaceful coexistence and cooperation take hold in the minds of the Terran Archonate—and if ever, would it be in time?

The hawks on Terra had good answers. The shield was a back-up, that's all, and one that most probably wouldn't ever be necessary. They quite rightly pointed out that Earth below, in the end, even in the hands of the maniacs that supposedly ran the planet, realized that they had no option but to live with what Terra dictated. What alternative had they? Even if they could, even in worst-case scenarios, everyone on Earth knew what bringing down the Terran Ring would mean. For "bringing down" meant just that. Terra crashing to Earth would make the end of the dinosaurs at the K/T boundary sixty-five million years ago seem like a hiccup in the planet's history. As for attacks from other quarters, the Ring was massive enough to take incredible blows from Borealis or anyone else while barely flinching. If such madness ever were to take place, the shield could be deployed before any irreparable damage was done. So the Terrans built their shield—and, incredibly, never switched it on.

For the hawks, the shield meant something else though—something which churned a visceral anger in them. It was one thing to have to compromise with the couple hundred billion remnants of Earth's population beneath them. To have policies dictated to Terra by the insignificant mosquito bite festering on the Moon's North Pole, imperiously delivered by a couple hundred thousand of the most arrogant humans alive, was quite another. There would be a reckoning in store for these overconfident egotists, and it couldn't be far on the horizon. Challenging the Terran Ring was going to turn out to be the last chapter in Borelian history. They said as much openly, and they meant it categorically.

While the shuttle whirred along smoothly, the initial pleasantries faded and were replaced by an uncomfortable silence.

Sadhana was not without her social graces but was actually somewhat shy. Conversation, though, rarely flagged in Van Ulroy's presence and he immediately saw to the discomfiture.

"By the way, you're absolutely right, Doctor. 1729 is quite an interesting number after all."

Sadhana's face brightened. He'd said the right thing—as usual. "I asked my amanuensis about it. Amazing story," he said.

"But that was almost two years ago," Sadhana remarked, her eyes widened by his sharp memory.

Van Ulroy smiled sheepishly. "Well, I looked again this morning." He shook his head disparagingly. "I hope it's not age creeping up. I just don't remember things like I used to," he admitted.

Sadhana had seen Van Ulroy's amanuensis a few times. She remembered asking herself what his choice implied. There were a few ways to look at it. He'd opted for Alcibiades, the exemplar Athenian bad boy. The last time they'd met, at an award ceremony for Sadhana presided over by Dante Michelson himself, Van Ulroy had asked Alcibiades what the reference to 1729 had meant.

Alcibiades pointed an omniscient finger and clicked open a virtual board from the early 1900s. Srinivasa Ramanujan was lying in bed in a London hospital room. The surroundings were quite Spartan and morose. Ramanujan was a young man, just thirty-two, but dying of tuberculosis. G. H. Hardy, the eminent British mathematician and Ramanujan's great friend, entered the room. A strained conversation ensued between the two, Hardy clearly at a loss for words seeing Ramanujan slowly expiring in front of his eyes.

"You know," Hardy said, trying to make chitchat, "I noticed the cab that brought me here was number 1729. I got to thinking and strangely started brooding about the amazingly nondescript and random nature of that number. Isn't it odd that some numbers aren't interesting in the least?" One could tell Hardy was only trying to fill the silence, but Ramanujan's reply was startling. Without the slightest pause the great savant gave a surprising rebuttal.

"Not at all, Hardy. Not at all. 1729 is the lowest integer which can be expressed as the sum of two cubed numbers, two different ways: 1 cubed plus 12 cubed equals 1729 and so does 9 cubed plus 10 cubed."

The expression on the virtual Hardy's face said that he wasn't just awe-struck that his comrade could do such calculations in his head, but that he could have seen the algorithm in his mind in the first place, and all within the space of a few seconds, seemed simply beyond the capacity of any human being.

"So you see, it's quite a unique number after all," the dying Ramanujan said.

TERRANS WERE PARTICULARLY ADDICTED to the use of their amanuenses and hardly ever closed them down. Psychologists proclaimed the more extreme cases a form of mental illness, and rightly so. There were many cases of people falling in love with their amanuensis, or whose best friend was virtual, or who refused to take a breath or step in life without their counsel, or who battled an amanuensis that was "out to get them." There were five billion people on the Terran Ring, but ten billion entities counting both human and virtual. Here was a closer mechanical bond than many humans shared with other individuals. According to many experts in ethics, this was far past the beginning of the end. No matter who preached what though, nothing could get people to turn their amanuenses off.

Truly alarming though was what *else* they could read about the people in the wearer's vicinity, and the dramatic changes this caused in society. An amanuensis could also scan the blood pressure, perspiration levels, and changes in voice patterns that indicated stress—or deception—of anyone within effective range. This played havoc with every aspect of human interaction in society, because the great shock was that there was very little that people did that was free of deception.

To dare to interact in public without one's amanuensis on "block" was inconceivable. Aside from having one's veracity verified at every step, one's identity, health status, state of sexual arousal, and many other personal secrets were open to anyone with the desire to scan them. Only excepting the saintly with nothing to hide, or the scandalous with nothing left to expose, the rest of humanity went about its business with their amanuenses most assuredly blinking red on block.

THE SHUTTLE SLOWED TO a stop and without saying a word the security officers exited. Simultaneously a leather-faced man in his mid-forties entered. He had an Earth tan, a deep one. The dark brown brow was framed by jet black hair combed back over the shoulders and falling almost to his belt. And, just as if stepping out of a time capsule of some sort, he *was* wearing a belt, and trousers too. They were denim; as a materials specialist, Sadhana knew the antique fabric. Around his neck was clasped a silver and turquoise choker. To say this fellow was dressed "old style" was an understatement. If he had been wearing a cape he wouldn't have looked any stranger. Sadhana recognized him immediately, but then anyone would have. Nonetheless, Van Ulroy made the introductions.

Roland Lighthorse was one of the last full-blooded Creek Indians alive. He was a prolific writer—everything from philosophy and history to anthropology and linguistics. He was known though for one audacious theory that he'd proposed that put him clearly and irretrievably outside the mainstream. His interpretations of the Pre-Mayan glyphs discovered in the

Yucatan Peninsula superseded everything he'd published, and then some. Those postulations had catapulted him into the realm of one of the most famous kooks in existence.

Lighthorse had ruined quite a promising career. He studied under the very archaeologists who'd uncovered the stelae and scrolls in their youths, and who even now in old age were locked in strident academic disputes about this translation and that one. Still no one could read all the inscriptions and about the only thing agreed on by all was that they were very, very old. The ancient folios had changed, nonetheless, the very foundation of human pre-history, and few doubted that they didn't contain a few bombshells. Lighthorse's hypothesis though was simply a bridge too far.

When a thorough ground-penetrating radar survey of the mounds around the Yucatan indicated that they were anything but hills, the scientific community had gone wild with enthusiasm. Half a dozen pyramids were unearthed and a treasure trove of thousands of inscriptions and codices came with them. Immediately, though, the firestorm exploded. These weren't Maya glyphs, or Zapotec, or Olmec, or anything else known. What was uncovered were the remains of a civilization far, far older, and completely unknown heretofore. Many names had been proposed for the lost people but even a common name couldn't be agreed upon. The culture was simply called "Pre-Mayan," and it was confidently dated sometime around . . . 12,000 BC.

What was surprising about this sea change in human history was how quickly it was accepted. The Fertile Crescent lost its preeminent position as the cradle of civilization. After the initial astonishment wore off, everyone just seemed to shrug their collective shoulders and gave in to the idea that Earth was home to a great civilization—thousands of years before the date previously held as the birth of agriculture itself.

Lighthorse had spent the best part of his adult life struggling to decipher the true meaning of the glyphs. By painstakingly juxtaposing them, symbol by symbol, with later Mesoamerican script, he'd made quite a number of glottochronological breakthroughs—many of them accepted as absolutely accurate. The tenor of what the codices said though, in the main, was where his colleagues took exception—vigorous exception.

"The narrative, almost all of it, is a chronicle of our ancestors' interaction with a race of incredibly advanced visitors," Lighthorse told assemblages of Mayanists and archaeologists. Pained silence and blank stares allowed him to continue at length. Lighthorse connected the pieces of this exceedingly arcane puzzle with brilliant insights, and everything indeed did seem to fit. As the years passed though, the restrained applause dampened to smatterings of sarcastic, perfunctory clapping that only called attention to the prevailing disdainful hush with which most specialists responded. And that later was replaced by catcalls and snickers.

"All discoverers have had to overcome similar obstacles," Lighthorse told the press. "Some were burnt at the stake, others simply booed off the podiums. In the end though, my interpretation is the correct one and history will prove it." Lighthorse's colleagues hadn't come for him with pitchforks and torches but neither was he invited to any more of their seminars. Sadhana wondered what in the world he was doing . . . *here?*

Sadhana politely took his outstretched hand. "It's a great honor to meet you," Lighthorse said.

"Roland Lighthorse is . . . " Van Ulroy began.

She cut him off. "I'm aware of who Mr. Lighthorse is."

She didn't say it with derision—more just matter of fact. But now she gave Van Ulroy a look that he took as petulant;

she meant it that way too. Her request to meet with "a representative of the Terran Archonate" concerning a subject "of great importance" and directing her to discuss the matter "with absolutely no party whatsoever" was a missive she'd never received before. That the representative turned out to be the aide-de-camp of the Chief Archon—"first among equals" of the nine men who ruled Terra—was sufficient to cause a case of rattled nerves. Seeing that Roland Lighthorse was also involved was enough to push her beyond coy politeness and to demand some clear-cut answers.

"What's this all about, Mr. Van Ulroy?" she blurted out.

The shuttle reacted instantly to Van Ulroy's voice command, "Stop." Now Sadhana was passed rattled nerves. Countless hyper-secret conferences were supposed to have taken place on shuttles in transit between offices in the Terran Archonate. She knew better than anyone why. A new generation of splicers was making a serious come-back. Splicing had its roots in admirable motives—originally at least. It was a technique for people under scrutiny—activists, politicos, intellectuals—to interact surreptitiously, completely unseen and unheard by the System. Suspended in the middle of a cavernous volume, with massive metal bulwarks, miles of conduit, and millions of semiconductors and electrical apparatuses all kept at the furthest distance possible, this was where one stood the best chance to protect a secret. Sadhana, of whom it could be said knew a few things about electronics, and no friend of the current administration on the Ring, had pulled off a few splices in her time. She knew exactly why they halted here.

"You must have something very important to say to me, Mr. Van Ulroy."

Van Ulroy changed visibly, instantly. He no longer wore the charming diplomatic face of a business-like bureaucracy but now made clear he represented a deadly serious, unlimitedly powerful entity whose self-interest would be maintained even if the Sun itself ceased shining. He now spoke to her in a far different tone; the law required it.

"As per Terran sedition and security codes, I must inform you, Dr. Ramanujan, that the information with which you are to be provided is of the utmost sensitive nature, within the confines of the highest level of classification, and may be shared with no one—in any way, shape, or form." He paused for the words to sink in. Her puzzled look told him they hadn't.

"But, I've been through all this, Mr. Van Ulroy," her voice slightly piqued. "I've had the highest security clearance, for many, many years now."

Van Ulroy was shaking his head in the negative. "This is strictly 'word of mouth.' Do you understand what that means?"

Of course she couldn't understand it, since only a handful of people on Terra even knew of such a security classification.

"This matter isn't in the System; it doesn't exist. Incredible measures have been taken to accomplish that. Even any allusion or implied acknowledgment of what you're going to be told—to anyone, by any means—will be considered a breach of the oath you're going to be required to take and will carry the most severe penalties for transgression."

He paused and furrowed his brow. "Let me rephrase. It doesn't carry the most severe penalties—it *mandates* them. Before I go on I'll have to ask you for your oath again."

Sadhana Ramanujan swore again, and this time the words were even heavier and more somber. It was more humbling this time. For all her status she was being made aware that she—like any Terran—was nothing more than a cog in a giant machine. She might be a famous and brilliant gear, but a mere cog nonetheless, and one that could and *would* be disengaged and tossed away should it cause any damage.

"Well, that's always a bit unpleasant," Van Ulroy said afterwards, smiling again. "Good to put that behind us."

Sadhana declined to agree and asked flatly again, "So what's this all about?"

He motioned to Roland Lighthorse. "Mr. Lighthorse's presence here must certainly give you some idea of the matter at hand?" It did but she indicated otherwise, slightly shrugging her shoulders and shaking her head. Van Ulroy was quite disposed to answer her now, actually rubbing his palms together anxiously.

"Well, Doctor, where to begin?" He paused for the right words. "Your input is requested on a project that is important enough to quite plausibly change the calendar. I'm guessing future historians are going to categorize every epoch from before and after this event." Sadhana could tell he hadn't fished for words; he'd obviously planned this speech. "We'd like you to simply take a look at an incredible item, and just, well... just tell us anything you can about it."

Sadhana frowned. "Just anything I can tell you about it, is that it?"

Van Ulroy was shaking his head in agreement. "Yes."

Lighthorse helped out. "It's an artifact, Dr. Ramanujan." His voice was deep and mellifluous. He spoke slowly, enunciating perfectly. "An artifact."

"What sort of artifact?" she asked bluntly.

"From the Yucatan," Lighthorse answered just as bluntly.

In an instant everything became clear as glass, even though at the same time hardly possible.

"The Bacalar Device?! Is that what we're talking about?"

Legends and rumors about an artifact found in a pyramid under a hill near the town of Bacalar in the Yucatan had surfaced, been quashed, and resurfaced again. Sadhana, like everyone else, put the device in the same category as unicorns.

It took her a while to form her next sentence. It barely qualified as a sentence.

"It exists?"

"It not only exists," Van Ulroy declared, "but it's in our possession and you'll be examining it shortly." Now he was smiling from ear to ear. "Exciting, no?"

Sadhana wasn't smiling yet. She thought carefully, for quite a while, as she composed her next question. The two men sat quietly as she formulated it.

"Yes, very exciting. However you've skipped a few steps. How did such an artifact come into our possession, from the Yucatan on Earth? And why isn't this common knowledge?"

Van Ulroy was a good judge of character and had already decided that in Dr. Ramanujan's case he would have to be more forthcoming than was his custom. He gave her part of the truth.

"It's a convoluted tale, Doctor, and I'm not sure about all the particulars myself. But it's amazing how closely the story mirrors other Mesoamerican finds in the past—the Dresden Codex, for example."

Lighthorse could see she missed the analogy so he explained. "The Dresden Codex was one of only four books left of the Maya's writings after the Spanish conquistadors finished their auto-da-fé of the 16th century. This plucky manuscript, having survived the fires of the Inquisition, wound up under the boot of a Russian major poking around the smoldering ruins of the State Library in Dresden, Germany, during the Second World War—from which it *also* escaped.

"Warfare, Doctor," Van Ulroy philosophized, "it closes doors, yes, but always opens others. The Western Alliance had the device since its discovery but kept it secretly in the Mexico City State. The Great Planetary War brought such chaos that in the tumult it bounced around the planet, like the

Dresden Codex had, until thankfully, it wound up safe here on the Terran Ring."

Now the doctor was even more confused. "But, the Mexico City State was . . . completely destroyed . . . "

"Oh no, Dr. Ramanujan," Van Ulroy almost chuckled at the misunderstanding. "The *Second* Planetary War, not the Third, thank goodness. Or else there'd be no device probably, would there?"

Tittering about the horrific fate of Mexico sent a quick pang of irritation through her and pushed her mind into high gear. Her next question came fast.

"But that was half a century ago, Mr. Van Ulroy. Terra has had this artifact in her possession since then, is that the case?"

"Forty years, Doctor," he corrected her, and he wasn't smiling in the least now.

Sadhana's mouth turned down. "Not very forthcoming of us, you'd agree?"

Van Ulroy didn't like that very much. "I wouldn't know about that. I wasn't even born when that decision was made," he snapped back.

Now Sadhana took a deep breath, and slowly exhaled through pursed lips. She was looking at neither man, simply thinking deeply for a moment. Then she let loose.

"Mr. Van Ulroy, you quite properly set the ground rules for me, and now I'm going to set them for you. If the Terran Archonate requires my expertise about some important matter—now I see having to do with the Bacalar Device—I'll be happy to do my civic duty. If, however, it's your intention to start things off with a pack of half-truths that quite possibly will make my job more difficult, whatever that job is, in that case I'd simply have to respectfully decline and just be on my way."

Van Ulroy was shocked, Lighthorse amused. She was sure of that because he was chuckling to himself. She went on, making the ultimatum plain.

"I'd love to examine first hand such a rare object. But we'll work openly and honestly with each other, or you'll find someone else. Is that acceptable to you?"

Van Ulroy bit his lip and nodded, not signaling yes or no, but at least acknowledging her words. "I'm not at liberty to explain how Terra acquired the device, Doctor," he admitted in a defeated tone.

"Excellent!" Sadhana exclaimed. "Now, let's see if we can keep that up, shall we?"

She put her finger up, as if to say that what came next should be marked well. "And you can tell Dante Michelson himself that I have grave misgivings involving myself in what is obviously an unparalleled cultural theft. I'm going to have to have some indication that there are plans to return the device to the people of Earth." She flashed an accusing glance in Lighthorse's direction. "I assume you, of all people, must have made the same demand?"

Lighthorse ignored her, and spoke instead to the aide-de-camp. "Mr. Van Ulroy, please?"

Van Ulroy had both hands out, gesturing for her to slow down. "Dr. Ramanujan, you don't understand . . . "

She interrupted. "I *don't* understand," she agreed. "This device—from 12,000 BC, in Terra's hands for forty years without breathing a whisper about its existence—and I've only just been summoned to examine it now?" Van Ulroy started to answer, but she put up her hand. "Better question, though." She pointed to Lighthorse. "I can understand why an esteemed Mesoamerican scholar is sitting here. But I'm a materials physicist. How in the world could I shed any light?"

As soon as she posed the question, she answered it for herself. "It can't be that you want me to tell you what it's made of, could it? I'd have sent an intern if that were the case."

Van Ulroy now delivered a punch of his own.

"We know what it's made of, Doctor. What we'd like for you to tell us is how that's possible." He waited for the words to register properly. "Is that forthcoming enough? It's made of a material that . . . well . . . simply can't exist." He paused, he had to for something so important. "It's transuranian." He paused again. "It's transuranian, and somehow stable. It's made of element . . . number 137." The three sat wordlessly while Sadhana was allowed to absorb the blow. "It's composed of Feynmanium. Such a thing, it is seen now *can* exist," he added parenthetically. "It's the largest atomic structure possible in *this* universe anyway. Anything more massive, as you know as well as anyone alive, Doctor, would violate the Alpha constant and would dictate that the electrons in the inner shell orbit the nucleus faster than light."

Van Ulroy graciously gave her something prosaic to focus on, having just been struck with this incomparable thunderbolt. "It's very, very heavy."

"My God," she said in a whisper, "Feynmanium? I guess it would be."

URANIUM, THE HEAVIEST NATURAL element, number 92 had been overtopped as early as the 20th century when physicists had already learned to play demigod with the laws of the universe, creating heavier and heavier elements: californium, einsteinium, fermium, etc. The densest element ever cooked up in Terran laboratories was the unnamed element number 132, and unnamed for good reason maybe since its half life is something less than a trillionth of a second. Nature abhors these synthetic creations, and they are all radioactive and degrade quickly.

"It's stable? A nucleus that big, and stable?" She was still whispering.

"Absolutely stable, obviously. It's ancient. Looks like shiny purple iron," Van Ulroy said.

Sadhana quietly absorbed the rest of her briefing in mostly stunned silence. She tried to listen carefully but a hundred divergent thoughts raced across her mind. One that soon crowded to the front concerned the unusual progress that lately had been made in the production of ponderously weighty transuranian elements, with a sudden flurry of six having been fused in the last few years—numbers 127 to 132. She saw good reason now for the string of recent successes, and tried to imagine the sort of painstaking disassembly, examination, and reverse-engineering which must have garnered this and who knows whatever other great leaps forward.

She turned to Lighthorse and asked a very simple question.

"This device—what in the world is it?"

Lighthorse was wearing the look of satisfaction. Armies of scientists had either scoffed at or ignored his clarion call for years. Now he had the breathless and undivided attention of the most esteemed scientist on Terra—or anywhere else probably. This was the last laugh for which he'd waited so long; he didn't mask his relish in the least.

"I'm afraid that if I'm constrained to answer that question within the restricted limits of 'the world,' I'd be at a loss for an explanation. The short answer is that I don't know for sure, no one does. My best guess though is that it's a weapon, or more specifically, some component of a weapons system."

Sadhana's expression said absolutely nothing. She just sat quietly taking in the words.

"As I've been saying for many long years, Doctor, and as the codices discovered with the device strongly support, the Pre-Mayans played host to a race of visitors about which not much in the inscriptions goes by without referencing again and again a great war between the stars."

"Codices? It comes with an owners' manual?"

Lighthorse laughed. "Well, not quite."

Van Ulroy gave Lighthorse a cautionary glance; she noticed it out of the corner of her eye. Lighthorse was involved in the project to aid Ramanujan's thrusts and parries as she'd crack her head on this enigma. Maybe working together they'd be able to use the ancient clues and the physicist's razor sharp expertise to force some headway. The device was the seed around which the greatest single project in the history of mankind had grown. After making some good progress in the beginning, it was clear that the mammoth—yet secret—undertaking had languished at a dead-end for some time.

"I don't want to put any thoughts in your head, Dr. Ramanujan. I'd rather you examine the device for yourself, read what's been gleaned about it already, and then we can speak about it."

Now all the science was eclipsed by the pure human emotion that flooded out of her overwhelmed mind, into her breast, and out through her vocal chords.

"Where were they from?" She asked the question plaintively, almost in a child's voice.

Lighthorse answered soothingly. "There are certain places in the sky that we might talk about later, Doctor. Right now, just best to say that we think the civilization that built the device calls or called the extreme far side of the galaxy home. To be located any further away from them would necessitate leaving the Milky Way."

Van Ulroy, seeing Sadhana rendered speechless beyond simple queries, chose the moment to drive home the State's now clearly seen appropriate reprimand for her lapse in confidence in the Terran Archonate. "I'll consider the request you just made for me to relay to the Chief Archon retracted, yes, Doctor?"

The idea of the Archonate letting loose of the most important find in the history of the human race was positively ludicrous—and beyond that; it was insane. But to hand it back to Earth—that roiling, unstable, suicidal confederation of fratricidal nihilists—well there was no adjective for that. Entropy would decrease, light speed would be superseded, time would run backward, before that happened.

"Yes, of course," she answered in a humbled voice. "Thank you for ignoring it. I had no idea . . . "

"I understand, Doctor." Van Ulroy breathed a sigh of relief. "Trust that I do."

CHAPTER SIX

THUS SPAKE ZARATHUSTRA

WALKING THROUGH BORELIAN CUSTOMS wasn't the easiest task. The best-selling "Declined"—beamed everywhere and setting sales records year after year—catalogued the jaw-dropping list of people to whom the Borelians had flatly said "no." In perusing the list of princes, gold medalists, politicians, and magnates who'd been turned down, the reader was constrained to ask himself what chance *he* had to visit Borealis. And the answer was simple: none. Such hopeless folly even entered the lexicon. Teachers from Earth to the Outer Solar System scolded their daydreaming students not by asking them if they were on "Cloud Nine," but now more often if they were "strolling on Borealis." Sadly, it was next to impossible to visit Borealis for simple pleasure, as a tourist. If the floodgates were opened a stampede of billions would ensue, trampling to dust this jewel of humanity by virtue of the weight alone. To receive official permission from Customs for transit wasn't just rare, it was the surest proof that one was indeed among the few of the most powerful and important persons alive.

The tortuous process of acquiring a valid Borelian permit always granted transit times thirty-six hours beyond the duration requested. Such a generous but seemingly incongruous boon made sense though. It would have been inhuman to allow anyone on Borealis without giving them time to take the city in with their own eyes. One of those exceptional individuals was Zarathustra, alighting on the Moon and passing through the least crowded visa office in the Solar System.

Zarathustra was Persian like his name but he wasn't from Earth. His was one of those rare *in vacuo* births out in the Big Black. The moon Ganymede was nearest but the vessel carrying his mother was registered to Europa, so he called himself "Galilean," as if just one single Jovian satellite were not enough for the likes of him. Zarathustra, a state visitor, would be granted an official tour of the city, a rite of passage for the lucky few from all parts of the Solar System. Borelians had little trouble spotting the few august visitors in their midst: stunned Terrans and Earthlings stumbling through their streets on feet unaccustomed to the light gravity, open-mouthed and yet dumb-struck. It was said that if one stripped the frieze from Trajan's Column and wrapped it in precious metals and jewelry around a five-layer wedding cake, and were it then made large enough to accommodate two hundred and fifty thousand, this would be Borealis. So, politically, the Borelians couldn't imagine a better prelude before an important conference with adversaries and competitors than simply by giving the visiting diplomats and businessmen some free time to take in the sights of the city.

"So, how do you find Borealis?" The Council never opened their discussions any other way, knowing of course that their visitors would be quite speechless to answer. Realizing this was just the treasure squandered on the aesthetics of the city, rivals were forced to weigh the wealth and power resulting from almost two centuries of sheer determination that had transformed the Lunar North Pole into the single most important power source fueling the entire Solar System.

One of the Borelians sent to meet his arriving ship asked the question Zarathustra had fielded a thousand times. What his very pregnant mother was doing speeding between moons a million kilometers above Jupiter was a story in progress, so many in the distinguished party were curious what the Borelian version would be.

"Oh, what a chronicle!" he began, but laid into it nonetheless, chapter and verse, non-stop, all the way from Customs to Althing Gallery, Borealis' great performing hall. He'd be entertaining here tomorrow. Now he was being escorted to the restricted suite within for important guests. The party made slow progress, with so many citizens they passed along the way interacting with the celebrity. That gave him plenty of time to expand on every detail of his nativity. When the door to the lounge slid open he was nowhere near the end of the tale, but abruptly broke off, putting his hands to his head as if to help keep it from exploding from the surprise.

Nerissa was to one side, among other important dignitaries, representing the Pilots' Guild. Rittener was standing against the far wall. Having never seen "The Fresco" before, Clinton was entranced by it, of course. This exquisite piece was the work of every artist who'd visited Borealis over the decades. Each virtuoso left his mark however he saw fit. Instead of leaving their scribbles with markers and paints though, the state had made available to them any quantity of Callistan onyx, diamonds, precious stones and metals, and other priceless glitter. It had turned out well, to say the least. It was meant to be an eye-catcher for visitors. But this masterpiece hadn't caught Zarathustra's; he was looking back and forth at something, someone, else.

"I'm sorry, commodore," he said to Rittener, shaking his head to indicate that it was a hard choice, "but there she is, in the flesh!" Zarathustra made a great show of prancing up to Nerissa. Whether it was a wand or a scepter he carried, he used it to punctuate his steps, waving the baton as a conductor would syncopate his heel-clicks on the immaculate Tethysean marble floor. He bowed, sweeping his crop-carrying arm so low.

"I had everything planned out. I practiced what I was going to say to you, and I've forgotten everything now!" He looked around the room and laughed. It was an odd, shrill, hooting laugh. The dignitaries smiled politely.

"Yes, I am made of flesh," Nerissa answered. That was clear because she was blushing a little. "On behalf of the Borelian Pilots' Guild," she began to welcome him but he cut her off.

"Oh, I *do* remember this though." He reached into his breech pockets. They were huge, but well-tailored and disguised properly within the folds of the pants. Such voluminous pockets elicited a remarkably tiny gift. "What do you get the Borelian princess who has everything?" He bowed again, just not so low this time. "Please, accept this with my sincerest compliments, Nerissa." It was a small compact of mascara.

"It's the kind I wear." He pointed to his eyes and put on a very solemn expression. "I'm serious. Please take a good look. You have to appreciate what this does with the light. This isn't just any mascara. Look closely."

Nerissa gave a quick smirk to her colleagues. The regular welcome routine was off the table. This was Zarathustra, after all. She was up to it though, the smile said. She stepped forward, put both her hands on his shoulders and drew him very close to her. She moved her head to the side, almost sensuously, as if approaching to kiss, but only examined his eyes.

Zarathustra was the one blushing now, Nerissa's coolness and self-assurance taking some of the pepper out of his façade. He was just explaining now, not boasting, and in a much quieter voice, hyper aware of Nerissa's proximity.

"There's nothing like it. It's made from the ash belching from fumaroles on the floor of Europa's ocean. They dry it in the radiation field between the Moon and the Old Man," he used the Jovian moon slang for Jupiter. "It's supposed to accentuate the look the eye has during the throes of passion." He shrugged his shoulders and turned up a weak grin. "It should. Cleopatra would have had trouble picking up the tab for this stuff."

Nerissa was genuinely appreciative. "Thank you, Zarathustra. I've never had such a gift." He was beaming now. It truly was next to impossible to put something in Nerissa's hands that she'd never touched before. He told himself that he'd done pretty well.

"Zari. I prefer that you call me Zari."

"Thank you, Zari."

"You're welcome, Nerissa. That's Clinton Rittener standing over there, isn't it?" He brought the two disparate sentences together without missing a beat, recovering his flair. "Do you see him?"

"I see him," she admitted gamely. "He's a new arrival on Borealis. He'll be taking the tour with us."

"You'll excuse me?" Zari asked.

"Of course," she answered.

Zari was back on stage, this time with even more flamboyance if that were possible, boldly inserting what was meant to be a few military strides into the swagger. He put both hands up.

"Don't shoot; I surrender, admiral." His baton was hanging in the air, yet didn't have the feel of capitulation, so he offered it to Rittener as if it were the saber of a defeated officer.

Rittener declined. "I've been to the bottom of the Europan ocean. If that's my gift, you're not going to convince me that it came from there."

It had been a few weeks since Clinton had arrived on Borealis and he'd questioned why this invitation for a formal tour had come just now, so late. And he wondered about something else. The powers that be on Borealis had apparently waited for the perfect, high-strung, loquacious eccentric to pass through so that Rittener should enjoy some excitable company during the excursion. The odd choice struck him as peculiar.

"Touché, mon capitaine." Zari struck a fencing pose, waving the baton like a sword, but then dropped his guard crestfallen. "But then that means I've come empty-handed." A bright idea burst onto his face suddenly. "Unless, of course . . . " He patted one pocket, then the next, finally shrugging his shoulders. "No, I haven't any more," he said, sadly. Narrowing his eyes to focus on Rittener's face and leaning toward him to make the examination more obvious, he gave his opinion. "But, I don't think the mascara would work anyway. I think the eyes are just right the way they are." He gave another look and pursed his lips he was concentrating so hard. "I love what you've done with the face," he said, referencing the scars. "It's very masculine. It really works for you."

He turned back to Nerissa for support. "Don't you agree? I mean, about Clinton Rittener's face. It's very unique and quite handsome, don't you think?"

The Borelian welcoming crew weren't horrified yet, but a few more remarks of this kind and they'd be there. Nerissa had long since given up hiding her smile, and gave in all the way.

"Yes, Zari, I agree. Clinton Rittener has a very unique and handsome face."

Zari put his hand on Rittener's shoulder. "Only tell me this, general," he said in a conspiratorial tone, looking behind and around himself. "No offense, but from what I know of you, well . . . how to say this delicately . . . things have a way of going pop and bang around you. Have you noticed that?" He aspirated a puff of air as if to say that it didn't require great powers of perception to discern that.

Rittener couldn't help observing Nerissa's delight. She wasn't concealing the fact that these were the words she wished she could find so plainly.

"There have been a few dust-ups that I've not managed to avoid," Rittener gave him that.

Zari shook his head in an understanding way. "That's why I'm not political, commissar. So just tell me what to say. Are we cheering freedom for the Asteroid Belt? Is that it? Up the Asteroid Belt! Hurrah for meteors!" He pirouetted smartly, sending his flowing locks whirling. Two deep widow's peaks were artistically shaved into his mane of dense, black hair, the exposed pate given over to tattoos and glitter, accentuated with a top knot at the crown.

"And if that changes tomorrow, just let me know. Deal? I'm a musician, not a soldier."

Rittener answered him with a hand signal, silent slang for insiders from the Old Man's family of satellites. He knew how to show off too. "Oh, that's classic!" Zari complimented. "Very well done! You *have* been around, haven't you?"

SINCE THE CORE WAS a labyrinth of elevators, tubes, chutes, escalators, and moving walkways, it was easy to lose oneself in the beehive. Everything sooner or later popped out at the surface at one or another of the levels between Alpha and Epsilon. With the most expert guides on the Moon in charge, the distinguished party emerged at the perfect place. It was a fine day on Borealis, but there could be nothing else. The dayglow was bright and crisp, yet gentle. It reflected richly off a city created in fantasy, a city where the only rare patches of concrete were those exposed purposefully so as to hold fast the sapphire and topazes in place for mosaic sidewalks. A million beams of light bounced off a million points of jewels, polished marble, gleaming gold, lustrous silver and rebounded into Zari's stunned pupils.

"Jupiter's beard." He barely got out the phrase. No Borelian uttered a word; this moment was left alone for the visitor. The only sound for the next moments was the odd combination of footsteps on hundreds of thousands of encrusted jewels underfoot and Zari's dazed mantra. "Jupiter's beard," he kept mumbling softly to himself. There were occasions when guests had to turn back from tours, finding the panorama too overwhelming.

"Here, you look like you could use a little of this." Nerissa handed him a generously filled goblet of nectar. It was right at hand since the docents had been often asked for something to fortify shaky guests. He downed it in a gulp and stretched the cup out for more. None of the lecturers told him to go easy, that nectar had a way of sneaking up, and fast.

"It's delicious!" was Zari's only comment, but the rest of his body was quite a bit more expressive—a short drama of twisting, stomach-rubbing, lip-licking, and head-turning. Nectar was mead distilled from matchless Borelian honey, itself like no other due to genetically engineered blessings in the Garden. It couldn't be sampled anywhere else since nothing was exported from Borealis—save one product, helium-3. The master distillers here spent their days and lives doing nothing but attempting to improve it, and that for the benefit of just themselves and their fellow few citizens.

Passing by the tongue-in-groove series of consummate palaces and mansions, where millions of pounds of gold, platinum, silver, and precious stones were treated as nothing more than stucco, they spiraled their way up to Beta. The Titan Consortium dominated this level, opting for a work depicting the Rings of Saturn. To represent the detritus swirling around that gas giant, tens of thousands of diamonds, rubies, and sapphires had been inlaid in a monolithic slab of pure black titanium. There were many others on this level equally as awe-inspiring: Phidippides running to Athens after Marathon, Columbus landing in the Americas, Adam and Eve in the Garden of Eden.

On Gamma Level the party arrived at Nerissa's uncle's humble residence. "This is Dr. Stanislaus' home. He's the Surgeon General of Borealis and one of our eleven councilors." Stanislaus had chosen a clean motif for his façade, but one hardly real. It required some time for the eyes to realize what they were taking in. The frontage was cut from two twenty-foot-high towering pieces of translucent chalcedony quartz. Between them an entrance was created in the shape of two strands of DNA separating, the base pairs created by matching fused bars of awesome shanks of other vivid, multihued quartzes: purple amethyst, yellow citrine, red carnelian onyx, green chrysoprase.

"He named it 'Mitosis,'" Nerissa said in a dry tone, not too impressed at all. A look up and down the level confirmed that this was indeed hardly the most extravagant house on the block.

"Nectar," Zari called out, unable to formulate any other comment. Nerissa smiled and saw to the request herself. He was stumbling by the time the Old City Museum was reached. Rittener remembered Darda's warning and had his eyes open; Zari had no idea, so the docent explained.

"Botanists, gardeners, cooks, and hobbyists in the Old City were determined to explore the limits of agriculture on the Moon," she began the saga. "They rigged hermetically sealed planters with the offspring of quite bizarre cross-breeds—utilizing the gene pool of the most resilient plants. After fits and starts and trials and errors, the survivors were placed in the blistering sunlight, shielded to a degree by well-designed solar screens that at least blocked some of the scorching rays. Each hobbyist had his own highly guarded secrets to protect—the just perfect percentage of carbon dioxide in the ambience being the most hotly debated—and that competition exists to this day." On cue a troupe of servers from the museum's restaurant stepped forward with sample trays. "The mature plants are processed with synthetic emulsifiers and taste additives, and boiled into a paste that is extruded and served. It may be eaten hot, cold, frozen, fried—even broiled in the Sun." With a broad smile and with some unmasked pride she handed the guests their menus. "Borelian flux, gentlemen."

Nerissa ordered her favorite, amber flux, and dug in. "This is the one I recommend you choose," she advised Zari between spoonfuls. Zari ignored her suggestion, a little upset that he'd come to his first roadblock. Even here they existed after all, judging by his distressed look.

"I want chartreuse," he slurred the word. "There's no chartreuse?"

Nerissa ignored the complaint. "Not for you though, Clinton Rittener." She intimated that his new citizenship carried responsibilities with it. "You're no novice now. You should be more adventurous. I think maybe red is a good next step." A mischievous sparkle in her eyes made him wonder.

"Is it anything like blue-green? I've tasted that. It's different from blue-green, right?"

Clinton was watching her eat amber flux and with no ill effect whatsoever.

"I'll just go with amber," he decided.

Nerissa was adamant and ordered for him. "Red. It's spicy."

"Spicy?" he repeated and asked at the same time.

No one answered him but Zari's query was quickly put right now. "Chartreuse flux, as you please," the head chef himself was presenting it to Zari with élan. Nerissa appeared surprised as did everyone else. "Well, it required a bit of color mixing," he explained, "but you've got quite the palette of flavors in there. *Bon appétit.*"

Zari gave Rittener a friendly slap on the back. "Chartreuse flux, satrap, can you imagine that? Quick as Mercury they cook it right up." He snapped his fingers, but with some difficulty thanks to the nectar. Zari's companion was too busy staring at his red flux to answer.

"Everything is possible on the Moon," the chef repeated the now hackneyed slogan, beaming.

Nerissa felt someone ought to say it. Zari had been addressing Rittener as everything from "alderman" to "zookeeper" thinking one of them might hit the mark.

"Clinton Rittener has no rank on Borealis. He is a private citizen."

It took a while for the words to sink in. Zari flared his nostrils and furrowed his brow, outwardly dumbfounded. He needed confirmation. "A citizen? Him? You're saying he's not going anywhere? He's not simply passing through, like me?"

Nerissa repeated. "Provisional, for specificity."

Zarathustra exploded.

"Oh, that's it! It's all over! Where's the panic button to push? Is it that emerald-encrusted switch, or the pure white gold one over there?" He was full-fledged drunk and everything he said was almost screamed and entirely slurred.

With one hand he waved his absurd scepter in Rittener's direction, while the other held the swaying spoonful of flux he'd been brandishing for some time.

"Don't you know who that fellow is?" He gave Nerissa some time to think it over, finally putting the chartreuse concoction in his mouth.

"Jupiter's beard!" He spit it back, leaned over his bowl and bathed his tongue with nectar, gurgling and cursing.

Nerissa handed him another goblet of Borelian mead, filled to the brim. "Here, let's replace that. No harm done." She didn't say "speak up" but Rittener could plainly see she certainly intended it. When he caught his breath Zari went on.

"He's one of the four horsemen of the apocalypse. Where ever he rides he leaves a trail of skeletons behind." He turned to Rittener and tried to soften it a bit. "Not literally, that's speaking metaphorically."

His head wavered back to Nerissa. "When I first saw him here, I knew it, just like that." He tried snapping his fingers and failed completely. "Hasn't any one of you stopped to ask yourselves what he's doing here? Or to ask . . . him?"

Those had been Nerissa's first words to Rittener, on the pilots' pad, before the race.

"Look, I'm going to perform tomorrow," he elucidated drunkenly, "fly out of here with more credits than I could ever spend in ten lifetimes, and I'm sure I'll never be back." He straightened up, shrugged his shoulders as if to prove he was still thinking correctly, and said it. "Who ever plays Borealis . . . twice?"

Nerissa was agreeing with him. "Not many, Zarathustra. Not many."

"That's right." He put his finger up; she should listen to this. "You see, I just passed through five long AUs of space from the Old Man to Borealis and have heard nothing but..." he lowered his voice, " . . . whispers." Too much emotion had taken hold of the artiste. He had to stand. He wobbled back and forth, using randomly selected and stunned Borelian shoulders for support. "And now I arrive to find the right hand man of the grim reaper here?" The dam broke. It was too much. Zarathustra wept openly, his priceless mascara turning back to mud and running down his cheeks.

"I told myself I hadn't cared, that it wasn't my concern, but that was before I'd seen this place with my own eyes. By the plumes of Io, nothing can happen to this place. It's too beautiful. It's just too awful to think of this all being destroyed."

Nerissa was in complete charge, calmly taking Zari by the hand and leading him back to his seat. "There now," she comforted, "nothing terrible is going to befall Borealis. Tell him, Clinton Rittener."

A long, long silence followed, uncomfortable enough that every unfortunate lecturer blindsided by this particular duty took the opportunity to avail themselves of exits in every direction. This highly unusual tour was over. "Won't you tell him that?" The three of them were alone now, seated at a table soiled with spilled nectar and spit-up flux. "Won't you tell *me* that?"

Rittener had been sitting quietly, stone-faced, allowing all the slights and horrific comparisons to pass unchallenged, his only reaction to fidget with the ring on his right hand. Zarathustra sported earrings, a necklace, several bracelets, and had rings on every finger, two on some. This was the only jewelry Clinton wore. Nerissa had spotted the token from the first time she'd laid eyes on him.

"Does that, the ring, mean something?" she asked.

"It was my father's." He at least answered that.

"A great man, your father." Zari had composed himself, wiping away all the smudges. Zarathustra emptied his cup as if in his honor. "He always played fairly with the Galilean Moons. The ambassador was well-respected there."

Rittener nodded his thanks for the kind words. Zarathustra reached across the table and took Clinton's hand. He said the next like no drunken fool ever had.

"If you know something, brother, or are able to act in some way, now is the time to speak up, Clinton Rittener."

The vestibule abruptly filled with the sounds of Zari's first great mega-hit, as the schedule had provided, an *homage* to Borealis' famous guest. The gaffe didn't surprise Clinton. This tour was running itself now on auto-pilot; all the conductors had leapt off the train. Zarathustra gave a shrill, hooting cry of glee, jumped to his feet and began dancing to it, shambling from one side of the reception hall to the other, leaving Nerissa and Clinton alone. They shared some candid observations.

"You could just as simply have asked me, you know, straight out," Rittener said sharply to Nerissa. "Put all the ridiculousness to the side and simply asked me."

"I've *been* asking you," she countered back, just as sharply. "You have a tendency to answer things in ways that make them more confused after all."

"You Borelians have a way of confusing things yourselves, you can trust that."

"*You* Borelians? Shouldn't that be *we* Borelians, citizen?"

"Provisional," he corrected her. "For specificity."

"That changes tomorrow," she reminded him. "My uncle, Dr. Stanislaus, asked me to deliver his request that you present yourself in his offices before you take the oath. He'll be the one to inscribe you as pilot—*if* he decides you're made for it—so I suggest you leave the double entendres and sophistry at home tomorrow. He's a man who expects and appreciates very direct language."

Rittener widened his eyes in mock surprise. "There's someone here, one, at least, like that?"

ZARATHUSTRA SLID BACK TO their table, his foot-long black braided beard swaying from his chin, out of breath but ready for more.

"Dance with me, Nerissa of Borealis. I'd give up a year of my life for a dance with you," Zari begged. His beard was plaited with more than copper wires gracefully wrapped around fine Ganymedan diamantes. There were also beads of the chartreuse appetizer, splashed with glistening amber honey mead.

"Keep the year," she said, gracefully rising to her feet, not taking her eyes off Rittener. "I accept."

"You, too, brother," Zari invited Rittener. "Let's dance, the three of us."

Nerissa unbuttoned her Borelian caraco-cloak, letting it fall to the marble while she reached back and took the needle pearl Madeau clip out of her shiny obsidian black hair. It exploded over her shoulders and down her back. A slight downward positioning of her face gave the seductive impression that she was unsure how to do this, a look so practiced and expertly effected, sufficient to shred through any male flesh as easily and surely as gamma ray bursts through tissue paper.

"Yes, brother, dance with us?" She used Zari's phrase.

"I admire that you'd do anything for your country," Clinton said to her, making his point by sending a disapproving frown in Zarathustra's direction, "but I'll decline." He'd been taking incoming flak all day while holding his fire but now would discharge the final fusillade, the one that counted, and he'd do it in his language of choice for serious combat. "Homo qui saltat, aut inebrius aut insanus est."

She had a "What, that again?" look on her face, so he translated for her. "A man found dancing must either be drunk or insane." He picked up her cloak and laid it folded on the table. "That's Cicero or Cato, one of those two."

She quickly put the proverb to the test. "That makes your opinion of me clear, but which does that say about him?"

Zarathustra was talking to himself. "But I'm right here, why should I be a 'him'?"

"Him?" Clinton gave a look that said there were things, men too, through which even gamma rays must struggle to pierce, turning on his heel and walking out.

"Both," Clinton answered in disgust.

CHAPTER SEVEN

CITIZEN OF BOREALIS

THE COUNCIL CHAMBERS OF Borealis were not as one would expect. As glittering and beautiful and rich as the exterior of the city was, the original Old City was left just as it had been. The Borelian Council sat in a man-made cavern, nothing more, the rock-hewn walls left rough, the utility pipes, shafts, vents and electrical conduits unabashedly on display. The ambiance was more that of a grand meeting place of some lost Mesolithic tribe from Earth's distant Stone Age. This was the seat of the unusual democracy that ruled Borealis.

The eleven councilors were the cabinet, supreme court, and legislators of Borealis. They wielded absolute power, yet could be replaced quite easily, almost at the whim of the citizens. Politics was a never-ending affair on Borealis and most of the current councilors had been elected, dismissed, and re-elected again—many, many times. Statecraft here was like sailing a ship in the raging waters around Cape Horn at the tip of South America. More often than not a councilor was pushed back twice as far as whatever headway he could make, and sooner or later his entire ship must capsize. Only freshmen councilors could boast of never having been defeated; they hadn't served long enough.

Every 180 days every citizen on Borealis voted. It was a simple matter. Each civilian just had a brief chat with his or her amanuensis, as if one were talking to a fellow resident over coffee about the important affairs of the city. The amalgamated opinions were collated, set against an algorithm which took into account a wide range of each councilor's statistics, the current needs of the city, and then juxtaposed them with the names of potential opposition candidates of whom mention was made during the "voting." Presto, the election results were then declared—Borelian style. Such fluidity in government should have produced chaos, yet it didn't. There was a core group of leaders who more or less took turns at the helm, sometimes in power when their ideas were in the ascendant with the population, sometimes out when their initiatives weren't. Terra said the place was run like a buccaneers' town, its Council "part-time pirates," but Borelians wouldn't have it any other way.

Opinion rebounding so quickly and constantly infused Borelian government with fast-acting flexibility. One of the unusual effects of such a tumultuous system was that councilors were always just a few months away from going back to the status of private citizen, and so their professions were maintained. Everyone had a job on Borealis, of course, meaning that generals elected to the Council didn't surrender their commands, nor professors their tenure, nor any councilor anything else. The Council didn't have the time then, or the inclination, to sit and bang gavels. It convened regularly though, to make the executive decisions that weren't already taken care of by the quite efficient bureaucracy—and did so in rapid-fire fashion. So there was no king, nor president, nor chief councilor on Borealis, but Stanislaus was the closest thing to it. He had been elected and confirmed to his seat forty-two times, while suffering defeat and losing his councillorship in twelve other sessions. When people on Earth, or Terra, or Mars or anywhere else thought about Borealis, his face was likelier than not to be one of the first images conjured.

Stanislaus came from a long line of physicians and was the Surgeon General of Borealis. His family emigrated from the Protectorate of Bohemia centuries ago when the Czech Republic was dissolved. In fact, his family—the Navrakovas—were one of the founding families. All prior Surgeon Generals had been charged with the health and safety of the citizenry. Stanislaus—on the Council for twenty-one of the last twenty-eight years—had expanded his bailiwick greatly.

Borealis' water, he'd made clear over many years as the heart of his policy, was its most important resource. He'd taken recycling to almost ridiculous levels, refusing to allow the city to part with scant drops for even the most seemingly necessary procedures. If water were irretrievably converted, in any process which would leave it at end outside the boundaries of the potable supply, he was against it—and vociferously. That worked to his advantage every 180 days when people could say anything they liked about him to their amanuensis yet always end it with, "though he sure does look after the water, you know?" Borealis' Central System Amanuensis, "Diana," would plug in quite a bit of electoral weight behind those accumulated opinions, because as everyone knew and understood, Borelians had a primal fear of running out of water.

Stanislaus had his hands in many other places, too. His powerful voice could be heard in current reproductive laws, in the genetic engineering that was and wasn't practiced in the Garden, to promulgating sports and exercises that conformed with and yet counteracted the long-term effects of the weakened lunar gravity. He was the quintessential physician: sixty-two, fit, salt and pepper hair and beard, both the same length and neat and trimmed. He wore a smock almost everywhere, an expensive impeccably tailored medical smock, but really only an unpretentious tunic. He was never to be seen though, anywhere, ever, without his gold Surgeon General's caduceus clasped on his collar. The flamboyant insignia was the only nod the doctor made toward ostentation and it wasn't too much to ask. Stanislaus was much more proud to be the Surgeon General of Borealis than to sit on its Council, as hard as that might be to believe.

CLINTON RITTENER AND STANISLAUS had never met, but each knew quite a bit about the other before they shook hands for the first time in the councilor's private office, a rather airy but austere space directly adjacent to the Council Chamber itself. Here was the man Stanislaus had recently voted to grace with honorary Borelian citizenship. Clasping hands, Stanislaus felt immediately that he'd voted wisely.

Rittener's mutiny was the spark that ignited a firestorm of resistance to Terra's recent imperial tactics. Flotillas of "pirates" coalesced as fighting groups. These weren't freebooters, as Terran propaganda led on, but were instead a united armed militia of the many states of the Asteroid Belt. They did exact a percentage of the metals trade as tribute for protection, but even these buccaneers blushed at the staggering theft of 50 percent which Terra was trying to grab. When a few other Terran "privateers" followed orders that Rittener's conscience refused, annihilating mining colonies across the Asteroid Belt, this confederate fleet went into action. They went after the purloined shipments of metals, vaporizing every last gram of booty en route to Terra, from friend or foe, and starving Terra like no boycott ever had.

Terra stuck to her guns even as Borealis weighed in. Borealis dispatched her fleet to the "disputed arena" ostensibly on a peace-keeping mission "to disengage the warring parties." Borealis' next punch she delivered with the gloves off: helium-3 shipments were suspended to all parties involved in the dispute. Borealis could not, in good conscience, provide the means for this brutal war of annihilation on humanity's frontier. That was a blow that caused energy-addicted Terra to cave in, but in a way that boded ill for the future. Terra saw every power in the Solar System, from the alliances on Earth to the combined confederation of the states of the Outer System, now buttressed by Borealis too, all ranged against her.

Stanislaus had committed to memory every glowering expression, all the subtle tones of menace that Dante Michelson had presented to the Borelian Council during the peace negotiations. "I want the *Peerless* back—immediately! Along with her crew." Michelson paused so that his next words might be weighed separately. "And we demand that Borealis surrender to Terra the stateless pirate known as Clinton Rittener." Rittener had already been tried—and convicted in absentia—and the Terran Ring only had to iron out the last little detail of putting the miscreant to death. Unfortunately, Borealis wouldn't be able to comply.

Daiyu, Borealis' Mandarin-born councilor and foreign minister, poetess laureate and honorary citizen herself, delivered the bad news. As was her custom, she spoke the simple words with the same dignity that infused her Gongfu tea ceremony conversations about art and humanity.

"Your classification of Clinton Rittener as 'stateless' is in error, Archon. He has been granted Borelian citizenship." She allowed a brief silence, long enough for her to answer the next question even before it was posed. "By spontaneous public acclamation," she declared, and with the appropriate solemnity. That was that. If Mephistopheles had shown up with a warrant for Rittener, or any other citizen, signed by Lucifer himself, the answer would be the same. No Borelian citizen had ever been surrendered, to anyone, ever, for anything, in the entire history of Borealis.

Daiyu was speaking truthfully. The citizens of Borealis went absolutely wild with admiration for this earthy European who cavalierly bet his life, counting on the honor and nobility of Borealis to vouchsafe it. Within the lacerating scorn Borelians heaped upon anyone or anything from Earth, there were to be found hints of a strange and grudging respect nonetheless. Rittener's exploits touched an ancient familial nerve. They didn't go chatting with their amanuenses about him, they screamed it, so stridently and repeatedly that it echoed to Diana, who informed the Council. It *was* possible to ignore a spontaneous public acclamation, but it was also stupid, and rarely, rarely done. The Council affirmed it unanimously.

The Terran Ring got her ship back, along with Lieutenant Andrews and two other crewmen who had refused to go along with the rebellion and survived by sitting out the mutiny in *Peerless'* brig. The throw-away crew that the Terran Archonate had hand-picked for the mission to Valerian-3, with its lackluster history and predisposition for acquiescence to questionable orders, turned out to be a double-edged weapon. They had acquiesced alright, to the formidable will of their mutinous captain, who stunned everyone by revealing something no one had assumed he had: a conscience. Ensign Gutierrez and the rest of the crew, who also found theirs, hit an amazingly rare jackpot, and were given indefinite resident alien status on Borealis, a boon denied previously to a Prince of Wales. And now, this was Clinton Rittener's big day, the day he'd take the oath of citizenship. The gavel for Council proceeding today, by luck of the draw, fell to Stanislaus, who'd summoned Rittener to his office just minutes before the ceremony.

"HAVE YOU EVER HAD yellow flux?"

That was the first thing Stanislaus said to him, beaming amicably and pointing to two steaming, jaundiced plates on a serving table next to a nearby settee. Before Rittener could answer Stanislaus upped the ante.

"My wife made that for you; yellow flux is her specialty. This *is* the Mc Coy." He smiled and shrugged his shoulders. "She admires you, Clinton Rittener, and made me promise." He motioned for the two of them to be seated for lunch. "Would you join me?"

Rittener didn't hesitate at an answer. "How kind of your wife. I never get home cooking."

Dr. Stanislaus wanted to make sure this all turned out right. He solicitously offered a dollop of fresh, incomparably exquisite Borelian honey. "You have to try it this way." A few scoops later and Rittener was shaking his head in grudging admission, just a little faked. "That's got an interesting taste, not bad at all." He put his head to the side and pronounced, "It tastes a little like sweet mustard."

"Exactly," Slanislaus agreed. "You've tried others? You've had the red?"

"Yes, blue-green and red both." Rittener thought back to the unpleasant experiences. "Spicy," he commented off-handedly, but yet making the Galilean hand signal for "too much." This one had currency throughout the Solar System, including Borealis.

"Aside from the lack of home-cooked meals, everything else is well?" Stanislaus wasn't just being polite. Rittener, until he settled in and his status changed, was a guest of the Borelian government. He was being quartered in the Basement, a growing subterranean space beneath the Core and spreading under the Garden. Tourists never asked to see this section of Borealis—vast research, infrastructural, industrial, commercial, and government centers were located here. The great mansions that lined the terraces weren't for rent, and buying one was next to impossible, even if technically legal. Extended families lived in them for centuries and were planning to do so for centuries to come. So new arrivals, however few, were treated the same as legations, or business and trade delegates. There were no hotels on Borealis; one either lived here or was somebody the government deemed significant enough to have permitted to visit. Concerning such obviously important guests, their tab for room and board didn't figure in the least with regards to how visitors came and went on Borealis, and so everything was at the government's expense.

Rittener's quarters were spacious and well-lit by plenty of natural sunlight brought in with architecturally pleasing fiber optics skylights. The housing ombudsman instructed him to just ask his amanuensis for anything—anything at all—and any furnishings, artistic décor, and the rest would be subject to no limit save Rittener's satisfaction. His stipend of credits for food and any other incidentals far exceeded his expenses.

"Everything is well, thank you," Rittener answered.

Stanislaus was taking two scoops of flux for every one of his guest. Still, here was an opportunity to offer a genuine compliment.

"Best flux I've ever tasted," Rittener complimented honestly. "Please tell your wife I said so?"

Stanislaus liked that of course but he didn't say so. Instead he put his spoon down, folded his hands in front of him, and got straight to the point.

"Everyone has a job on Borealis," Stanislaus said it as a matter of fact and as the slogan it was. This wasn't Earth, for goodness sake. Unemployment didn't exist on Borealis and hadn't for centuries. "So what will you do? Soldier, surveyor, gardener, miner, or something else? You've given some thought to this, no?"

Rittener didn't hesitate for an instant. "I want to pilot. If I live the rest of my days flying on Borealis I'll end up being a very happy man."

Stanislaus was rubbing his mustache with his index finger. "Piloting? Well, you've set the bar quite high, even for a man like yourself." He civilly kept his opinion about Rittener's age to himself and how a piloting career, at best, would be measured into the future in months, not years. Now he stroked the facial hair with his whole hand; he was thinking deeper. "Of course, I do have a thing or two to say about sports on Borealis." Then he added politely, "I saw you fly; you're an exceptional pilot." Rittener knew he was mediocre compared to the talent on Borealis but it was in his interest to play along too. Stanislaus' next question came unexpected.

"How did you manage to save that girl, Darda, at Tartarus?" he asked, practically in monotone, impressed but with a slight reluctance to accept the facts. "And live through it?"

Rittener described how he'd backed air when reaching Darda, gripping her around the waist with both legs, using explicit piloting parlance so Stanislaus should see it correctly. It was some tricky piloting, Rittener admitted. "It might have been the best flying I've done in a while."

"Please," Stanislaus held up his right hand and almost challenged, as if asking a magician to explain a trick. "I'm a fair judge of what constitutes expert flying. This hand has inscribed every pilot on Borealis. I know how you did it, but would like to know *how* you did it."

Rittener said it so matter of fact. "I expected sooner or later one or the other of the maintenance or emergency locks would be opened."

This didn't clarify at all for Stanislaus. "So you gambled your life on this?"

"In a way, if you insist . . . " Clinton made light of the odds. "But really, Doctor, how high would you rate the probabilities of the System ignoring three human beings flying, and suffocating, inside a carbon dioxide tube, even in such a far-flung locale as Tartarus?"

"Makes sense," Stanislaus almost groused. Now he worked his beard with real purpose, making it lay smooth. "Still, you made it half-way back up, even dragging Darda with you, and uphill." There was a mixture of amazement and admiration in the words. "Do you think you'd have made it to the top?"

Rittener's blue eye had seemingly come to life at the query. As a doctor, Stanislaus knew that was impossible. The rest of Rittener's bearing though at the same time went flat and drained. The pause that followed was interminable—literally. Clinton didn't answer, and yet it wasn't an insolent silence, just hush for a question that was neither asked nor answered. He'd watched and learned first-hand how to make quiet speak with great effect from one of the best tacticians—his father.

Stanislaus gave in finally and moved on. "Daiyu and I have spoken about you."

Stanislaus and the poetess Daiyu were the moderates on the Council, Rittener knew. They worked together, voted together, and were courted by the other coalitions wishing to acquire the all-important six-vote majority. "I'm sure a place could be found for you in the diplomatic corps as well." Daiyu was in charge of Borealis' foreign ministry, and from the conspiratorial tone Stanislaus was using, it was being made clear that "pilot" and "agent" were very close to synonymous on Borealis. The councilor's next remark took on a chummy air. "That's quite an offer to consider, Mr. Rittener. An assistant attaché is a high station, and doesn't come without quite generous credits."

Rittener hadn't come to Borealis for the credits. And the offer of Borelian diplomatic credentials, something that meant nothing less than entry into the most rarified heights in existence, even this wasn't it either. Rittener's expression of mild interest in both Stanislaus judged sincere, as incomprehensible as that was, and that made him a bit nervous. He regretted offering both like that now but it was his policy to just say things plainly. Humility wasn't a Borelian virtue and its councilors ate flux, not humble pie. He bit down on his lower lip, squirmed a little in his chair, and then slowly came out with it.

"Or, maybe, Mr. Rittener," he paused. "Maybe you're just a genuine friend of Borealis. Maybe you're one of the last people in the Solar System that aren't merely bought and sold. Maybe you're here of your own volition, nothing ulterior. A pilot would be able to explain that."

"Living correctly," Rittener repeated the pilot code.

Rittener's expression had changed; it was perceptible.

"That's right," Stanislaus continued, "maybe you're here because you think it's the right thing to do. And if that's the case, with your history on Mars, the Asteroid Belt, and the rest of the Outer, not to mention your connections on the Terran Ring and with the alliances on Earth, I'm guessing what you might be able to share your first day could be worth an entire diplomatic career."

That sounded weighty enough so he thinned it out with a joke. "Who knows? I'm a fair man. I might vote to credential *and* retire you on the same day if that's the case."

Rittener smiled at the silliness. "Hired and retired on the same day? Is that legal?"

Stanislaus smiled back. "It would require some wrangling . . . but yes, I guess it is." Rittener knew he was going to say it. "Everything, you know, is possible on the Moon." He almost guessed the next words too. "Your opinions, especially, about the Terran Ring are of particular importance to us."

Stanislaus had imagined he was in charge of this conversation. Rittener leaned forward now and let him know he wasn't. It struck like a punch, immediately disabusing Stanislaus of the error in his appraisal.

"Councilor, I *am* here as a friend of Borealis. And as a friend I'm telling you that your worst enemy now is yourselves. Borealis can't win a war with Terra—the idea itself is ludicrous. It simply can't be done. I know what they're capable of and how strong the hawks on the Ring are now. You're playing right into their hands by acting the flint for their steel. These are sparks you should want to see extinguished."

The councilor was caught off-guard but recovered quickly and jabbed back. "That's a clever turn of phrase," Stanislaus wasn't complimenting though. "There are a number of powers maneuvering to pounce on Borealis' resources who send us far less flowing ultimatums. Perhaps you wouldn't mind saying what you mean more plainly. I assume you're referring to helium-3?

"Borealis has been an honest broker, posting in every interplanetary forum the accurate figures of the h3 mined and shipped, revealing the evidence our explorers have meticulously compiled, explaining the disappointingly finite supply left. I don't know if the Terrans are simply blind or if their thinly veiled threats imply other disabilities. You rather know them; what's your opinion?"

"Well," Rittener pointed out, "there's an outstanding Terran capital warrant with my name on it so I'll vouch that they make mistakes from time to time."

Stanislaus matched Clinton's black humor on the death warrant, "It's nothing personal, I'm sure.

"Just because prospectors have been rubbing their hands together at what they expected to find as they moved south doesn't mean things had to turn out that way. Everyone in the Solar System had better get used to the fact—and quickly." He sounded like a teacher scolding a middle school class. "There'll be fresh supplies soon at hand, around the equator and further down into the temperate zone of the southern hemisphere." Stanislaus put on the same face of exasperation Rittener had seen on Rufinus talking about Australis. "But, as Borealis had said so often, there is none to be found in a vast area cupping the Lunar South Pole, extending up to the 65th parallel. This helium-3 wasteland is real and all those from Earth to Titan still wearing tinfoil hats about this need to take them off and to start thinking constructively."

He finished his lecture, sat back and punctuated it. "We don't have a wand to wave so that Terra's energy problems can be solved."

"With all due respect, Dr. Stanislaus," Rittener said, "I believe the Terran Ring is asking for something less than that. Their claim is that they should have some say in their own future."

That future was being jeopardized by the rationing plan the Borelians seemed determined to implement. It was going to hurt, but the pain was to be spread around, and it was the only option available—other than war, of course. Earth, Terra, and all the smaller states were to receive a fixed share of the supply. The most renowned economists, mathematicians, engineers, planners, and logisticians alive had done their best to calculate how that burden should be shared fairly. No one was to be cut off, yet no party would be able to satisfy all of its former demands. According to the calculus, a few decades of steadily shrinking supplies were left—for all. This was the clarion call. Earth and Terra should have complained the least, so close to the giant ball of fusing hydrogen they'd almost ignored for so long. There was their future—Sol—and the plan put them on notice to either make the switch or stumble back into pre-telegraphic times. As for Mars, the Asteroid Belt, and the rest of the Outer—well, the future was a little less secure for them. Further out from the Sun they'd have to solve some monumental engineering problems to get at the helium-3 on the gas giants of the Outer Solar System. It looked impossible now, but it wasn't wise to bet against human ingenuity, especially when pushed into a corner.

"The Terrans have their own figures they'd like considered," Rittener said politely. "It's their view that Borealis' distribution graphs were crafted more by the armies of lobbyists and teams of deal-making legations that flooded in to help Borealis with the plan." There was no polite way to say that. "It couldn't hurt to look at the figures again, could it?" Rittener left off saying, "especially if it avoids a war."

"That old saw, again? There isn't a scintilla of truth to that." Rittener didn't need to consult an amanuensis to determine if he were lying. But the flushed redness in Stanislaus' face betrayed something else too. He was flabbergasted that Clinton Rittener, of all people, should be putting forward Terra's case on Borealis. He needed clarification.

"Is Terra's view," Stanislaus demanded to know, "your view?"

The Terran view was the Lunar Partition Doctrine. For their part, nothing could be more fair and equitable. There was obviously a helium-3 shortage and Terra would be more than happy to lend a hand. The Lunar Equator was proposed as a demarcation line. The Terran Ring would see to acquiring its own helium-3, tapping the fields in the southern hemisphere. Borealis could go on mining those in the north and sell the production to the rest of the interplanetary market. There it was, plain and simple, problem solved. The plan surprised no one. Terra had always just grabbed whatever it wanted, and the heavy-handed fingerprints of the Ring were easily discernible on this proposal too. The generous accord to leave the rapidly dwindling stakes in the northern hemisphere to Borealis while they expropriated the rest was actually offered with straight faces by Terran diplomats.

When the plan was unveiled it produced snickers everywhere—except on Borealis. Borealis took it for what it was and started growling back. They'd come to regard the Terrans as thankless and insulting. Borealis had powered the tens of thousands of fusion reactors on the Ring, and had done so for generations. Now that a crisis loomed—and yet one that could be peaceably solved if but Borealis' steady hand be trusted—the Terrans weren't replying as faithful comrades and allies. They were snarling instead, barking directives and threats that made it quite clear the Terrans didn't view them as equals at all.

"And these proposed Terran settlements on the Moon," the Borelian ambassador had said in the Forum, "from whence will they receive their water and food?"

The Terran ambassador bristled. "If you are threatening to withhold those supplies, Terra has the ability to ship them in. They would be small operations that wouldn't require that much."

All the delegates laughed at the idea of water-starved Terra exporting H2O to the broiling lunar surface. The laughter was punctuated with cat-calls from the delegates of the Alliances on Earth, mindful of another great bone of contention. "So pilfering Earth's fresh water for yourselves isn't good enough? Will you leave us our oceans at least, or do you have plans for that too?" The Alliances on Earth had every reason to complain bitterly. Terran long-wave, very low frequency technology, broadcast into the ionosphere with blistering amplitudes, created pressure cells in the atmosphere below that moved the jet streams anywhere the Ring liked. They mostly liked them at absurd heights where much of the moisture could be sucked into intake scoops the size of the base of the Great Pyramid at Giza. This had greatly expanded desertification of the planet and helped spawn the desperate wars that wracked the parched planet. The Terran Ring looked like a halo from Borealis, but from Earth it looked like a noose.

The Borelian ambassador's retort was considered a casus belli on Terra. "Well, they'd better not be *too* small. Anyone entering Borelian sovereign territory without valid documentation is subject to immediate arrest. Hopefully, you're considering logistics which includes a security force, too."

There is where matters stood—on the brink of war. Terra had sent Demetrius Sehene to participate in the recent piloting match and Borealis had pretended to welcome him. But both sides were maintaining a diplomatic pretense that hardly disguised that the adversaries were on the edge of a precipice.

"YOU TALK MUCH LIKE the jingoists on the Ring, Mr. Rittener," Stanislaus accused. "Whose side are you on anyway?"

"I'm on the side of common sense, Dr. Stanislaus," Clinton elucidated. "You must realize Borealis plays right into their hands with all your provocations."

That animated the councilor quickly. He didn't like Rittener's choice of words in the least.

"Provocations?! You can't be serious," he said in a loud, angry voice. "It's just the reverse." Stanislaus' face was sapped of any power for subterfuge, frowning and staring in offended disbelief.

Rittener waited for some composure to return, and then held up a fair-minded hand. "Be that as it may, it really doesn't matter which side is pushing harder. The Terran Ring has always pulled its punches with Borealis. I'm telling you— they're willing to hit you as hard as they can right now." He said the next sentence very quietly, very honestly, as amicably as he could. "Councilor, you don't have to buy me. If you're asking if I have good reasons for my beliefs about Terra's intentions, formally swearing me into your service isn't required."

Stanislaus was still stuck on the word. "Provocations?" He laughed aloud. "You mean like the provocation we offered them when we refused to hand you over to Terra?" Stanislaus' left eyebrow raised. By his exasperated expression Rittener could see quite easily that many a heated debate about just that must have raged within the Council lately.

Rittener didn't utter a sound, allowing the councilor to nod affirmatively to his own question.

"But if you're here as a friend and you have some knowledge that poses a danger to Borealis . . . " Stanislaus paused, trying to bring the right words out. "Then it's the request of the Council that you make us aware of it."

Rittener replied as simply as he could. "The old policy of 'inviolable Borealis' . . . well, Councilor, you're going to need a defense stronger than that."

That had been Borealis' great protection against powerful neighbors: her incomparable allure. Paris wasn't destroyed in the World Wars for the same reason. To obliterate Borealis, though, would be as unconscionable as burning down a hundred Parises. The Borelians had let this go to their heads though, imagining themselves bullet-proof. They were at times petulant and uncompromising and their adversaries were tired of it. "Who *does* own the Moon?" was now accompanied by another question. "Why *shouldn't* the Borelians get exactly what they deserve?" Many people on Terra were saying out loud for the first time what sort of treatment was best suited for the unspeakably arrogant Borelians.

"Mr. Rittener, I must tell you," Stanislaus was shaking his head 'no' as he spoke, "if you've come so far to advise surrender, you might just as well have stayed on Mars. I have to deal with plenty here who are entertaining the same thought."

Rittener was shaking his head 'yes' as he spoke. "I'm aware of that. Was that stunt involving Nerissa during the previous race concocted to depreciate their counsel?" That might have been too blunt. He *was* speaking to a Borelian councilor—and Nerissa *was* his niece.

"Explain yourself," Stanislaus growled.

Since it was too late to do otherwise, Rittener did. He had determined already that it was time for Borelians to experience first-hand what bare knuckles felt like. Maybe they'd come to their senses after all?

"I've trained flying virtually with Nerissa a hundred times. But I've never seen her fly so clumsily and recklessly. I have to say I was a bit embarrassed for Borealis, watching such an amateurish display." He stopped for a moment and shrugged. "It might have pushed subliminal buttons with a few fence-straddlers still unsure about the faithless nature of Terrans, true. That's the wrong medicine right now."

Stanislaus had determined something of his own: that Rittener had passed into the realm of impertinence. He was sure about that, but since that never happened— ever—he wasn't quite so sure how to react. He sat there staring wordlessly.

"And how surprising that all those tangles should have involved Demetrius Sehene," Rittener added sarcastically. "He's a Terran spy, you know, don't you?" Everyone in the

Inner knew that. Having all this pointed out was the final straw though.

With that the interview was concluded. Stanislaus made that clear when he called his amanuensis' name, Hippocrates.

"Yes, Councilor?" He appeared instantly—bald, bearded, clad in a toga—with stylus and papyrus at the ready, just as if it were 400 BC.

"Ask Daiyu to schedule a meeting with Clinton Rittener, at her earliest convenience. It's about that matter we discussed."

"Immediately, Councilor." Hippocrates gently tried to remind him about some color code for the message but Stanislaus ignored the prompt. He rose and motioned Rittener to follow him. "The Council will be waiting. It's time for your oath."

As the two men strode in the gentle gravity through the stone-cleaved corridor between Stanislaus' office and the Council Chambers, Rittener, out of the blue, told him the rest. Rittener had chosen to take the councilor into his deepest, personal confidence at the very last moment, when it was too late for any discussion. It was cheeky in the extreme but it was powerfully delivered, and when Stanislaus had time to think about it, taking his seat on the dais, it didn't surprise him after all. This particular *condottiero* was famous for being impossible to predict.

"I'm quite well-informed about the question you were afraid to ask. As a matter of fact, I know the whole thing—and a bit more, too."

Stanislaus detected nerves in his voice, for the first time. That assured him that Rittener was telling the truth more than anything. "I *did* come to Borealis for no reason other than to live correctly." Rittener paused. Stanislaus couldn't really make out the expression in the dimly lit corridor, the voice sounded pained though. "And, maybe to make up for the parts of my life when I didn't live correctly."

Rittener pointed to Stanislaus' golden caduceus. It gleamed even in the low light. "Fate has put you here and now, just like me. It won't do for either of us to pretend otherwise. Think about what that insignia means to you as you listen to me speak before the Council. And then support me."

The impractical, childish part of Stanislaus told the doctor that Rittener's words, certainly unusual and strangely delivered, still meant nothing more than what tension and emotion might produce. Rittener was a man who had been escaping death regularly for many years and now had found himself safe and sound in the unassailable harbor of Borelian citizenship. Why shouldn't he be giving voice to strange, garbled utterances?

Sitting in his august councilor's chair, going over syllable by syllable what Rittener had just told him, that's what Stanislaus told himself, anyway.

CHAPTER EIGHT

IMMINENT DANGER

IT WAS STANDING ROOM only for Clinton Rittener's swearing-in ceremony. A vacant seat would have been unusual for any session of the Council, though. Borelians were keen on politics and the Council rarely sat unless under the eyes of a full house. The chamber itself wasn't that big—about the size of an arenaball auditorium, and in the design of an ancient semicircular theater, the rows of seats carved in the rock itself, rising one on the other at a noticeably steep angle. The councilors sat on a raised dais against the far wall, in the center.

Above the councilors, ascending a good portion of the height between them and the ceiling, stood—or rather floated—a ten-foot-tall, three-dimensional, holographic representation of the goddess of the Moon: Borealis' Central System Amanuensis, Diana. She wasn't dressed in the flowing regal gowns that Hera and Athena wore, nor in the noble robes worn by queens in images stamped on coins or cut into marble. It was a rather perky Diana, a deity in her early twenties, perpetually. She wore a huntress' tunic, cut well above the knees and made of a material silky and still rustic, translucently diaphanous and yet opaque. The programmers had played other tricks to infuse her with convincing divine characteristics. Her skin radiated a heavenly glow, her lips painted in a red too rubicund for reality, her eyes the color and sheen of the finest sapphires in the Titan Consortium's mural of the Rings of Saturn. At her hip hung a quiver of arrows, and over her shoulder she wore her bow.

Diana's hair was modestly restrained, pulled back in a Hellenic twist into a flaxen braid that fell down her back. And, for certain, one look into Diana's face is all that is required to tell that Borealis had something other than a coquette in mind when they crafted their amanuensis. She wore the same expression the goddess in myth had shown to the hunter Orion, who had accidentally come upon the deity bathing in her sacred pool one midnight in the sylvan thickets of the woods. Diana had set the wild dogs of the forest to tear Orion limb from limb—not spending a thought on the hunter's blamelessness. She was upholding the common sense dictum that embarrassing a goddess would be the last act of any human—innocent *or* guilty.

Borealis had meant to send a similar message with the look they'd given Diana, and the air desired was well conveyed. Here was a gilded city, beautiful and rich, cultured and open-minded, and unique in all of creation; that's what Diana's body said. Here was a state with the muscle to tame any inimical force in space, a people that had conquered every challenge put in their path, a power on the ascendant, young enough to be perhaps reckless with that strength. That's what the face said.

Diana made the formal announcement. "Councilors, next on the agenda: Clinton Rittener, taking an oath of citizenship, matter number AE 1432-C." The five hundred Borelians in attendance erupted, applauding fiercely. By the time Rittener had reached his place in the witness' platform in front of one of the podiums, the crowd was on its feet. The ovation was strong enough and lasted long enough to require that Rittener bow politely to the audience behind him, and then turn to the Council. He could see, as could many nearby, that even though decorum prevented the councilors from clapping had they wanted to, one of them, Daiyu, was gently wiping away tears. It had been a long time since the last honorary citizen was sworn in—Daiyu herself—twelve years ago. Everyone understood her feelings.

The emotions that drove Rittener's supporters were much more complicated. For starters, where *did* loyalties lie with Clinton Rittener? Every time a close look was taken at him he was in the service of some different power. Everything about him was in dichotomy. He was born on Earth and fought with the Eastern Alliance, yet as a liaison of the European Union. He was both a privateer of the Terran Ring while at the same time currently a wanted fugitive of Terran power, convicted of mutiny and treason. Between all this he'd rubbed elbows with the riff-raff of Mars and the underground, lightless world of the Outer. Now here he was on Borealis, piloting, of all things, and becoming a citizen.

For as beautiful, rich, exciting, and splendid as living on Borealis was, the plain fact was that a profound and abiding homesickness afflicted Borelians. After so many centuries, the people really just missed Earth. Blue skies, weather, rain, fog, sweat, humidity, and more—all the good, along with all the bad—but mostly the freedom of uncertainty was missed over everything. Rittener possessed the swashbuckling hubris that Borelians found earthy and appealing, that mixture of thinking and irrational, cowardly and brave, honorable and dastardly that humans used to make sense of the cacophony of life on Mother Earth. And, for better or worse, wasn't Clinton Rittener the best, at what he did and was? Hadn't Borealis been the harbor of the most superlative personalities in the Solar System, for centuries now? Lastly, not a few of the pilot-crazed aficionados on Borealis stuck up for him for no other reason than that. Many of them were calling out piloting slogans and catch phrases. So he got quite a reception from the live audience taking in the proceedings; many other Borelians were watching through their amanuenses.

When the applause abated, Stanislaus directed him to raise his right hand and had Rittener repeat an ancient promise to uphold, protect, honor, and defend Borealis, over all others, unto death. "I do swear," Rittener repeated at the end.

"Then the Council of Borealis recognizes you, Clinton Rittener, as a citizen of Borealis, from this moment forward, entitled to all the rights, privileges, and protections thereto, unto death."

Now a real ovation broke out. It was long enough that Stanislaus had to bring his gavel down a few times. Diana was attempting to move things along too, repeating to the Council, but actually addressing the onlookers, "Mr. Rittener has requested to make a citizen's oration." Indeed, there was an old-fashioned, genteel part in the ceremony, going back to Settlement Times, where the new citizen should say a few words about his feelings for his new home. The audience was hushed, and five hundred fellow citizens listened intently to what the newest should have to say. The councilors were keen to listen too, each guaranteed to hear the words through their own particular filters.

THERE WERE FIVE "HAWKS" on the Council, led by two military men: the admiral of the Borelian fleet, Albrecht, and the commandant of the Security Forces, General Gellhinger. Two CEOs of the largest helium-3 concerns in existence, along with the very eccentric philosopher-artiste, Mariah, made up the rest of the voting bloc. Four "doves" opposed them currently. The Caretaker General of the Garden, Breonia, spoke for them, because hardly a more pleasant voice could be heard. She acted the part of everyone's green-thumbed, well-intentioned, nurturing grandmother on Borealis. The commissioner of the Goldilocks Array's workers voted with her. So did two labor representatives from the most at-risk areas on the Moon—those operators in the Field working to mine helium-3 and sunlight—and outside the protection of shields. Stanislaus and Daiyu were the tenth and eleventh councilors, the swing vote.

Rittener signaled this was going to be more than the usual citizen's declaration when he silently, slowly pulled his amanuensis from his thumb, clicked it off, and placed it on display on the podium. This was absolutely voluntary, as it was illegal in any court, deposition, or legal session of any kind in Borealis, or any other civilized place, to demand testimony "naked"—that is, scanned without wearing an amanuensis. Diana would definitely scrutinize for honesty and candidness by default. It made an impression, sending a quizzical murmur through the assemblage and changing the expression on the faces of the councilors.

"What I have to say to the Council and people of Borealis is important enough that there can be no doubt about its veracity." He looked over his shoulder at his fellow citizens in attendance; he was talking to them too. "As per the first article of the first section of the Health and Safety Code," Rittener cleared his throat, quoting a law written back in the very oldest of Settlement Times, "I invoke the 'imminent danger' clause." He looked at each of the eleven members. Not one of them had really understood him. Of course his words made sense, but they were so incongruous, so unexpected. Admiral Albrecht was as puzzled as the rest and seemed on the point of words to Rittener, frowning and pulling himself straight up in his chair. "So I am requesting that the Council take my citizen's declaration as both that, and also as fulfilling my responsibility in bringing the most extreme emergency to the attention of the Council."

That certainly made things clear for the admiral, who addressed him now.

"Mr. Rittener, first, welcome to Borealis." He didn't say it like the Chamber of Commerce did; he was offended already, and deeply. "I commend your knowledge of our legal system. I'm not a lawyer but I am something of an historian, and I don't believe there is a case of anyone ever being granted Borelian citizenship and then putting it at risk within the first minute.

"Diana?" he asked.

"Never." She responded a few microseconds later. Diana had read the admiral's mind almost, from his dour expression, from the anger detected in the first syllable of the first word he uttered. She guessed correctly that the councilor was quite interested in the witness, yet not in a friendly way. She was all over Rittener, this unusual testifier sans amanuensis.

Albrecht lectured him. "Our ancestors were wise enough to put the responsibility for public safety in every citizen's hand, especially in those old days when disasters could and did strike so often. They were also sensible enough to craft the law so that it shouldn't be abused." The admiral fixed Rittener with an extremely frosty look of disapproval. "You are also aware of the risks attendant to misusing this right?"

Rittener knew that crying wolf could ultimately wind up getting one banished. But that was for repeated infractions, and the few times it had ever been used, candid histories admit, it was more akin to ostracism—for mostly political reasons.

"Yes, I am aware, Councilor," Rittener responded without emotion. "May I continue?"

Admiral Albrecht made an airy wave of his arm in Stanislaus' direction. "The Chair gives and takes permission to speak," he said plainly, completely unbiased, as if simply reading from the rules book. The admiral was a crew-cut, spit and polished, old-fashioned military man. He didn't even look to Stanislaus but kept his icy stare on the witness. The admiral's expression said he wasn't sure what was going on but that he didn't like it already.

Stanislaus wasn't absolutely certain how much more Rittener might know beyond what he'd already shared, but based off their previous conversation, he knew the direction Rittener's declaration would certainly take. That was enough to cause the nerves to be written right across his face, making clear to everyone, including the hundreds of citizens who were silently transfixed by the unbelievably strange turn of events, that he really didn't want Rittener to say another word at all.

"What are they talking about?" a few voices could be heard to say. No one told them to quiet down because everyone in the crowd was thinking the same thing. The "Twelfth Councilor," that's what the congregations of citizens at Council meetings were called. Sometimes the atmosphere could become quite raucous, but that was patently Borelian, too. There were so few citizens on Borealis that a gathering a few hundred strong, if sentiments within this "twelfth member" were united, was a force unto itself, and one that even the Council didn't anger without care and concern. "Is Clinton Rittener going to give his citizen's oration or not?" other annoyed voices were asking.

"It seems to me," Stanislaus offered, "that what you might have to say to the Council would better be heard in a closed session. I'll see that this matter is put on the agenda of the next meeting." Stanislaus said it with such evenhandedness that the finality which came with it sounded equally appropriate. Rittener's response to this seemingly fair decision, on the other hand, was unexpected and close to an open declaration of war.

"If you'd rather not accept my next comments as both my citizen's declaration *and* an official 'imminent danger' warning, then just consider it the first. But I don't intend to appear before any secret meetings of the Council, Dr. Stanislaus. What I have to say is going to be said here and now." The Surgeon General seemed to be physically knocked back by the words, and leaned in his chair. The rest of the councilors too sucked in their cheeks at the audacity.

"Then you're dismissed, Clinton Rittener."

Rittener demurred, twice more, quoting the law, emphasizing the importance of his remarks. Stanislaus stood his ground, and invited him to step away from the witness' podium—twice more.

That was supposed to be that, and it was—sort of.

The irritated grumbling that had punctuated the crowd now metastasized—and quickly. "What's going on? He's not being allowed to speak?!" The outraged queries started coming fast, furious, and loudly. The pilots weren't saying anything. They were too incensed to speak, now standing and sending incredulous stares down at the councilors. Before he turned to address his fellow citizens, he told Stanislaus that the die was cast, delivering the battle cry in Latin, as he had before so many other clashes: "Alea jacta est." The rest he said in his second language, in perfect New English, to the eager crowd on their feet, and pressing forward.

"Citizens of Borealis, I *do* have an imminent danger warning to convey. If the Council won't hear it, I'll deliver it to the citizenry instead." That's as far as he got when the Council—although stunned at the astonishingly rude challenge to its authority—regained its composure quickly enough.

Stanislaus took to his feet, brought the gavel down, twice, while calling out in a loud, disagreeable voice. "Mr. Rittener . . . Mr. Rittener . . . You are excused!"

Clinton turned to answer him but the words were drowned out by a quickly building roar of disapproval that swept from behind him and crashed on the councilors' dais. Two events occurred now simultaneously. Admiral Albrecht, beyond restraint at this point, barked an order to the bailiffs to remove Clinton Rittener. Five rows up, Alexandrine, an old-timer in the Field, a grizzled engineer and helium-3 rocketeer, at almost the exact same moment gave an emotional cry. "My nephew was at Valerian-3! By God, he'll be allowed to give his citizen's oration!" Those two conflicting projectiles, "Remove him!" and "He'll speak!" crashed together in the crowd's midst, setting off a chain reaction which rippled through the assembly. The collective decision was made instantly, and an angry human wave surged over the banisters and through the aisle barricades, surrounding Rittener on all sides. The pilots who led the assault seemed to have blood in their eyes, so different from the look of reluctance on the faces of the bailiffs, whose tardy reactions now put the matter in another realm altogether. Before weapons were drawn and a full-scale riot touched off, Breonia, the grand dame of Borealis, brought back sanity and decorum, and snuffed out the fuse. She scolded both sides, insisting that the citizenry retreat, demanding order, and charging the bailiffs to stand down.

Breonia's people had originally come from the Caribbean side of Costa Rica—from its Garifuna community—and she spoke both Spanish and New English with a delightfully pleasing accent. "Cuando menos piensa!" she started in Spanish, and then finished the thought in the patois English heard in Jamaica. "Cree! My goodness, but how quickly things often happen when you least expect them! Stand down!"

She silently caused her orders to be obeyed, glowering at any in attendance not ready yet to heed her lawful command, using her baleful countenance to subdue and pacify the unruly. While she waited for the proper comportment to be restored, she gave Rittener a long, silent look, and then addressed her fellow councilors with an honest query.

"The law entitles him to speak; that's simple enough, isn't it?" That she followed with an open admission. "There's the obvious concern among some councilors here, myself included, that Mr. Rittener might be preparing to allude to something classified." She paused with her head down for a moment and then faced her peers. "I've asked myself if the time for secrecy has passed." She scrambled slightly the old English proverb, "and if he's going to be putting the cat out of the bag, whether I should vote to let him speak anyway."

While Breonia and the other councilors were ruminating about this issue in front of them, only Diana was speaking. The amanuensis had never seen anything happen like *this* before and was certain that the councilors would be thankful for the panoply of information she was graphing out for them on her giant holographic console, whilst quoting the pertinent statutes concerning classified information.

"Shut up, Diana," Breonia said calmly, and then turned to Rittener.

"You have information about a matter that poses an imminent danger to Borealis, young man?" she asked Rittener plainly.

"I do," he answered just as plainly.

"Very well, I vote to allow him to speak, and demand a vote all around." There it was; as simple as that.

THE PILOTS OF BOREALIS

As the councilors deliberated and voted, Rittener caught sight of Nerissa. She had attended too, after all, with the other pilots. She was avoiding his eyes, he thought at first, but that wasn't the case, he could see now. He realized she was staring at someone in particular with that downcast look. She was frowning at her uncle who had just voted—"no." How odd, he thought, that she should have the power to capture his attention at such a moment, and much more strange that it should please him too.

It was six to five—to *allow* Rittener to speak. Three of the hawks were so enraged and disgusted by the vote that they decamped en masse. That changed little though. Clinton Rittener gave his citizen's oration, and invoked the safety clause—at the same time for the remainder of the Borelian Council, his fellow citizens in open session, the rest of the city via their amanuenses, and out into space and most importantly to the Terran Ring, by spies too stunned at the ease by which the news came.

Nerissa was listening intently too.

IT IS UNKNOWN FROM whence it came or how many eons it drifted in proximity to Sol's environs in the somewhat boring outskirts of one of the spiral arms of the Milky Way. After many thousands of years of coasting and silently listening, a signal was finally perceived, a signal and reception for which it was built: the first radio transmissions ever propagated by humanity. How it propelled itself toward the system from which the radio transmissions came is also unknown for certain, although it was a means not only beyond human engineering but barely dreamed of as yet. It merged unobtrusively within the trillions of comets and frozen detritus swirling in slow motion at the absolute limits of the Sun's gravity, arriving at its destination within the Oort Cloud. It focused its beacon on the obvious source of the electromagnetic signals, the third planet from the G-type, main sequence star a light year away, and began hailing. It had been hailing non-stop for many, many years—and finally had been answered.

The "Object," as it was called by the few who knew of its existence, had been broadcasting in a medium that had only recently been discovered to exist. The detection of this medium alone was enough to set physicists back on their heels. But if it weren't enough to discover a new type of neutrino, j-neutrinos—so infinitesimally small and ethereal, yet particles so staggeringly profuse—the real shock was that no sooner was a giant j-neutrino receptor brought on line on Luna then the astoundingly powerful drumbeat was heard loud and clear, coming from the Oort Cloud. The moment was at hand, stunned researchers realized, the scene imagined for centuries now reality. It pushed the subject of j-neutrinos not only out of the spotlight but right off the stage. These newly discovered subatomic particles, whether or not part of the answers to questions about dark matter and whether the universe were closed or open, were now one thing and nothing else: the vehicle that brought the first and long-awaited extraterrestrial message to human ears.

The greatest dialogue that could ever be shared was opened—with intelligences about whom nothing was known at first. Nothing mattered, even to include the clues of highly advanced information the Object was sending, so much as the earth-shaking, history-changing fact that a real salutation had been received—from alien minds. How they reasoned, what they thought and wished to convey, where they were from, or even more basically, how they counted and whether they had four, five, six, or more senses—everything had to be prised from the transmissions. They were cleverly constructed, packed with encoded information within concealed layers of data, which was interlaced and dovetailed with more obvious layers. One of the first things discovered about them was that they counted and did their math in base-11, unlike our base-10 system. The initial message made that clear in a number of ways. As with everything else nestled within the messages, the number was shouted straight out and also intelligently embedded.

The opening transmission, the original hail from the Oort Cloud, Borealis answered with a carefully measured and patterned burst of one hundred and forty four j-neutrino pulses directed at the Object. The scientists couldn't hold their breaths that long while they waited for a response; the Oort Cloud was too far away. The light-lag back and forth was two years, a duration of the greatest nail-biting and head-scratching in human history. During the long wait the message was received over and over. It was 3.35 minutes long—200.8663092 seconds long to be more exact. It was repeated again and again, with a 3.35-minute pause between rounds. The Fibonacci sequence was being beamed at the Earth system, dashed out in j-neutrino pulses—the first eleven digits of the sequence anyway—from one to eighty-nine.

One, added to itself, makes two. Two, added to the prior number—one—makes three. Three, added to the previous integer, two, in the sequence before it, makes five. So the pattern goes. The Fibonacci sequence is found everywhere in Nature, from the growth pattern of plants, to the geometry of shells, to the shape of spiral galaxies—and was found to be the very first message beamed to mankind from another race of sentient beings. And so the Borelians beamed their response at the Object, the digits of the sequence itself composed of the golden ratio, *phi*, which separated the next number in the series, the construct being infused with the ideal of all structures, forms and proportions, whether cosmic or individual, the mathematical essence of perfection. Yet, there was more imbedded than just the Fibonacci sequence. Scientists discovered this by attacking the transmission from every possible angle using every possible algorithm. Human acumen was sufficient to the task of searching out basic "yardsticks" hidden in the message.

Hydrogen was the key to unlocking other clues. This simplest of elements is by far the most abundant in the universe. Hydrogen is everywhere. It's the matter being fused in the cores of stars. Hydrogen is the yin to oxygen's yang in every drop of water in every ocean on every planet and moon. Great nebulas of the gas, many times the size of the Solar System, stretch across every section of the galaxy, sending out hydrogen's natural microwave emanations, radio waves attuned to 1420 megahertz. Hydrogen's signature, across the universe, everywhere, is a pulse of electromagnetic radiation moving outward at the speed of light and with the waves cresting 1,420,405,800 times per second. Since Earth's seconds would have meant nothing to the Object's builders, Borelian scientists juxtaposed countless possible combinations—one of which was the duration of the message with the wavelength and frequency of hydrogen. The first lock on the first door was opened. At almost one and a half billion cycles per second, in 200.8663092 seconds a hydrogen "clock" would have clicked off 285,311,670,000 ticks. This wasn't as random a number as one might think at first glance. It was eleven to the eleventh power—exactly. Theoreticians were numb with delight and satisfaction. Not only was the mathematic base of the Object's creators inferred, here was independent corroboration—independent, indeed!—of one of the central "crossroads integers" in the 11th dimensional matrix-vectors they insisted explained the universe at the Plank level—ten spatial directions with an eleventh temporal bearing, time itself.

THE PILOTS OF BOREALIS

Two years after Borealis beamed its response—sending one hundred and forty four j-neutrino bursts, the *next* Fibonacci number—the transmission ceased briefly, then restarted. This time the Object was broadcasting its tutorial, satisfied that it had a bona fide listener. Borealis frantically pressed into service every single one of the newest, fastest quantum computers at its disposal in order to interpret the messages, throwing all other research into an immediate moratorium. That wasn't all though. It put itself into motion, loosing its orbital mooring in the Oort Cloud and falling toward the Inner Solar System. The Sun's feeble gravitational pull at these distant regions, a light year from its surface, was far too weak to be accelerating the Object to the velocity it reached. Borealis watched close to utter disbelief as it attained 99.999 percent of the speed of light by the time it crossed the Solar System's heliopause on its way—obviously, it seemed to flabbergasted observers— to the Moon, and Borealis.

How such speed could be realized was, of course, of great interest to Borealis. The tutorial seemed to indicate a space-drive powered by quantum fluctuations in the vacuum itself. The tiny ripples in the froth of the fabric of the universe were the result of infinitesimal explosions of matter and antimatter virtual particles that came into being and then annihilated each other. This bizarre background of existence on the Plank level was an antique discovery—the Casimir effect, from the middle of the 20th century. The advanced physics of the race that constructed the Object could access the smallest reaches of space-time itself and play amazing games with the laws at the heart of everything, temporarily thwarting even the bosons in the Higgs Field that gave their vessels—and everything else in the universe—mass. They'd learned to manipulate space in eleven dimensional vectors in such a way that their crafts moved through areas rendered temporarily devoid of the normal rules for inertia and mass. They didn't break either Newton's or Einstein's bylaws; they simply manipulated them so that their ships—seemingly without mass insofar as Nature were concerned—could cruise through sections of space which suspended the standard demands required for building up light speed.

It wasn't so easy for Clinton Rittener to tell the whole story, even stripped of details. The narration was interrupted many times. The citizens of Borealis, at first thunderstruck and rendered speechless, quickly came around with dozens of questions they called out to the Council, to Rittener, and quite understandably, to no one in particular. One of the councilors himself, the most garrulous and talkative Stephanangelo, was casting back and forth of his fellow adjudicators, wearing a puzzled, hurt, and angry look. "Was I the only one not informed of this?" By the looks on the other councilors' faces it was embarrassingly apparent that this gossipy, voluble Italian, a liberal today but a conservative yesterday and who knows what tomorrow, had outrageously—and illegally—been left out of the loop. No one bothered to answer him. "What about that, Diana?" Stephanangelo asked.

"Shut up, Diana," Breonia said again quite calmly.

The Borelian Council's State Amanuensis hadn't opened her virtual mouth since being ordered to shut it the first time. Diana had to ignore the face Stephanangelo made and the accompanying pained bleating; Rittener found it comical, but had politely stifled the smirk. But now the electronic palpitations that were wracking Diana—recording the details of a meeting during which the minutiae of the highest-classified esoterica was bandied about openly—gave her an aspect her programmers never imagined her using. Asked a question by one councilor and told not to answer by another, programmed to maintain state secrets as one of her primal functions, and yet posting these pernicious data entries in her banks at the same time, well, if such an entity as an amanuensis could look confused, Diana did. She wore the same expression she might have displayed as when the hero Orion caught her off guard—only this time as if he'd brought Jason and all the Argonauts with him to peek at her while exposed bathing. That *did* bring a little smirk to life, a little levity that felt like a tonic to him right now. Just as his lips turned up he glanced at Nerissa again. She wasn't looking at her uncle now, or anyone else; she was staring straight back at him. Without thinking, automatically, he shrugged a little and crinkled his brow, as if to say, "Well?"

Stanislaus was banging his gavel, for once with gusto, with necessity. He was shouting for the boisterous assembly to return to their places, and for order to be reinstated. When the last unruly citizen was shown to his seat and decorum restored, the sole remaining hawk addressed Rittener.

There was a "Philip" on Borealis, of course. Here he was: the lantern-jawed, ruggedly handsome, sixty-year-old corporate dynamo of the Borelian helium-3 market. He was labeled a hawk by most, but possessed quite an opinion of himself, one too grand to fit into any one word. When Admiral Albrecht and the others stormed out they didn't seem the least surprised that Philip not only hadn't followed suit, but made it clear immediately that he'd be led around like that just as soon as water froze at noon in the Field. This councilor didn't mince words at all.

"Clinton Rittener, time is going to tell whether what you've already said is going to be sufficient to warrant your arrest. You can be assured that is being investigated as we speak. You understand that, of course, do you not?" He said it so plainly, seemingly without bearing ill will, not as a threat—even though that's exactly what it was. Rittener's nods told him that he did, so he went on. "You insisted on invoking the 'imminent danger' clause of Settlement Times codes." Philip put both hands up as if requesting aid. "I've heard nothing of the danger of which you wish to apprise the Council."

There was always a slight chance that Borealis could have pulled it off—without coming to blows with the Terran Ring. The odds now on that possibility were becoming astronomical. On the plus side, here was a relatively small target, so far away, radio silent, and broadcasting in the most arcane, hardly believable, just discovered medium. The hope was that Borealis could physically seize the Object before any other party were aware of it, or at least before any other effort could be mounted. The coup had to be attempted at least. Here was the future of the entire Solar System, the next great step for mankind, a shortcut to who knows how many centuries or millennia into the future.

"This is the property of Borealis," the hawks had declared so clearly in secret meetings, the sub rosa trysts to which Stephanangelo wasn't invited. "Borealis discovered it, hailed it, caused it to put itself en route to Borealis." Their logic seemed unassailable. Rittener decided he'd use the other side of the argument, as the doves most certainly must have brought up in those same clandestine meetings. Rittener steeled himself to finish, to broach this extremely unpleasant business, well aware that every step further was most definitely on illegal, seditious, life-changing ground. In a last moment of uncertainty and weakness he looked around himself at his newly adopted countrymen. Of a sudden he found the strength to let go the last restraint to which self-interest had clung, and it was in the faces of the Borelians around him that he saw what braced him. Their faces merged with so many others: with the confused, scared, disbelieving faces of too many humans he'd seen from the valleys of Asia on Earth to Valerian-3 in the Asteroid Belt. An innate yet evil power, humankind's will to self destruction, had been sucking the soul out of him his entire adult life, and changing him into someone he was not intended to be. That ended today, forever, he thought to himself as he gathered his thoughts.

"You couldn't have imagined that something like this would have transpired unnoticed by others?" Rittener asked the Council.

The Borelians in attendance had stopped fiddling with their amanuenses some time back during these amazing proceedings, realizing that the Council had quietly changed the status of the meeting from open to closed. All channels out were unceremoniously blocked, it was quite clear. It was too little, too late, and too ineffective though. Five hundred Borelians were still listening, and quite intently now as they realized what the councilors' look of dismay and apprehension meant.

Philip wasn't backing water at all. "To which parties are you referring?"

Rittener gave him an exasperated look. It was an excellent wager that any object, no matter the size, no matter from as far away as the Oort Cloud or the Andromeda Galaxy for that matter, which hurtled toward the Inner Solar System at the speed of light, and then braked at just as a shockingly unbelievable deceleration to invite contact, would certainly register on a data console—somewhere. As it was, the *son et lumière* of the Object had set off bells and whistles—everywhere.

"The Terran fleet, on a heading to engage the Borelian squadron sent to rendezvous with the Object, I'd say is fairly good evidence that the Terran Ring qualifies as one of those parties. Would you not agree, Councilor?"

Philip was engrossed in the virtual panel he'd asked Diana to open in front of him. His eyes never left it, his fingers deftly manipulating data in what from Rittener's point of view looked like nothing but thin air. "We'll ask the questions, Mr. Rittener," Philip answered, as if he'd hardly heard what Clinton had said. He had heard though.

Without looking up he fired what was meant to be a lethal shot. "I'm going to have charges prepared against you, for that last comment." Now he raised up and glared straight at Rittener. "Your audacity in coming before the Council, declaring state secrets in public in this chamber . . . " Since sedition was a capital offense Rittener realized this was going to be a fight to the death. There were no rules in such combat so he interrupted the councilor.

"Audacious? I'm an amateur. Only experts could think to withhold news of the greatest event in history and then turn it into just another excuse for another round of yet another war." There was no fear for himself detected in his words, only disgust. "Both Borealis and Terra have behaved shamelessly, stupidly—dangerously," he accused, and then went on to explain how.

There was a peace faction on Terra that wanted to share and solve problems with Borealis, Rittener reminded the Council. There was a war party too, who wanted nothing less than the destruction of Borealis as an independent state. The cloak and dagger scenario had greatly helped bring the crisis to the point of all-out war, with two great fleets now streaking toward each other, set to collide near the orbit of Jupiter. Both sides had relied on the absurd strategy of mute silence, neither saying a word to the other, both pretending that nothing at all was happening, with the populations of both powers kept completely in the dark. Borealis, though, it was clear was desperate to claim her prize, and Terra just as determined to snatch it for herself.

"You're doing exactly what those who wish the worst for Borealis would hope you'd do," Rittener warned, "and draining the political life out of your allies on the Terran Ring with the actions you've chosen."

"Allies? On the Terran Ring?" Philip sneered. "Is that who you speak for, these allies on Terra?"

Admiral Albrecht and General Gellhinger re-entered the Council Chambers as Philip spoke. They were accompanied by an armed squadron of security guardsmen who, like always, were wearing the same expression of pure, deadly serious business. Rittener's citizen's oration was at an end.

Albrecht spoke as he and the general took their seats. "Clinton Rittener, you are both excused and directed to appear at a closed meeting of the Borelian Council next session to be fully debriefed." He was so obviously furious that he had a hard time getting the words out without showing his anger. He glanced around at his fellow councilors who were all shaking their heads in agreement.

Rittener gave a respectful nod and repeated submissively, "Of course, Admiral." He had lodged most of the points he'd wanted to make. All Borealis, all the Solar System, would be talking about the rumors of an unknown extraterrestrial Object and the impending clash between the Terran and Borelian fleets, and how both were stunningly true, how both led down two clearly marked paths, one for peace and the other for war. He'd missed though with one last important piece of news that more than anything else made sense of his "imminent danger" speech. Borealis might be challenging Terra to an all out gunfight—armed herself only with a pathetic little derringer. He would be able to apprise the Admiral and the Council about the most alarming part of his testimony behind closed doors, and hopefully, in time to make a difference. "It is a rare privilege to be heard by the Council," he said politely, bowing to some extent. Then, after just the slightest pause, he added, almost as an afterthought. "I do have one more request to make of the Council—a purely personal one, if I may?"

The Borelian Council, all of them, friend and foe, had had enough of Clinton Rittener. Not one of them even wanted to respond formally to any of his requests, personal or otherwise. Their collective silent stares he, strangely enough, interpreted as his leave to continue.

"Dr. Stanislaus, it would be a great honor to fly with your niece, Nerissa. As I told you before, Councilor, I came to Borealis to pilot. I have admired her, greatly, for some time. If you would convey my request, I would be very much in your debt."

It started almost immediately, though slowly—then, very quickly, it built. All the pilots and many others in the crowd were whistling, that particularly lunar, high-pitched whistle in the slightly alien air. It was another thing that pilots did that couldn't be explained exactly. The idea, though, was that the sky might be falling, but Rittener, by Diana, had kept his priorities in order. This scarred, amply repaired, over-the-hill mercenary from Earth was sure acting like a pilot—and on no other place in existence was such behavior respected more than Borealis. And so the chamber reverberated with their whistles.

From the gallery, even though the noise drowned out her words, he could read her lips. "I *will* fly with you, Clinton Rittener," she was saying.

And, for the first time, she gave him an entirely genuine smile.

CHAPTER NINE

THE PILOTS' CODE

THE NEXT MORNING HE had already arrived at the base of the piloting elevator and was waiting for her. She was rarely without a memorable opening remark, and this was no exception.

"Asking permission from my uncle was such a quaint and Earthly thing to do," Nerissa said, her words accompanied by a wry smile. The mild sarcasm was more than paid for though by her next sentence. "But I have never seen such a courageous case made in the Council, and I want to apologize for having misjudged you."

"Well, that comment about you doing anything for your country," he was apologizing as well, "I know that didn't come out right."

She opened her eyes wider and parted her lips in surprise. "But I would. I'm flying with you, aren't I?"

She held out her hand.

"Apology accepted," he said, taking it. Her fingers, like her limbs, were long and sleek, the nails brushed with glitter that sparkled in the dayglow.

She'd only just awoken, Rittener could tell, her hair still uncombed, braided quickly for flying.

Strolling next to him, her step in graceful harmony with the lunar gravity, she stood only half an inch shorter than him, and Rittener was a very tall man. Such an imposing frame was somehow yet delicately constructed. Nerissa's allure though, her uniqueness, came from those kinds of dichotomies because she was a complex creature of diametrically opposed qualities, somehow contained within the same beautiful female animus. Her delicacy was yet another contradiction, for that was appearance alone; her stamina and will were absolutely unbounded. Nerissa used the contradictions and dualities that animated her personality to quite an effect, sufficient to take men's feet out from under them. This princess, the niece of one of the Borelian councilors, the most famous flyer alive, and most probably a former or current spy to some degree, was also this sweet-smelling, hair-tousled coquette in front of him. Even that had its mirror image because she'd worn a particularly modest leotard, one so proper and reserved that it had to have been chosen quite purposefully. As she took his hand again she seemed shy and coy, and yet possessed of an eagerness barely hidden for dignity's sake.

"Something else I think I've had to change about you, too. You came here to fly, didn't you? You're a real pilot, aren't you, Clinton Rittener?"

This was even more personal and flattering, because pilots, well, they were a breed unto themselves.

DIFFERENT COLORED RACING CHARIOTEERS, in ancient times, each led their rival factions in Rome, Alexandria, and elsewhere. They were powerful enough to almost bring down emperors. During the Nika Riots in Constantinople, Justinian had to flee from them to the city's harbor on the Bosporus to take ship, and was only turned back at the last minute by his steel-hearted, cold-blooded wife, the Empress Theodora, who told him famously that "royal purple doesn't run!" Gladiators' sweat sold for such a price that only high-born patrician maidens could afford it, and centuries later the perspiration of rival knights and chevaliers who jousted soiled the kerchiefs of swooning countesses and marchionesses. Sport had always shaped society, and society done so with sport, since the beginning. Golfers had been businessmen, and cricketers, gentlemen. It was ruffians who played by the rules they created for ice hockey and rugby, and footloose partying surfers who invented a dialect to go with theirs. Pilots, too, had their own culture and etiquette, but it was much, much more than that. To many it was a unique bond among an insular band of brothers and sisters, and to some it was almost a religion.

Pilots believed in absolutes, since they faced them constantly as they flew: exhilaration, endurance, confidence, and the rest. Each of these and every other quality existed somewhere, a perfect good and bad that suffused the universe, perhaps, many pilots believed, embedded in the very fabric of the nothingness of the vacuum of space. People had known this void since Old Modern times, but in the current era, with the realm of humanity measured much less as solid ground and so much more as the vast, empty expanse of the Solar System, the effect of that sea change was seen in a thousand places, piloting but one. The piloting code was pure simplicity, but roiling at the same time with an infinity of agreements and contradictions within, just like the incomprehensible quantum froth that lay beneath the surface of nothingness itself.

Pilots just "lived correctly." If that meant lying were the path that produced the real good, a pilot would be expected to lie. If truth did more good, nothing could induce a lie then. That same simplicity ruled every other action. Everything was allowed, up to murder and beyond, while anything might be forbidden at the same time. The basic philosophy was that every sane human knew instinctively what course to take to preserve dignity, to uphold the affirmative interior view of self, in short, to live one's life as a positive rather than a negative force. Their audacious claim was that hints of this simple maxim—their code—was to be found in Egypt's Book of the Dead, Isaac Newton's little-read million-word treatise on biblical code, Vedic texts, Dead Sea Scrolls, and in a thousand other places where humanity had left a mark distinguishing itself from every other thing in this wide Solar System, or any other. They were the current vessel for this dogma.

Pilots didn't waste too many words describing it; the code was something that should come naturally to the flyer. Part of the shorthand was that as rare as it was for a person to venture into the public arena without an amanuensis, it really wasn't that unusual for pilots to "go naked" like that. Neither Clinton nor Nerissa were wearing theirs. It was a statement that said that deception—among many other things—was really self-deception at heart.

They boarded the piloting elevator and touched the tab to the expert level. Ascending presented yet another breathtaking panorama of wondrous Borealis.

"Where would a poet promise to steal a Borelian woman away to?" Rittener asked the question in all seriousness, quietly, staring in awe at the vista before them. "Doesn't that present a problem as a literary device—with paradise right here?"

Nerissa, native-born but not yet jaded with the city's beauty, was transfixed too. "It's going to be better in a while," she answered simply.

There were no words to describe the bird's-eye view of a pilot flitting around the gilded city of Borealis. Powered by one's own muscles, truly flying like Icarus, or even much older myths and fantasies—as human winged figures painted in Neolithic cave dwellings showed—indeed, just calling such dreamlike ecstasy "better" didn't really do, but then no words would.

When they reached the launch platform and Rittener was helping her buckle on her wings he asked her the same favor everyone did. "If you've got any advice for me, before we start . . . ?"

She looked at him blankly. "Well, I'd have to see you fly first, Clinton Rittener." She waited for the wisecrack to sink in, hiding her smirks, tugging at the buckles and straps, checking her kit. And then she looked at him with an expression of realization. "Oh, you're wondering about the last times, during our races," and then added, "I can't see behind me when I fly." He wasn't sure if Nerissa of Borealis was flirting with him, but she certainly was joking with him, even if it was at his expense, and soon—would be flying with him.

"That's true," Rittener agreed. "Keep an eye on my dives, though, if you would? I'm already pretty much an expert at crashing into people." The minute he said it, he almost wanted to pull the words back, not sure if he should have referenced her tangles with Demetrius Sehene with his tongue in his cheek. But Nerissa took it good-naturedly. And, she was determined to have the last riposte.

"Diving? That comes at the home stretch." She made a Galilean hand gesture of her own; she'd been there too. It suggested that was a long way down the path for Rittener.

SITTING AND CATCHING THEIR breaths under Kepler's Arch, recuperating after the flight, they talked of many things. Not a word though passed between them about anything he'd said in the Council Chambers, he too certain he'd already spoken far enough out of turn to last a lifetime on Borealis, she unwilling now to tempt him to do more damage. She too had good reasons for reticence; she was still Stanislaus' niece. There were plenty of other things of which to speak. They talked about the marvels of the Solar System they'd both been fortunate enough to see for themselves, and laughed about the strangest habits and customs of those far-off places.

"Speaking of the most unusual customs, you *are* sitting under Kepler's Arch, you know." Nerissa asked him if he'd made his wish yet. The arch was the largest single piece of solid gold in existence. Anyone fortunate enough to sit underneath it could make a single wish, but only once in an entire lifetime. She interpreted by his disbelieving chuckle that he hadn't.

"Well, don't wait too long," she lectured him like one of the city's guides. "There are cases of people who lived their entire lives on Borealis and had died without wishing. They hadn't wanted to waste it, and waited for the perfect time that never came."

Wishes, and things that came true or didn't, and the fatigue that overtook both of them now as they sat and collected themselves—this had both of them sharing a quiet moment. Sitting next to him, she boldly took his hand, enticing it toward her.

"This was your father's, you said?" she asked him. It was an unusual ring, on its face embossed a red salmon leaping over three blue waves. He pulled it off and handed it to her.

"Have a look at it. It's very, very old. From the beginning of the twentieth century—1914, to be exact."

Nerissa was enthralled. "I love antiquities!" The enthusiasm in her eyes was real. "This must have an amazing story. Does it?" If it hadn't, Rittener would have had to make one up for her on the spot rather than disappoint her.

"A very amazing story, actually," Rittener said confidently. "My father's side of the family is from southern Denmark, an area that was once part of Germany. One of my ancestors exchanged buttons with an English Tommie during the World Wars, the first one. That fish, and the waves, that's the insignia of the British Second Corp. It was passed down all these years, someone made a ring out of it, and here it winds up on the Moon under Kepler's Arch."

Of course, the ring and story had more than piqued her interest. She held it up to the dayglow reflecting off the Dome to get a better look at it.

"Why were they exchanging buttons?" she asked. "Was that when the war ended?"

He answered her first with a contradictory, disconcerted puff of air. "It's a sad story, Nerissa," he warned her, wincing his green eye a little. "You sure you want to hear it?"

The Christmas Truce on the Western Front in 1914 was more than a poignant story. It was the title page of an epic of carnage and slaughter that had been the history of bleeding Earth from then on, and *still* at it. German and English troops, dug into opposing trenches and having just undergone the most horrific six months ever experienced in warfare, of their own accord on both sides, against their officers' wishes, exhausted by the killing, just put down their weapons on Christmas Eve, 1914.

"So, they met in the no man's land between the wires, exchanging gifts, trading cigarettes, singing holiday songs, playing soccer—and swapping insignia." Rittener was going to go on, but left it right there. It was just as well since Nerissa didn't care to hear any more.

"Oh, I don't want to know the rest," she said, closing her eyes and crinkling her nose. "They, of course, had to go back to it the next day, right? They went back to killing each other the very next day, that's how the story ends?"

She took his hand and pushed the ring back onto his finger, shaking her head in distress. "You've got a relic of a nightmare here, Clinton Rittener."

He nodded his head in agreement but had a good answer. "It was my father's. It's really one of the very few things of his that I have."

Nerissa was still holding his hand when he said that. Now she took the other one too, sitting so close to him that he could smell her damp hair and the slightly sweet scent of her perspiration on her leotard.

Her next words went straight inside him, to the deepest place. "That change in you that you spoke of in the Council," she was looking straight into his eyes, "that made a great impression on me. This is part of that, isn't it?"

Rittener looked confused. "But I never said anything about any change that's come over me."

Nerissa lifted an eyebrow. She could see inside men, her look said. She could see inside him, at least. That's what her words said too.

"No, you didn't say that outright. But I heard everything you were saying, Clinton Rittener."

Maybe it was possible for women like her to peer within and see the wounds inside him. A change *had* built in him, growing for a long time now, and overpowering him finally at Valerian-3. It pleased him greatly to think that Nerissa could actually perceive it. She must have seen something, though, because a tear was almost welling in her eyes.

"I want you to know that we might disagree on some important things—but I'm on your side. As a Borelian, as a pilot, as a friend."

Rittener reached over and wiped the tear from her cheek. "You're not wasting a wish on me, are you?" he asked.

She pushed his hand away and laughed. "Diana! You are arrogant, aren't you? And that's perspiration. Of course not, I made my wish a long, long time ago."

She squeezed his hand and said it again though.

"But I'm on your side, Clinton Rittener. I swear it."

He heard her promise, under Kepler's Arch, listening to her sweet words—while making a silent wish of his own.

CHAPTER TEN

POLISHED GEMS

BRIGHT AND EARLY THE next morning—even though the bright-
ness never changed and morning was just an archaic term
attached to the *ante meridian* itinerary on Borealis—the sergeant-at-arms of the Council presented himself at Rittener's
quarters. He was accompanied by two smartly attired officers
from Security Forces. It wasn't made clear whether by invitation or compulsion.

"The full Council is in session. I'm here to escort you."

From the Basement to Council Chambers was a completely interior trip, accomplished with very little effort
through the honeycomb series of elevators, escalators, and
moving walkways. Passersby either kept their distance or
moved out of the way of this party—the officers in the lead
with the same air as lictors of Old Earth bearing fasces to
advertise the footsteps of an imperial magistrate. The Council,
however, didn't consider itself in the same category as Russian
politburos or French directories, shuffling endless lines of vic-
tims off to gulags or guillotines with bored indifference. The
sergeant offered Rittener a token of the Council's humanity
and courtesy.

"It's early and with no prior notice the councilors were concerned you'd miss your breakfast." Borelian tarts, delicious concoctions of pecans, marzipan, and honey, were meant to be eaten on the run. They were addictive but Rittener couldn't be tempted. "In training," he declined. Noticing the sergeant's eyes lingering on the delectable treats, he added, "But there's no reason they should go to waste." The sergeant-at-arms was wiping away sticky crumbs as they entered chambers.

This second appearance before Borealis' Council was more daunting in some ways than the first. Rittener stood before the eleven ministers and no one else, the closed session absolutely blocked, the chambers vacant. The only other entity privy to the proceedings was—Diana. She initiated the hearing, banging her virtual gavel.

"Councilors, now to the matter of Clinton Rittener, docket number CR 2346-E." She paused, and with surprising human affectation, fixed him with silent and uncomfortable scrutiny, hesitating just long enough to let Rittener know she had indeed remembered him, and with her next words to apprise him that the memory was less than pleasant.

"This session is . . . classified." She paused, yet again, before the last word, and put even more emphasis by raising her volume. The next few minutes Diana spent advising the witness regarding the minutiae of the legal strictures and responsibilities that applied. Rittener purposefully refused to look at the amanuensis and really was only half-listening. Daiyu, he could plainly see, by luck or design, occupied the Chair. Rittener probably knew her better than even her fellow councilors, even though he'd never exchanged a single word with her. Clinton had left his former soul in her country on Earth, dreamed often in her language, had read most of her Mandarin literary works and memorized the gems. The last time he'd been in Hell the people there looked and acted a lot like her. Daiyu, of course, knew all of this as well.

Diana's litany about all the ways Clinton could lose his life by loosing his lips very quickly turned to background noise. He and Daiyu had locked eyes and seemed to be sharing something both sublime—and yet painful.

Still, Diana demanded a response. "Is all that clear? Does the witness have any questions before the session begins?" Rittener's lack of attention became apparent to Diana as it was now obvious he'd been thinking about something else all the while. The look in her virtual eyes suggested that amanuenses could in fact feel anger and other emotions. It gave the impression she'd be happy to have her holographic hands around his neck.

"Mr. Rittener," now a soft, feminine voice caressed the rock-hewn chamber walls. Such a small and mellifluous accent reverberating off the lunar stone piqued Clinton's ears. "Is that how I should address you?" Daiyu asked. "You're a Borelian citizen now. Your name is to be inscribed in the Roll. Is it to be Clinton? Or something else?"

Clinton started and stopped an explanation that quickly went nowhere. There were too many very personal details to share. Daiyu smiled and shook her head. She'd been born on Earth too. It was indeed hard to sever every tie to the ancient home.

"That's for another time," she waved it off. "We have other matters before us." Then glancing toward a glowering Diana, "Please indicate to us, Mr. Rittener, that you understand how important it is that you keep the confidence of the Borelian Council. Every word said during this session is classified." She said the next in a way that said she had to. "To repeat it is to potentially invite the sternest punishment."

"I understand everything the state's amanuensis has just elucidated," Clinton replied.

The poetess laureate noted his choice of three words instead of a simple "Diana" and smiled. "No, I don't think you do understand." She leaned forward from her position at Chair as if they were speaking across an accent table at one of her soirees at her mansion on Gamma Level instead of him standing in the docket, she raised across and above him on the dais. What she said though did seem like dinner conversation.

"You've over the last days been the subject of two most remarkable contradictory developments. There's a saying in my language." And then she continued in Mandarin, "The gem cannot be polished without friction . . . " Rittener interrupted and finished it in her own language, "Nor the man perfected without trials."

"*Yu shu da*," she complimented in Mandarin. Then she overruled herself. "*Hen how*," she praised, meaning "excellent." Clinton could sense immediately that it gave her great pleasure to speak in her native tongue. Her life for many years now had been surrendered to New English. This offered him an advantage. He could listen to her—in a language she longed to speak.

Mandarin—for Clinton Rittener—meant something else though. It was the language of death, destruction, abomination, pain, and horror. There were so many phrases that he'd given voice to in Mandarin that he couldn't imagine saying in any other tongue. Listening to her made him think back to some of his own directives in that language. "The current level of assaults on civilians has become insufferable and must cease. Rapists and outright murderers henceforth will be summarily executed." He'd never said that or anything remotely like it in Danish or German, but had many times in Mandarin. "There'll be no quarter given. Kill everything in the town that moves." That also was not a common sentiment given out in Spanish or Arabic. Actually, even Clinton Rittener didn't know how to say "no quarter" in Swahili. But he could be polite in Mandarin too.

"Thank you. To hear that from you . . . " He didn't finish but offered a slight bow, which she returned. His eyes told her that he knew more about her than she about him.

Daiyu in her youth had been a great beauty. Even if her loveliness didn't launch a thousand ships, twice that number of her family's great shipping fleet were sunk in the wars on Earth from which she'd been swept away and avoided just in time. Harbin's most desired debutante, at the interface between Russia and China on the Songhua River, had fallen in love far below her station and had to choose between the immense wealth and power of her father and uncles or eloping with a man with no prospects whatsoever, but in whom she recognized instantly the true reflection of her own soul.

Her life had been compared to the princess Cusi Coyllur, abducted by the low-born commander of the army of her father, the great Inca Pachacutec. In Ollantaytambo in Peru, where her father and husband settled things with two great armies, the Earth itself is said to remember the tragic encounter, with the setting Sun's image of the distraught Pachacutec frozen in the shadows that play against the out-cropping above the ancient city. Daiyu's affair was preserved in something as long-lasting as a mountain in the Andes. She and her husband's impassioned adventuring took them to every corner of the Solar System, their treks giving birth to a book of sonnets, *Wandervogel*, said to contain some of the most poignant couplets ever written. "Wandervogel" were footloose German youth who said goodbye to prosaic society after the first world war of the 20th century and instead simply roamed around Europe. The second war crushed their movement; the Great Eastern War did that and more. It sent billions fleeing, with the smallest number drawn to it, and of those few, hardly any surviving to see its end. Daiyu's husband was one of those volunteers, desperate to return to his China in the hour of crisis. Theirs was one of the great and tragic love stories of the age.

She was in her middle age now and certainly past the time to drive men mad with plain desire. The maturing Daiyu, however, was something to behold nonetheless, exuding everything and anything one could imagine of the woman who possessed the hands that penned *Wandervogel*. Her face was at the far edge of youthful—bright, clear, a languorous and exotic admixture of White Russian, Chinese, and Japanese. The hair was so straight, so charcoal black, the perfect frame for skin as white and fair as a chrysanthemum. Her most attractive feature though wasn't bestowed upon her through her genes. It was her grace. She seemed never to spoil the ideals of the precepts of *tribangha*, the Buddhist pose of three bends: hips, waist, and breast. Her every movement cut a swath through the rest of humanity, giving an exhibition of poise in motion. To many it was ironic that she should now go through life alone. Many more realized that it was unthinkable that Isolde should find another love after Tristan, or Juliet after Romeo. There was an often referenced meeting once between her and the lothario governor-general of the tiny Martian moon, Phobos, who was curious as to when her grieving should end and her next romance begin. Her answer was enduring. "Love is a blade both to conquer like a sword and yet to inflict the defeat of hara-kiri. Having known both edges I feel no regret." There was simply no man on Borealis to step up to such a woman as Daiyu. And if such a man didn't exist on Borealis, he'd be found nowhere else in the universe.

THE CHAIR NOW GOT to business. "Keeping in mind how trials do serve in life, I regret to inform you that an accusation of sedition has been lodged against you. We are the body to adjudicate such cases. The Council is investigating and deliberating whether to formally indict or dismiss the charge."

Rittener's lack of surprise said he'd expected as much. There was one thing that did require clarification. "I hadn't realized you were required to inform potential defendants in advance. Are your laws so accommodating?"

She answered in New English; a less friendly mien went with the tongue. "The entire city has spoken of nothing else since your last appearance here." She stopped and corrected herself. "The entire Solar System is speaking of nothing else." She put an elbow on the mahogany desk top and a thoughtful fist under chin. "That must have been what you wanted. Whether it's sedition or not is for some other day."

Admiral Albrecht interrupted. "There are other charges too." The admiral wasn't speaking to anyone in particular. He simply grumbled the reminder out loud. Since it required no attention, it got none.

Daiyu went on. "On the other side of this is the polish. You are the subject of a spontaneous public acclamation—yet another one—that has reached the Council. The citizens of Borealis want you to have a seat on the Borelian Council." She paused and restrained a wry smile that almost escaped. "I *am* required by law to tell you that."

Rittener was taken aback. "But there is no election currently; there won't be for another two months."

Now Admiral Albrecht spoke right up and loudly. "That's absolutely correct. It's also a cock-eyed piece of nonsense." He looked at his fellow colleagues for support. "Who ever heard of such a thing? It's ridiculous on its very face and nothing more than an emotional reaction that will pass just as quickly as it came."

Philip evidently agreed with the admiral. He was shaking his head from side to side while letting out barely audible chuckles. He seemed nonplussed to have to explain the obvious.

"The Council has ignored acclamations in the past and this is an example of one that definitely should be placed in the same trash bin. What if it were the collective desire of the citizens of Borealis that we should present them with a unicorn, and that it should be polka-dotted?" He turned to all-knowing Diana, the oracle, the very receptacle by which this strange portend came to the councilors' ears. "It's your opinion, isn't it, Diana, that there are quite a number of ambiguities regarding this acclamation? Didn't you yourself advise that there was a degree of uncertainty as to what the citizenry actually meant?"

Now Breonia interrupted. "Cheese on bread! Rass! But this is no time for wizardry—or circuitry. I won't have Diana bringing us the news and then interpreting it for us. Good God, Philip."

Philip threw his hands up. "Fine. Let's confirm it then. Whose seat shall he take? Yours, Breonia? Or yours, Daiyu?"

All the councilors had a turn, and at the same time. It left Daiyu with no choice other than to sound her gavel repeatedly. When the Chair's requests for restraint were finally obeyed, the only one speaking was Rittener. He'd been trying to be heard and repeated himself.

"But I have no wish to sit on the Council."

Daiyu feigned surprise and made it seem believable. "What's that? No wish to sit on the Council? That's an odd reaction to such a high honor." Now she frowned. "It's almost insulting you could decide something like that on the spot."

"I'm not the right choice. There are eleven good choices right here, right now," he answered.

"If so," she asked the obvious, "what then will you do here on Borealis?"

"I am a pilot."

"A pilot? Nothing more?" Her tone had been drifting toward curt; it was there now.

"Nothing more," he answered.

"You're fit, uninjured, prepared to fly?"

"I could fly today if I had to."

"Not today—day after tomorrow."

Now she leaned back in her chair and gave him what he took as a look of satisfaction. "The Council is sending a diplomatic mission to Terra to see if some détente can't be reached regarding the uproar caused by your citizen's oration." She waved her hand as if to say that the next was of no great consequence now that other things were taking precedence. "You're aware that there were some irregularities in the recent games. We had lodged a prior request for another contest, a rematch, to confirm things, and the Terrans had already amicably agreed. You and a team of pilots therefore will accompany the legation; you'll leave for the Ring in forty-two hours."

Rittener was speechless. Daiyu took his silence in contrived puzzlement. After an uncomfortable pause she asked, almost exasperatedly, "That's exactly what you wanted. This suits you well?"

"The match is on Terra—and it's being held, even now?" Rittener asked.

"Yes, on Terra," Daiyu answered, not bothering to respond to the other question.

"There might be a small problem is all," Rittener reminded her. "I have a sentence of death waiting for me on Terra."

Daiyu brushed her hair back slowly with both palms; she was thinking. "Yes, that's right. That does present a problem, doesn't it?" She put her finger in the air as though she just realized something. "But here's a worse problem." She half-smiled at the joke to come, even though it was at his expense. "Perhaps not worse from your point of view of course," she said, referring to the Terran ruling, "but what good is a pilot to Borealis who can't fly at Terra?" She wasn't Borealis' high foreign minister because her iambic pentameter thrilled. She was as sharp-witted and skilled in statecraft as any retainer who'd navigated the stormiest waters in any regal court. "Would you fly only on Tuesdays and Thursdays also? Is Titan or Mars also off your itinerary?"

Now she gave a biting riposte. "Really, Mr. Rittener, to turn down a seat on this council and to offer instead your services as part-time pilot is . . . " She paused. The worst was yet to come and required the advertisement. "It's absurd." She said it both literally and to signal to her fellow councilors that this béte-noire could be handled.

Clinton tried to parry; it was automatic after so many duels. "What you said about my name, I think I might like the idea of going by Clinton-Rittener, with a hyphen. Are hyphens allowed?" He immediately both regretted and wondered why he'd said it. Daiyu spoke the next quickly, sharply.

"That sort of cheek I find infuriating. Now you'll listen and closely, and provide me with an answer devoid of everything save complete sincerity or you'll be reading a transcript of the rest of these proceedings in immediate custody. You've come to Borealis with about the same effect as a comet striking. I congratulate you, putting yourself in the center of what will doubtlessly turn out to be a great watershed in human history. I don't know if you belong there, but I do know that you're not going to simply dust yourself off and just stroll away."

She walked him down a simple path of inescapable logic. "You came to Borealis to be a pilot. Stanislaus has already inscribed you. Pilots compete. I've just given you the venue of the next match. This is where and when you'll fly and you will acquit yourself equal to the state you represent."

No one was daring to even breathe, either in or out. Daiyu, having her say, softened her gaze perceptibly and leaned back. "Of course, you'll need diplomatic immunity. Envoy-at-large is the lowest-ranking status I can confer that yet carries with it that protection and entitles you to take part in the negotiations as well." She looked side to side at all the councilors then back to Rittener. "You accept?"

Now Clinton chuckled out loud, a soldier's laugh, but a friendly one, the kind people make when faced with life's ironies. His mind had composed a comical synopsis of the proposal. "I'll be an envoy-at-large, condemned to death on the Ring, and under accusation on Borealis for sedition. None of that will be noted in the credentials, I assume?"

Daiyu understood and appreciated the wit. "That's not to mention how the Terrans will take it. Their sense of humor isn't usually that keen." She added a response to what was on everyone's mind. "To harm a Borelian diplomat though would mean war. I assume they'll honor your credentials; they'll have to, won't they?" She used the tone of someone who really didn't know the answer herself.

"Or not?" Admiral Albrecht volunteered, interrupting again. His timbre was easily understood. From his point of view it mattered very little if Rittener were to return or meet his end by arrogantly presenting a get-out-of-jail-free card to the Terran authorities.

"You accept?" she asked again.

"If survival is reacting to the future in advance," Clinton admitted to her, "here I must tell you that I am blind to see a thing."

"If you're paraphrasing Sun Tzu, that's still neither a yes nor a no."

"I'm quoting my father," he told her in Mandarin. Daiyu, Borealis' top diplomat, and yet like any other billions of Chinese, had a whole series of terribly vivid images in her mind about the murdered ambassador. That day in Shanghai was the beginning of the end of everything she had known of her childhood China. Her face flushed involuntarily.

"We are all blind to some extent," she allowed. "That's the business of the foreign service—to go and see."

"And if you're citing your father," she said this in Mandarin, "then I believe I already have your answer."

Rittener nodded. "I accept."

"Good flying, then, Clinton Rittener." She'd gone back to the same sweet and friendly tone, the same smile, as from the start.

"One more thing." She acted as if the addendum wasn't that important. It was though.

"The Object, what do you think it is?"

He answered in Mandarin since this couldn't be an official question. The Borelian Council knew more about the Object than everyone else in the Solar System combined. It had to be a personal query.

"It's the end of something, and the beginning of another."

FORTY-TWO HOURS LATER THE state's ferry, *Pegasus*, passed through a momentary aperture in the Gravitonic Shield with a bearing for the Terran Ring. She'd make quick work of the short journey, pulled harder and faster by Earth's gravity the closer she came and pushed from behind by a laser emitted from an orbiting solar collector that tracked the frozen volatiles in her stern, converting the waste sludge into useful jets.

Clinton-Rittener, Borelian envoy-at-large, was one of the official passengers listed on the transit manifest. He'd been given a bare-bones briefing, and in his experience that usually turned out to augur that he'd unfortunately been the most informed person in the room. What troubled him more than that was who was leading the delegation. It wasn't Daiyu, Borealis' foreign minister; it was Stephanangelo, the one councilor who until now hadn't even been informed where square one was. Indeed, he was an important magistrate and on paper as high-ranking a representative as could be sent. He was also something of an engaging buffoon, and Rittener realized that the Council's choice boded ill for any real diplomatic breakthroughs.

"Neither confirm nor deny; keep them guessing." He shared this astute game plan with Rittener several times while elaborating little beyond it. At least this much was plain though. Clinton was tasked to find a way to meet with one of Borealis' operatives on the Terran Ring, a pilot by the name of . . . Adem Sulcus.

"Do you know anything about the man?" Stephanangelo asked.

"Our paths have crossed in the past," Rittener replied.

How, where, or when that might be accomplished however was hardly spelled out. Rittener's retinue was equally thin: two Nepalese bodyguards, twin brothers from Earth. Ram Dahadur Limbu was the clever, taciturn, reserved one, and Tam Dahadur Limbu, the outspoken, good-natured, but fairly slow-witted sibling. They weren't citizens of Borealis, nor were they resident aliens. As Gurkha warriors in the direct service of the Council, they held a special and singular status: *perioikoi*. Borealis used the selfsame term that ancient Hellenic city states conferred upon indispensible members of their communities, vested with all protections and rights but still not quite full citizens.

For the Gurkha there were some caveats that went the other way round too. In taking their oaths they insisted on the phrase, "excepting in any assaults against her Majesty, the Queen," as they swore their allegiance. Borealis had no plans, conceivable or otherwise, for an offensive against Buckingham Palace, and acceded to the addendum. That they still hadn't forgotten their pledge to England's sovereign was proof that the loyalty of the Gurkha was legendary. They were the most fearless, steadfast, ferocious fighters in existence. Rittener was assigned only two of them, but he reckoned that would be quite enough. They'd be with him every single moment spent on Terra, so for now left him alone gazing out *Pegasus'* port viewing window as it filled with Earth and the Terran Ring. It was a colossal and awe-inspiring sight as they grew toward their true sizes.

"All the pilots will refuse to fly if you're arrested." Nerissa took a seat next to him and delivered the news, trying to cheer him. "There's not one who isn't willing to turn it into an interplanetary incident if that happens." She'd obviously seen to this herself.

Rittener was unconcerned with that and just tapped the Borelian diplomatic badge he was wearing. It was real.

"They're not going to arrest me but they're not going to let me off a leash either." Clinton wasn't so sure about the rest, changing the subject but doing it awkwardly. "I may need you to do something for me on the Ring."

Nerissa waited for him to continue. He didn't.

"And, that would be?" she invited him to explain.

"Well, that's the thing. I don't know myself just yet."

Nerissa pretended she understood. "So you want me to do something for you, have no idea what it is, but I should tell you I'll do it?" There was a petite smirk that accompanied the asinine appraisal.

"For your country?" he joked.

Rittener agreed it sounded ridiculous when put that way but reminded her that there'd be no square centimeter on Terra where they'd be able to say a word, exchange a note, or do anything else without being seen and heard. "I may need your help and we'd best have a way to communicate that."

"Alright, then," she concurred reasonably, "how will we do that?"

"Well, you'll just know. It will seem natural that way," Clinton said simply. "That's the best way."

With that she looked him over closely, letting him see her do it. Her eyes moved down the long scar on his face. She let him see her do that too. "You're putting a lot on my powers of perception, aren't you?" He realized her eyes were on his face, on the interesting but damaged parts.

"If my course of action is natural," he explained, "but yet brought about unnaturally, you'll know I'm asking you to do something vitally important."

"Unnaturally natural? What a contradiction in terms," she chided. "That's an oxymoron."

Clinton smiled. "That's a wonderful word, in many languages. It's a valuable and powerful word too. May I tell you something about it?" He leaned closer and lowered his voice. "They say it's a key to training the mind. There's a practice pilots supposedly learn in the Outer. It begins with forcing your mind to think in doubles, like oxymorons."

Nerissa had heard, of course, of esoteric *yanta*. She was both genuinely impressed and eager to know more. It gave a palpable thrill to think the man in front of her might know more about it than almost anyone. "Once they've mastered doubles they add permutations, variations, and other chains— all in the mind—building on each other," he revealed.

"Can that really be done? Why would anyone train to do that?" she asked.

"It confuses alpha waves." He sidled closer to share the true reason. "Just as importantly, it confuses sensors." He answered the other too. "They say there are some who can."

She had summoned just enough pluck to ask him about the scar, but veered off at the last.

"You're one of them?" she asked instead.

He laughed as if the question were silly. "I'm an envoy-at-large of Borealis, a former *yuan shuai*, high marshal, of the coalition of Jiangsu, Shanxi, and Fujian. Unfortunately, everything there is to know has already been broadcast about me."

She doubted that. She had never entertained it and was convinced of it now. Her mind was forming an oxymoron of its own about this engaging, interesting charmer, someone who'd seen everything—including, against all sense or reason, genocide, his scars plainly declared.

"There's a certain uncertainty about you, Clinton Rittener."

He liked that. "I knew you'd be a fast learner."

"Teach me then," she said.

The starlight played across Clinton's face through the viewport at an odd angle. For a moment he looked almost frightening, the patchwork on his face visible. A movement to the side and he came back, almost the way he'd looked in his youth; fine hair, strong cheeks, cleft chin. He nodded his assent.

"You're a pilot. It's allowed."

For the rest of the transit they remained at the observation port, Rittener initiating her into the beginning mysteries of the arcana perfected in the abysmal loneliness of the Great Outer. There were secrets said to exist out there and nowhere else in the universe. Even someone like Nerissa felt special to be permitted to hear of it—and from such a man as her guide.

CHAPTER ELEVEN

WHISPERED EQUATIONS

TERRA HAD SPARED NO expense for the state dinner to be held to welcome the Borelian pilots. It was held in a majestic dining hall within the Borelian diplomatic sector, lavishly decorated in the style of Bhutanese architecture of the Himalayas. Ethan Van Ulroy and many great officials, magnates, jurists, athletes, and other crème of Terran society were in attendance. Everyone was gathered in an enormous yet splendid anteroom—much, much too large to be considered a foyer, but with clever design tricks made to seem cozy and inviting nonetheless. Even permanent thick mist was created to hang as the same ceiling one might see trekking along the Gangtok Pass on the ancient Silk Road between Sikkim and Lhasa. Rittener had seen the real passes, holding the ground at Nathula and Jelepla. He wasn't there touring, but this was a good approximation as far as his memory could tell. The vestibule was laid out to resemble the courtyard complexes that sprang up around *dzongs*, the fortress-monasteries. Soon the massive gates to the hall would be opened and an incomparable feast would be served. For now this elite company simply drank, entertained themselves, made and lost supporters and rivals—and kept their hopes up that history should be made at this banquet, as it had at so many others.

The Terran Ring had responded in kind, earlier in the day, to Borealis' embassy headed by the maladroit Stephanangelo. Dante Michelson and his aide-de-camp, Van Ulroy, not only were missing, but there wasn't present a single liaison with the Chief Archon's office. In their place, Secretary of State Grace Karis was hosting, equal in every way to Stephanangelo's ineptitude.

Madame Karis was quite an elderly lady. Even though she'd been cosmetically re-done a dozen times, nothing could hide that. She was attractive though, in her way, the best an octogenarian beauty might accomplish. There was unfortunately no way to rekindle youthful sparks in the eyes though and certainly none to recharge the mind. Hers had never been a strong one, and hadn't aged well. She was famous now for contradicting herself within the same breath while talking in circles. It was said that adversaries sometimes capitulated to her in negotiations simply by virtue of the tide of incongruities she'd spout, and for such great lengths. There was reason in all of this. Under Dante Michelson's rule it was the Archonate with whom one did business with the Terran Ring. The state department was relegated for use as a stop gap for those the Archonate deemed next in line to meet another branch of their bureaucracy: defense. War, for the Terran Ring, began at State. If it was Madame Karis waiting across the negotiating table it meant Terra had judged coming to terms impossible. It signified The Ring was busy solving the problem in other ways as their foreign minister babbled away for as long as it took.

Rittener was aghast; Stephanangelo took it in his stride. "She's Cypriote, you know. We have the same temperament." It was true, the lady had Greek and Turkish blood; Stephanangelo's was from a neighboring island, Sicily. "We're both Mediterranean," he told Rittener. "We should be able to sort something out." Terra and Borealis both had their wish as two great bunglers walked each other around in circles for many hours, bringing a great dizziness to all forced to participate.

Clinton Rittener came to understand now that the Terran Ring and Borealis were going to actually have a go at each other, after all. It sent an anxious feeling through him, one that made him more determined to somehow find a way to hear what the Terran mole, Adem Sulcus, had to say.

FEW FAILED TO NOTICE when Sadhana Ramanujan entered the grand reception—that in itself beyond unexpected—and without saying a word to anyone else, made straight for . . . Clinton Rittener. She parted a path of open-eyed and closed-mouthed aristocrats as she went. Rittener's status, whether pilot, diplomat, or fugitive, Terra was pleased to leave unclear. Officially, he was simply being ignored. So when Sadhana made her way to arrive in front of him she didn't need to cut in line. No one was daring to bend an elbow with this particular enemy of the state. She didn't bother looking him over too closely; for identification purposes he looked like hardly any other man alive. She was a scientist, however, so she couldn't restrain the perfunctory challenge.

"Clinton Rittener, I presume?"

Rittener was less concerned to answer her and more anxious to signal to his guard that this woman posed no threat—for God's sake!—and that her obviously bellicose approach and stance should be simply disregarded. He, of course, recognized her for who she was; the Gurkhas only spied an angry Indian lady drawing near and threatening. Fate intervened and froze the men in their spots.

"I am Sadhana Ramanujan. Your forces destroyed my family's *haveli* in the Chettinad." She then slapped him, well and hard, right across the face. It made a loud sound, and set off a cacophony of gasps that moved over the crowd like a wave.

Rittener let a few seconds pass; he was collecting his thoughts. "I'm sorry to tell you that I don't remember the particular event; that probably makes it worse. I saw action at Chettinad, and unfortunately burned many ancient palaces and mansions. I ordered many awful things to transpire there. I truly wish it could have been different."

Sadhana had changed the look on her face. She wasn't listening to Rittener's response, her eyes instead were signaling that this was something much, much more important than a lost tea plantation years ago on another world. She had desperation and fear in her eyes, of that he was sure. He could recognize it better than a shark senses blood in water. Ethan Van Ulroy also was talented in that realm. He was the Terran magistrate hosting the function—even as he'd neglected the official talks—and reacted to the commotion before it happened, as soon as he'd caught sight of Dr. Ramanujan. He was cutting a path through the crowd to the scene as quickly as he could.

"You're two-faced." She said it strangely, even more oddly than the words themselves. "No, actually with your excuses, you're three-faced." Van Ulroy was yards away and nearly knocking over highborn party-goers when Sadhana gave her last rebuke. "There's no place for you under the Sun." She then turned and took the arm of the aide-de-camp who'd just arrived, breathing a little harder and his hair for once a bit disheveled. There was nothing for Van Ulroy to do but escort the distraught scientist away from the fuss. Sadhana had lost her appetite and insisted on going home. Van Ulroy also had a damper placed on his, but had no choice other than to smile and compliment the dishes throughout the whole of the evening. Clinton Rittener, on the other hand, acted as if nothing at all had happened. He was so gregarious and engaging that even the Terrans selected to sit next to and across from him couldn't help but surrender to enjoying his company. There was a reason for his excellent mood. He realized he might have already accomplished the hardest part of his mission from the minute Sadhana had stormed off, and was calling on a stunning talent he'd managed to groom like few men alive. He'd put it right out of his mind, literally.

Rittener knew that every breath, every heartbeat, every involuntary dilation of his pupils, every single of his words and deeds would be recorded and dissected for the slightest information it may reveal. Nothing could block the illegal but frighteningly intrusive surveillance of one's very persona—if Terra decided to bring to bear every electronic tool at its disposal to focus on one single individual. And, there had never been a person of interest like Clinton Rittener. He imagined—correctly—that everything from the chemical content of his urine to the timbre of his voice as he laughed at jokes was to wind up on a screen, somewhere, with a team of experts at the ready to determine what it meant. Clinton Rittener, though, was actually a living, breathing example of something even the Terran Ring's specialists couldn't crack. The tales about pilots from the Outer were true.

Rittener had command over those things that most humans simply assumed were beyond their control. He wasn't the only one alive who could do it. Anyone willing to spend years on Titan in the company of the most dangerous assassins in the Solar System could have a chance to learn it. A certain and tremendous inner strength was required though to attain one's *yanta*. There were pilots, indeed, whose breathing, concentrating, and other severe talents made them fairly impervious to scanning. Clinton Rittener wasn't just one of them, he was a most remarkable example of the best of them. He knew immediately that Sadhana had said far more to him than her literal words, and every indication of his surmisal—surprise, satisfaction, anxiety—was buried too deep to find, no matter how many knobs were turned on any number of machines.

The Terrans at his table warmed by the end of the evening, giving in to the once-in-a-lifetime chance to cross wits with the legendary mercenary. None dared to breathe a word of impending wars or extraterrestrial prizes, but not unlike many other talks around many other tables, the subject turned to military matters. Which were the warriors who were the best in all of history? Each in the company gave an opinion. Spartan hoplites, Japanese samurai, and Teutonic knights had already been put forth when it came to Rittener's turn to voice his choice.

"I think the best that ever were are still the best that are today." He gave a look over his shoulder at his guard. "A British colonel during the Second World War asked his Gurkha adjutant for volunteers to be airlifted and dropped behind enemy lines to destroy a bridge. To his amazement he was informed by the shamed adjutant that not one Gurkha would step forward. Never having witnessed cowardice from the battalion he led, the colonel flew into a rage, ordered the men assembled, and gave them a stern dressing down. Within the hour he had his volunteers. As the squad boarded the plane the colonel noticed that none of the men had the slightest look of unease. They seemed as ready and eager for battle as ever. He called the adjutant over and demanded an explanation. 'Oh, the men are in high spirits, Colonel,' he answered happily. 'They've been issued parachutes and now understand their use.'"

The youngest one at the table, an honors mathematician seated across from Rittener in case the conversation should go that way, was the first to understand the punch line. "You mean the men volunteered to jump out of an airplane, thinking they'd simply hurtle to the ground, before being told what a parachute was?"

Rittener didn't need to answer. Ram Dahadur did it for him. "Those must have been Magar or Tamang Gurkha. I am of the Limbu hill tribe. Limbu would never have hesitated."

Now the young mathematician was genuinely impressed and wanted to know. "Have you ever met men like that, Mr. Ambassador?" Rittener was a credentialed envoy. This was the first time anyone on Terra deigned to accede to it. Rittener had. He'd be flying against some of them tomorrow.

"No," he lied. "Men like that don't exist anymore."

THE PILOTS OCCUPIED PADS on a circular start wheel, each equidistant from the zero-G line that ran down the center of any section of the spinning Ring. Up here the gravity well was already quite weak, diminishing greatly the pilots' weight. Terra's best, Demetrius Sehene among them of course, would be making for and claiming a place on that line. Insiders were whispering under their breaths to watch Quince Xavaris, the newcomer to Terra. He didn't seem like quite that much, until one had a closer look. Xavaris was one of those men who Nature had deemed from the start to be lean, hard, and wiry. This particular flyer however, of the most extreme brand of Titanian pilots, had taken his profession to its limits. He was tight skin, rock hard bone, steel cable muscle—and nothing more. Clinton knew him, but only too well, from his years in the Outer. They both learned their *yanta* from the same master. Pilots on Titan had their own radical and secretive association—tracing their line supposedly back through yogis, knights Templar, *hassassins*, and back to Egyptian masons and beyond. Xavaris' mind and spirit therefore had to be as formidable as his body, the proof of which shone through extraordinarily piercing eyes.

When the flyers alit from the start there was to be assured a classically violent scrum. These super-fit gladiators pushed forward on almost weightless bodies in the Terran heights with the most powerful muscle engines in the Solar System. The fact that all of them possessed personalities more like Xavaris' than not, that all of them spent at least half their training time devoted to martial arts, guaranteed that the beginning of the match was world-class, no holds barred, close order combat—but among centaur-like creatures from mythology, half human and half eagle.

The Terrans began cheating immediately. One after the other came at Nerissa in angles that made no sense other than to put her out of the running. She gave the Terran audience a show of how she defended herself when the gloves were off, whirling and kicking almost too quickly to follow with the naked eye. The first Terran took a vicious foot to the Adam's apple and plummeted out of the sky. The second had his nose broken so badly that the spray of blood blinded him, causing him to inadvertently block the third. Her shoulder, if ever injured in the last match, was obviously much improved.

Clinton was cheating too. He was flying doped on cartazene. Just prior to the match, Ram Dahadur had approached him and blandly handed him the dose. "Dr. Stanislaus ordered me to make this available to you." When the Gurkha saw the look of evident reluctance on Rittener's face he followed through. "Dr. Stanislaus also has a personal request: protect his niece." Clinton still wasn't convinced.

"But there's no way to get away with this," he protested.

Ram had a perfect answer. "Only the winner is tested, sahib." He looked down for a moment out of respect. "You're too old to fly, sir. You have no chance. Everyone knows that." Then he bucked up and gave him a look straight in the eyes.

"Remember your code, sir."

The cartazene helped put Rittener into the leading pack and allowed him to give some support to Nerissa himself. Even with the dangerous chemical working its magic, Clinton couldn't make a cut to block a fourth swooping attack on Nerissa. It was countered however—by Demetrius Sehene. He obviously hadn't liked the way the last match had ended, and hadn't appreciated the aspersions that had come with it. The Emperor flew fairly, would take on all comers face to face, and hadn't any use at all for gutter tactics. As it was, and as he'd said many times, he admired Nerissa. The check was expertly effected, in as gentle a manner as possible so that Sehene could keep his forward impetus, dipping under the attacker and ripping up while shrugging him off to the side with his bull's shoulder. Rittener was close enough to hear what the Emperor cried out to his team-mates, "This is to be a race!" As if on cue, the pilots took the advice in unison. The contest was on.

The most dangerous piloting matches could only take place on Terra. Only on Terra did pilots fly in zero gravity. Here they could attain killing speed. But the great draw for the audiences on the Ring were the water obstacles—amazing and beautiful, perfectly spherical globs of millions of gallons of precious water suspended along the race course, quivering delightfully as they hung in the gravitational null zone. A torrent of pilots spilled either above, below, or to the sides of them, forming human slipstreams around this string of dazzlingly blue pearls floating in the sky.

Rittener was still in the thick of the pack of front-runners at the first, second, even at the fifth water obstacle. Flying with the most superlative pilots to be found though was an impossible task. Clinton was a good pilot, maybe even very good. Nothing though—not even if he willed it to his death—could prevent him losing ground against these flyers. So he didn't see himself how it happened. One of Terra's own pilots, none other than Quince Xavaris, was the cause of it, initiating a tangle with Adem Sulcus at the very circumference of the penultimate water obstacle and sending him face first to "belly flop" into it. The splat made a sound Rittener could hear, so he knew someone was in trouble. Sulcus was in more than just trouble. Hitting the surface tension of the water at such a speed rendered him unconscious. His body, slowed down by the abrupt and sudden halt, nonetheless retained enough inertia to thrust him completely within the liquid orb, his wings trailing behind him like a mosquito trapped in a globule of amber. As Rittener glided under he could see him twisting languorously just below the surface, knocked cold, subject to the chaotic currents of his own impact, and drowning. It was plain the Terran pilot would be dead in short order without assistance, and none, strangely, seemed to be forthcoming.

Before slipstreaming around the next obstacle Rittener dipped his right wing and gave another look back, catching sight of the rescue shuttle as it finally arrived on the scene. He had his misgivings about the reasons for its tardy appearance.

The distraction cost Rittener. He missed an unparalleled struggle at the sprint between the Emperor and Nerissa—all clean, all fair, a classic ending between two incomparable competitors. The official markers were being displayed. Nerissa had broken the line first—by .0003 of a second.

The Borelians were rejoicing wildly. The Terran audience was clapping politely, having witnessed something that could require nothing less. Then news of another blow came for Terra. Adem Sulcus was dead, expiring from a broken neck and other shocks. Rittener breathed in just such a way, and began meditating, flooding his mind with motifs learned from the great deceivers, and yet with room enough to answer when his fellow Borelian pilots came breathless with the report. Quite a number of enemies of the Terran state had coincidentally expired due to "shock" and Rittener deemed that his neck was likely as not broken in the shuttle while unconscious. That's not what Rittener said though.

"Poor fellow. He flew a good race. This is a dangerous course; it's really all too bad."

To anyone listening, for anyone monitoring his alpha wave patterns, for any army of amanuenses that might ferret out a different inner meaning, there was nothing but that: "Poor fellow. He flew a good race." Clinton knew better, of course. Sulcus was the operative with whom he was to rendezvous. The Borelian Council had risked Rittener's life to intercept the intelligence the Terran would now never share. If all were lost Rittener however now did something strange. The entire Borelian team went off to celebrate. All save Clinton, that is. He went straight to bed.

FOR THE NEXT FEW hours Ram Dahadur and Tam Dahadur took turns sleeping, dressed in full combat assault gear—including incongruous *kukris* sheathed at their waists—sitting in uncomfortable chairs on either side of Rittener's bed. Rittener was in meta-sleep, half meditation, half sleep. Neither had seen anything like it.

"What's that? What's he doing?" Tam asked his brother.

Ram frowned and motioned with his head that Tam should turn away. Ram didn't know either but realized it was inappropriate for them to look on. "He's a pilot—from the Outer. He's preparing." Then he added in a chiding way, "Obviously."

"What's he preparing for?" Tam asked.

"Anything," Ram snapped.

That made sense and the subject was closed. A moment later Tam muttered back some good advice though. "He should have done that *before* the race." He then sidled back and rested his eyes. Tam didn't drift off though; there was another inquiry.

"Do you think he knows what that thing is?"

"What thing?" his brother asked. Tam gave a look in the direction of where he thought space would be. On the spinning Ring though those types of nods couldn't miss.

Ram scolded his brother. "We've been given orders not to even mention that word. That's for Borelian diplomats."

"I didn't say 'Object,' I said 'thing,'" Tam protested.

"*Yo jhakana!*" Ram cursed under his breath. The rebuke was cut short though as Rittener's body made a short, quick jerk, released a few seconds of tremors, and then fell back quiet. Tam was watching wide-eyed, absorbed. His brother, the clever, intelligent one, was still unconvinced.

"He can't know that. No one does."

CLINTON ARRIVED AT NERISSA'S quarters utterly refreshed. Every single member of the Borelian team was making a time of it in the opulent accommodations the Terran Ring had respectfully provided, celebrating and breaking a significant number of rules. They'd been at it since the electric finish.

Without even congratulating her he instead made a lunatic request. "I'd like to invite you to see some Terran sights with me below."

For his Gurkha guard from Earth and himself too, a "dirt crawler" for most of his life, a foray off the Borelian levels to the Deck itself and into the 1.08 g's of standard Terran gravity would be a slightly uncomfortable outing. For Nerissa it would require everything she had to endure it for long. She was though now officially, for the moment, the pre-eminent pilot anywhere, so Rittener deemed her up to it.

"On the Deck?" she asked.

A stunned silence came down like a tarp. It was as if interrupting a party to ask the guest of honor to accompany one over the falls in a barrel. He certainly had dressed for the occasion, giving anyone watching the scene—or recording it—the impression that he fancied his invitation might actually be accepted. He'd shown up in a ten thousand credit, impeccably tailored, form-fitted bodysuit. Over his shoulder lay a matching sash, very impressively festooned with rarely achieved emblems, among them his badge as Borelian envoy.

Nerissa gave him a prolonged stare, during which time he said not a word, sufficient to convince that no matter the preposterous request, it was given out seriously. Then she looked herself up and down.

"And with me looking like this?" She bit her lip, wrinkled her forehead, and drew his eyes to the kimono she was wearing, a beautifully embroidered pure silk kimono, but still just a wrap. "I didn't pack anything for that."

Rittener stepped right in front of her, took her hand, slowly raised it to his lips, and kissed it.

"Please, we might never have this chance again." He was indeed making such a fool of himself, but his manner was so . . . unnaturally natural. She took her hand back and put it to her mouth, swept away.

"Such daring! But you're a previous high marshal of the coalition of Jiangsu, Shanxi, and I forget the rest. How could I refuse?"

Nerissa had some daring too. She reappeared wearing the only thing she could: the same flowing formal wear from the previous state dinner.

"Do you think anyone will notice?" she asked, biting her lip again.

It wasn't as simple as changing clothes though. A large, elite squad of Terran troopers immediately fell in around the couple as they left the compound. They weren't meant for the "envoy"; they were assigned to Nerissa's movements. Rittener had taken his frowning guard along too, so all in all the mixture was like gunpowder. When the destination was learned—down to the Deck—along with the identity of her escort, it put fire to the fuse. The Terran captain wasn't prepared for this tourist outing and didn't like it at all. Nerissa came on like a tiger at the right moment of indecision on his part.

"Outrageous. I'm not asking your permission; I don't require it. I'm a prisoner of no one. If you insinuate it even once more I promise I'll see you're placed in a brig before I leave Terra." Rittener was giving the captain helpful knowing glances in Nerissa's direction, as if to say, "Listen to her, brother. She'll do it."

Clinton held her hand as the shuttle descended. By the time a dozen levels had swept past and the gravity began to kick in, she was squeezing it as hard as she could.

RITTENER HAD DECIDED TO make it quick. It was the wrong choice, but the only one he had. A long, drawn-out misdirection would be much better. He cringed knowing he was going to put Sadhana Ramanujan at greater risk because of it. Nerissa would have to endure every moment of every false turn he might make and he knew he wouldn't be able to watch her suffer for long in the increased gravity. This would be the sloppiest—and yet perhaps the most important—work he'd ever done. It would be the most obvious "splice" of his life.

Splicing was not only possible, but transpired sufficiently often to rate as a serious and daunting problem. Putting in or taking out information completely unseen to the System was a hidden fact—in business, trade, diplomacy, the military, spying, and anything else. Rittener knew the rules as well as anyone. Splicers had their best chance during brief intervals when solar storms flared by. That's what Sadhana had meant by cursing him under the Sun. It told him when. The latest coronal mass ejection, though nothing much to speak of as they go, was rushing by the Terran Ring—just now—and interacting with the astronomical number of electrical fields at the Deck level. Now was when to sneak something in. Exactly *where* though had to be pin-point. Sadhana had been brilliantly coy in calling him two-faced—and then amending the insult to "three-faced." Such a silly hyperbole could be written off by Terran security monitors as the embellishment of an angry woman, and nothing more. But in reality, she was actually directing him to an exact locale on the Ring, but only in a parlance that could be understood by . . . a pilot. Rittener knew where the "three faces" were even before the sting of her slap had worn off.

Pilots thought of themselves as the sentinels of a secret treasure trove of knowledge and power that came to them through all the ages, and but for them would be lost. The mantra was fairly simple to follow in the main. No ziggurat or pyramid was constructed by chance. To the contrary, the unbending will of chosen men and women was to be seen throughout history. Their fingerprints were everywhere, in any place where the cosmos had surrendered. Enlightened pilots saw bushido not just in the hearts of Japanese daimyos of the shogunate, but also in the rishis who accompanied Alexander the Great. And Templar esoterica ran thick through the pilots' code. One of the charges against those medieval knights on that first unlucky Friday the thirteenth so long ago was a bizarre worship of a strange head: Baphomet. It was three faced, and there were a hundred metaphoric explanations for what the image meant. Rittener didn't particularly believe in any of them, but was versed in the allegories. And he knew full well where to find a cranium. There was only one famous head in this vicinity of the Ring, at the very foot of the Borelian diplomatic level, put there perhaps as a taunt. It was a colossal bust of Daniel Forrester, one of the Terran Ring's iconic founding fathers. It wasn't much to take in, and, especially in this gravity well, was on no Borelian tourist itinerary.

The incongruous party exited the shuttle and stood supposedly admiring one of the least interesting points of interest on the entire Ring. Clinton stood seemingly mesmerized, but his rapid eye movements and twitching lips were hints that far from just standing there, he was taking part in the most important conversation of his life. He had spliced into a number of fuzzy, clandestine messages in his time. This one though was much more clean and crisp. He recognized the lioness by her claw print. The fidelity of the electronics had to be the handiwork of one of the only people who could accomplish such mastery over an almost mythical solid state art: Sadhana Ramanujan. The splice signal was from amanuensis to amanuensis, Sadhana's to Rittener's in this case.

Struggling to keep her knees from buckling, Nerissa's blood had rushed out of her ashen cheeks and now matched the color of her magnolia evening wear. Her eyes and lips were twitching like Clinton's, but hers were from the strain of the gravational force weighing down on her. She was doing everything she could to keep a smile on her face.

The Gurkha guardsmen were attending to a series of different but building problems. There had been some sharp words and deadly glares exchanged with the Terran troopers, who weren't happy in the slightest that an envoy that included a man with an active death warrant out on his head has strayed so far from the confines of his resting quarters. It all made for quite the sight, even if the bust of Dan Forrester wasn't.

This was not a text-book, by-the-numbers kind of splice—hardly.

"Are you holding up alright?" Clinton asked Nerissa, looking over and noticing the strain. "You should be sitting down." But as he was saying this he was simultaneously asking Namagiri why he should trust Sadhana and to explain her purposes for contacting him. It was impossible to do both things at once.

Nerissa fainted. Ram saw her going down and made a sudden movement to catch her. A nearby Terran trooper who'd been crowding them mistook Ram's sudden movement for aggression. The trooper swung mightily from the Gurkha's blind side, delivering a terrific blow that knocked the diminutive soldier completely off his feet.

Tam reacted instantly and threw himself into the fray, elbows, fists, boots, and knees making vicious contacts with jaws, noses, ears, groins, shins. Rittener yelled desperately to call his guard to stand down while attempting to bluster the Terrans to back off by pointing to his absurd envoy's badge; both actions were abysmal failures. One of the troopers stumbled going down, trampling across an unconscious Nerissa.

Now it was on.

In under a minute, a military shuttle flashed onto the scene at breakneck speed, spilling out troopers before it even moored. A senior commander began bellowing orders, backing the Terran troopers away from the scene. Rittener was still—through all of it, thick and thin—now just making an end to a most complex and intense dialogue with Sadhana Ramanujan.

Nerissa was under her own duress, being brought back to consciousness with smelling salts.

"I've had enough sightseeing for one day," she said off-handedly, "if that's alright with you?" She was struggling to get the words out though, not speaking to the senior commander but to Rittener. The high-ranking officer hadn't waited for her or anyone else to answer. With one sweep of his arm Nerissa was being air-lifted back top, with another the subordinate captain was dismissed amid a torrent of stinging curses. The last gesture he sent in the Borelian envoy's direction. His sash was ripped, his formal suit spattered in someone's blood, his brawl-tousled coiffure more fit for a scarecrow than an ambassador, and to add insult, he was missing a shoe. The Terran looked him up and down with a mixture of dismay and disgust. "Maybe it's time for you to present your credentials." No consular invitation was ever given less diplomatically.

Rittener's guard couldn't be pried away for anything, and after quite a bit of persuading compromised by standing outside the doors of Ethan Van Ulroy's offices. They still were able to hear enough even where they were. The aide-de-camp sat between two sullen-faced men wearing uniforms and badges unfamiliar to Rittener. Whoever they were, they weren't diplomats.

"You're leaving Terra. Now." That was Van Ulroy's opening remark. He didn't wish to inspect any credentials. The authorities had made arrangements to jettison Rittener in a most disrespectful manner, pressing a D-class Borelian tramp into service. It was loaded with fertilizer for the Garden. Instead of going home on the state's *Pegasus* he'd be stuffed into the corner of a garbage scow. Van Ulroy flung a last piece of trash at him.

"You have one thing to tell the Council and just this. Call the Borelian fleet back. Do it immediately. Do it or face the gravest consequences."

Clinton got out only one question. "Is that a condition, request, or threat?" This was the real conference between Terra and Borealis, even though neither Stephanangelo or Madame Karis were present.

"Put it under any heading you like!" Van Ulroy thundered. "It will be heard by deaf ears but those are the exact words. Call back the fleet and stand down." He then dismissed him by standing suddenly and walking briskly straight out of the room.

Only half an hour later as they were taking their berth next to seventeen metric tons of manure Rittener heard Ram Dahadur grumbling. "They were exceedingly rude, sahib."

"Maybe not," Rittener answered. "They might just have been being honest."

Ram thought for a moment. "If that's Terran honesty, I'd rather have them lying to me," he reasoned.

On Borealis, in Daiyu's palatial mansion on Gamma Level, Stanislaus' broiling scowl at least warned him.

"I don't appreciate the liberty you took with my niece's safety," he rumbled. Stanislaus had been thinking about it long enough for the words to marinate and soak up anger. Rittener had little choice but to acknowledge them without much of a fight.

"I had no other option, Dr. Stanislaus. There was no way I could accomplish it without her help."

Daiyu nodded at Stanislaus. That was an acceptable answer. Another nod told Rittener to take his seat, a thin pillow placed on the tatami floor. Daiyu's *chashitsu* was an unusual venue for official business but an elegant and pleasing one nonetheless. Rittener's place was next to the hearth built into the floor and sidled up to the rustic, unfinished stone wall. The masonry curved behind him to an alcove where exquisite scrolls hung at his back. They were ancient, from Japan, and priceless. This was a simple *chakai* and Daiyu herself doled out confections and poured Rittener's tea. For all the trappings of an informal ceremony it was as if the entire Council were present nonetheless. The debriefing was being logged by Diana—not the ten-foot-tall version, but a less intimidating one, human-sized and simply present and listening.

"Especially after Adem Sulcus' death, Dr. Stanislaus, Clinton-Rittener should be praised for pulling things out of the fire. I think we owe him some latitude." Stanislaus had to acknowledge the truth of that, the logic pressing his lips together.

"So you bring us two messages: one from Sadhana Ramanujan and the other from Ethan Van Elroy," Daiyu started things off; Stanislaus interrupted immediately and corrected.

"One was from something or someone claiming to speak for Sadhana Ramanujan. That's more accurate, isn't it?" It was an ill-conceived idea. Rittener excused it.

"I'm quite sure that was Dr. Ramanujan. She was close enough to slap me." Stanislaus' face still radiated residual anger; his eyes reflected that he could certainly imagine doing that.

"For the Council," Daiyu motioned to Diana, "Clinton-Rittener, would you please recount it?"

Rittener took a deep breath, slowly. "She said Terra had a *wunderwaffe*, a wonder weapon, one that would change the outcome of any potential war, one that would leave Borealis powerless," Clinton said plainly.

"Huh!" Stanislaus gave his opinion immediately.

"What kind of weapon?" Daiyu asked.

Rittener shook his head negatively. "She didn't say." Then he corrected himself. "She wouldn't say. She made quite a point though about the fact that she shouldn't be seen as a traitor. She kept the details back because of her loyalty to Terra."

Rittener stopped for a moment, giving thought.

"I know it was just a splice and nothing to judge of her in person, but it was believable."

"Believable?" Daiyu cocked her head to the side. "And what makes you say that?"

"I just knew."

"Huh!" Stanislaus repeated, and louder this time. "Besides the ability to make Borealis helpless, was there anything else this splice of the amanuensis of someone claiming to be Sadhana Ramanujan said?"

That was the worst way to preface the remarks that followed, making them seem ridiculous.

"Terra had been working on the weapon since before I was born, from seeds that were . . . extraterrestrial."

Daiyu seemed not shocked in the least. "And why do you think she should have told you this when she held back all the rest?" Rittener knew. He'd heard the words himself, inside his head, and he had no doubt about their veracity.

"That we should know the extent between the chasm now that exists militarily between Terra and Borealis. That was her intent."

"A chasm," Daiyu repeated his term. She put down her tea and was shaking her head "no." "That seems to render our deliberations irrelevant. Perhaps we should have the Terran Archonate sort this all out for us and then simply await their communiqué." She said it somewhat facetiously. The sarcasm lit a fire.

"Excuse my digression, Madame Councilor. Here though might be a good place to deliver Ethan Van Ulroy's message. He said you had deaf ears and intimated strongly that Borealis would suffer for it." He looked at both of them with incredulous eyes. "You can't have already made your minds up to ignore this, have you?"

"This could be a perfect false-flag maneuver. The supreme art of war is to subdue the enemy, to break his resistance, without fighting." Diayu quoted Sun Tzu. Stanislaus agreed, almost grousing under his breath how absurd it would be to surrender based on an insubstantial splice. Neither councilor was having any of it.

"Certainly there can be no harm in at least attempting a compromise," Clinton petitioned. "I implore you to consider calling for further talks—real talks, substantive discussions. I make no mention of surrender."

"You imply it," Daiyu answered stubbornly.

"And all of it based on a flighty splice," Stanislaus supported her.

There it was again: Borealis' unbending, foolish arrogance, just beckoning hubris its way. Everyone in the Solar System had suborned to accept it, but not this time, not this man.

"What do you know of splices, Doctor?" Rittener snapped finally. "Your last splice was used to set a broken bone." He had an equally outrageous and insulting allusion for Daiyu's talents for poetry, as compared to her relative ignorance concerning modulating baud interstices in solar flux. Both remained stone silent. Not many had ever spoken to either of them like that.

Rittener wasn't one of many in the Solar System. He was still the mathematics genius of decades ago, the linguist prodigy turned diplomat turned general, a former *yuan shuai* of the coalition of Jiangsu, Shanxi, and Fujian, the son of an illustrious diplomat whose father held even greater stature. His flashing blue and green eyes, now sending out stares too glowering to endure for long without looking away, assured the Council that he suffered no self-doubt. "If only you knew how many speeches like yours I've heard. On Earth they come before every disaster, every annihilation. If only once there were a new wrinkle, a new slogan, a new preamble."

Now he stood. What came next he decided shouldn't be said sitting down.

"I've changed my mind. I'll take my seat on the Council. My first charge is to demand an open vote."

Daiyu shook her head. "That has been rescinded. The jurisprudence is clearly against that. The ruling is that charges against you must be settled before you can take a seat on the Council."

That was another excellent and self-interested reason to covet a councilor's seat. "And I'd certainly like a vote on *that* too!" Both Stanislaus' and Daiyu's unyielding and mute faces said that wouldn't be happening either. Rittener saw no reason to prolong the debriefing. No one was really listening to him anyway. He'd leave them with something to think about though.

"There's a species on Europa, under the ice, within that huge planet-girdling ocean, called skim shepherds. They're apex predators and fear nothing. But there's only one prey they take: skimmers. Schools of skimmers haunt the great cracks in the ice shield at the surface where nutrients enter the water, opened and closed by Jupiter's tides. So skim shepherds enjoy easy lives, expending no energy in the hunt yet certain that their meals will be provided like clockwork. You see, there's a unique symbiosis at work. The shepherds follow the schools, protect them, prevent anything from harming them. When they require sustenance, through a sense that no one understands fully as yet, the skimmers respond by pushing the old, the injured, the weak, the infirm out to be taken."

Both Daiyu and Stanislaus knew the story. Only Rittener though had actually seen it at work on the Jovian moon.

"Your point, Mr. Rittener?" Slanislaus asked, using his Earth moniker as a slight rebuke.

"Which is the dominant species, Dr. Stanislaus? Since the way of the world is not black and white but very grey, which is providing the greater service for the other? Can you answer me that?"

Daiyu had the answer. "We are neither skimmers nor their shepherds. But you've done your duty, Clinton Rittener. The Council thanks you for that."

Clinton clicked his right boot heel down hard and pounded his heart with a fist in the style of European Union officers. As he turned and strode out, he knew he hadn't.

CHAPTER TWELVE

GOTTERDAMMERUNG

LIKE MANY CATASTROPHES, THIS one too came without much warning. Borelians didn't see the fleet arrive with their own eyes, having scrambled en masse into the Core at the sound of the alarms. Unlike other disasters that struck other great cities in the past, there was no mad panic for one, as there had been at the dawn of the fourth day of 2053 in Los Angeles, for example, when it was leveled by the series of great earthquakes. The natural impulse to run scared and flee, which had emptied countless cities before countless invaders, was missing too. That didn't mean though that morale hadn't already been struck a mortal blow. Like a last stronghold of a crusading order now surrounded on all sides by a sea of enemies, Borealis saw her stark circumstances in the same light. There was no place to escape, and Borelians thought they might actually be glimpsing the arrival of the city's end, an idea that spread like a virus.

The population of Borealis had prepared for several war scenarios with the Terran Ring. Unfortunately, none of those were unfolding. Instead, the terrified population was being treated to an unending series of strong rumbles from tremendous explosions, and most disturbingly, from *within* the shielded perimeter. Clinton-Rittener was in his quarters in the Basement when it all started and could feel them quite strongly. Thousands of holographic replicas of Diana appeared instantly everywhere within the Core, at the juncture of every corridor, at every public place, in the private quarters of every citizen.

"Borealis is under attack. This is not a drill. Borealis is under attack." She said the words so calmly, so incongruously as to what was being declared. "Martial law is in effect, so do your part to maintain a safe and secure Borealis. Clear all corridors immediately, and above all, remain calm. The authorities are taking measures to ensure the security of the city. Remain calm."

Rittener didn't believe Diana was being totally honest though, and he was right. Borelian Security Forces weren't taking any measures at all but were simply riding out the disquieting jolts like everyone else, and wondering, like everyone else, what was going on.

The Terran fleet, taking an outwardly spiraling orbit centered above the Lunar North Pole, was leisurely pounding every square meter of the Shadow Zone between the ridge line at the edge of the crater supporting the Goldilocks Array, and the periphery of the Garden where the lush fields terminated against the air locks and sally points. There was nothing to destroy here, thank goodness, but the massive, pulsed particle beams, meant obviously to terrorize the citizenry, packed such a horrific punch that they brought down part of the city indirectly. In the places where the Shadow Zone lessened to a thin corridor, the blasts had undermined the crater walls and brought down some of the titanic mirrors anchored above. A few had crashed straight through the dextrite ceiling between the agricultural fields and the black, airless vacuum above. Efficient emergency airlocks did their job, cauterizing the wound, but a number of sections were gone. There'd be very little cucumber, peas, and okra on Borealis this season.

"What has happened to the shield?" Frightened voices were asking as they rushed past, making their way to the shelters. "And, where was the Borelian fleet?"

Diana wasn't addressing any of those important queries. "The authorities are doing everything in their power to take control of the situation. Please, above all, remain calm."

The Borelian Council, quite to the contrary, at that very moment, was having the last remnant of its control snatched from its grasp, and by someone who had striven for this moment with unceasing passion, the Chief Archon of the Terran Ring.

"HAVE OUR SHOTS ACROSS your bow got your attention, Admiral?" It was Dante Michelson himself, not the commander of the Terran fleet. He was being patched through from the Ring. That was the assumption anyway, since not even the pretense of the slightest diplomatic niceties was observed. That was Michelson's opening remark and it didn't bode well at all.

Dante Michelson was not blessed with a handsome appearance, and further, he'd not done the best with what Nature had allotted him. His skull was thick, asymmetrical, and knotty, and those unsightly characteristics were highlighted by the fact that he kept his hair trimmed so short that it possessed no style at all, just a stubble which covered the scalp, save for a wide bald patch that dominated the crown. Two thick, incongruous sideburns accentuated the fleshy jowls that made a naturally rectangular face seem far too square to please any eye.

Simply put, he had the face and bearing of an unattractive, airy, upper-crust bully, and that would have said it all, except for the stunning aspect of his eyes. They were nothing less than

intimidating; two giant, ebony pools that demanded the attention of anyone upon which he cast his gaze, a look part praying
mantis, part raptor, and which exuded a dangerous intelligence. For better or worse, one way or the other, by the sheer
force of unlimited will, this grocer's son had become the most
powerful man alive. In his company it was the rare individual
who didn't keep that fact in the very front of the mind.

Admiral Albrecht couldn't answer him, his lips trembling
with frustration but sealed tight by the force of sheer shock.
Breonia, who also was seething, responded for him.

"Even Genghis Khan declared war, Mr. Michelson." She
said it in as ugly a way as the words implied. "Is the Terran
Ring, sir, at war with Borealis?"

Michelson forced a fake laugh, the kind made by people
not very practiced in the real ones. "War is declared by one
state to another," he lectured. "You've obviously not been listening to us for the last few decades, have you? We're not here
to declare war, but to put an end to a rebellion, one that's
gone on for long enough."

Before she could answer Michelson had his hand up. It
was his way of signaling that this *was* the beginning of the end.

"There is to be no discussion about matters already end-
lessly debated. No negotiations are requested, nor will they
be entertained or tolerated. I'm here to deliver the terms
of your surrender." He paused, and in an odd tone of almost
friendly conviviality, as if allowing the councilors into his confidence when he certainly need not, the Archon let them in
on something.

"The fact that there *are* terms, that we *are* talking, says
volumes about the amazing restraint Terra shows, and the
reluctance to bring more force to bear on Borealis than is
necessary." In case the councilors didn't understand, he said
it right out for them. "There are some on Terra that wouldn't

have the Archonate offering any terms at all. So I strongly suggest that you consider wisely the articles of the accord we're sending along."

Breonia ignored the diktat and asked what Admiral Albrecht was too angry and distraught to put into words.

"This Terran reluctance to bring force to bear, does that explain the disappearance of half the Borelian home fleet?"

The Borelian fleet hadn't disappeared actually. Those ships which happened to be in lunar orbit on the Earthward side when the attack began were being scanned as millions of pieces of flotsam circling the Moon. Their shields also, for reasons completely unexplained, had failed too. Michelson was disposed to explain that and put the brightest spin he could on the annihilation.

"Those Borelian warships that made clear that their intentions were to exit the battle were allowed to withdraw from the Field." That was the diplomatic way to detail that Terra had destroyed half of the Borelian home fleet with all hands lost, and scattered the rest into space, in all directions outward.

The truth is that neither he nor anyone else was sure about the effective distance of the new technology which was operating so superbly, reverse-engineered by the mind of Sadhana Ramanujan from an alien artifact, creating "wormholes" in Borelian shields, and keeping them open long enough for pulses of death-dealing particle beams to vaporize warships, or to pound the lunar surface along Borealis' Shadow Zone. The eleven-dimensional magic which tipped the balance so completely in Terra's favor was being generated on the Terran Ring itself and the infrastructure which powered it couldn't be fit into a Valerian-sized asteroid, much less a Terran warship. But it was in Terra's interest to let Borealis wonder if her expeditionary fleet, closing in on both the Object and approaching Terran warships near Jupiter's orbit, might not also be heading for an equally calamitous tragedy as the home fleet had just suffered.

Not just Daiyu, but Michelson too had read *Art of War,* from China, from Earth's ancient past, realizing the unrivaled craft of any general was subduing the enemy without a fight. Michelson was paying homage to that dictum, and was leaving the Council in power just long enough to order her fleet to internment at Terra, their last act—before surrendering the city. There was a new reality to acknowledge and it was starting right now, the Archon's tone and glower said distinctly.

"The facts are quite simple," Michelson concluded with the silent, cowed councilors, "resistance or hostilities, here or anywhere else, will be met with severe and immediate consequences in Borealis." He made the threat and demand as plain as glass. The former ambassador, who'd been forced to sign a humbling agreement by these same Borelians, was back now—to tear up the accord.

There was to be a very different Borealis, indeed.

The arriving tram's doorways opened to debouch a silent, somber party. They walked briskly, all business, their synchronized military boot steps clicking on the polished metal floor of the corridor. Rittener, accompanied by a detail of heavily armed, expressionless Security guardsmen, knew he must be mere yards from the exact Lunar North Pole but didn't ask anything about it. He was more surprised and interested in the activity all around him; the bustle said that the maglev was still in operation, in a city completely locked down under martial law. Borealis' accelerator, built precisely at the pole to give the widest possible targeting range, shunted helium-3 to all parts of the Solar System. Unlike the old-fashioned cannons that explosively fired canisters to Earth and the Terran Ring, EMMA—electro-magnetic materials accelerator—used a wave of powerful magnetic pulses, pushing from behind, pulling from ahead, to reach escape velocity.

A last security lock slid open at the voice command of the subaltern escorting Rittener, to reveal a truly unexpected scene. Rittener at first had no idea what it all meant. EMMA's control room was a beehive. Two councilors—Stanislaus and Breonia—along with their staffs and a military contingent at their step, all crowded in with the engineers and stevedores who operated the maglev. His eye then went to Nerissa and he realized in an instant what everything meant. Even though his heart sank, he quickly found the strength to reach inside and right himself. He gave her a rakish smile, more for himself than for her, strode right up to Stanislaus and in the age-old tradition of fighter pilots, rodeo riders, gunslingers, gladiators, and all the others who never lost their nerve—joked.

"Am I under arrest, Councilor?"

Stanislaus' defeated, rest-deprived look told Rittener that the councilor was almost sleepwalking through a nightmare from which he wasn't going to wake. It was too late for debriefings and new rounds of talks, too late to discuss the solid intelligence Rittener had brought to the Council, that spooks and agents all the way out to Titan had been whispering about lately—a new Terran weapon which could, astonishingly, pierce shields. It was too late to extend a hand to the faction on Terra that wanted peace, who were themselves kept in the dark about most of what Terra did and didn't do. All that was left was for Rittener to end this the right way, courageously if he could.

Stanislaus responded with some gallows humor of his own. "I'm afraid it's worse than that. We've found a job for you, after all—a commission in the Service." Rittener thought for a second about which fate was more dangerous and silently cursed his luck.

With his right hand up and repeating the words, he couldn't help but be distracted by the mega-magnets operating so near, switching on and off in their billionths of a second, behind and in front of cartridges that hurtled down the electromagnetic sled. EMMA made an uncomfortable, scary sound, a "swoosh" that came from the walls around them, rather than the airless, soundless barrel, firing projectiles at escape velocity and higher.

Not that it probably mattered that much, but Rittener had to ask anyway. "What's my rank?"

"Commander," Stanislaus said.

Rittener frowned a little; that really wasn't that high. He made use of the frown, as long as it was there, nodding his head in the direction of the breech of the giant accelerator.

"Is one of those cargo canisters going to be my first command?"

Nerissa now had tears in her eyes. He could see them welling up the minute he entered EMMA's control chamber, and now they were streaming down her face. She was wearing a *dress*—so old-fashioned, so feminine, so girlish, and crying just like that. But her hair, well, it was unbraided, cascading freely off her cheeks and flowing past her shoulders, with the strands pushed away from her face, damp with salty tears. It was more than he, or any other man, could honestly be expected to resist, even with the sound of EMMA punching the heavens with kilometer-per-second blows dominating the background.

"You have the most beautiful hair I've ever seen in my life," he said, stupidly, humanly, honestly—mostly realizing that he'd probably never be able to say that if not now. He had more to tell her, but it caught in his throat. And she'd stepped to him anyway, taken his hands—both of them, the way Borelians do with close friends—and was doing all the speaking.

"They specifically asked for you. Turning you over to them is on the list of demands they've made." She stumbled through the words, reluctant to repeat Rittener's death warrant to him. Then she wiped her cheek and put on a braver face. "You're to join our fleet in the Field. You're going to be part of Borealis' last chance, Clinton." It was the first time, he realized, that she'd ever called him by just his Christian name.

Breonia had been taking everything in wordlessly. She now shared some advice with Rittener, her grand-maternal bearing quite alive and well, only now showing the kind of teeth an experienced, old lioness bares.

"You should know Borealis has nothing to gain or lose with Terra in handing you over, or in sending you off to the center of the galaxy, either one. They've made it clear; they're taking everything." She paused and then repeated for emphasis. "Everything."

It wasn't just for pure spite either that Borealis was giving Rittener this dangerously unlikely glimmer of the hope of escape. "But there is that too," Breonia admitted to Rittener, almost cursing Terra under her breath.

"Mostly, and you should thank your stars for this, you're only getting in this poppy show because this young lady begged her uncle, and her godmother too, for your life."

Stanislaus thought Rittener understood her, so he added his piece, too.

"You're going to have to beat big odds, Commander, for even the possibility of following these orders. The Borelian fleet's last directive is to scatter, to save itself, to survive, to live long enough to fight another day." He pointed to EMMA. "You have to realize your chances are terrible, yes?"

"Cha! Cho!" Breonia scolded Stanislaus. "*Valgame, Dios!* What are you scaring him for? The young man will be alright, or else how will he come back for her?"

215

She looked at Rittener and stunned no one by winking at him. That worked for her, a lot. Her aquiline, *mestizo* nose, perfectly shaped and noble-looking in an antique way, sat between two aged yet clear eyes that said they had seen everything.

"I don't suspect patriotism will cause you to scour the Solar System, finding a way to oppose Terra and rescue Borealis' fortunes." She gave a tender, familial look in Nerissa's direction. "But I don't doubt that something will bring you back here, and that such a day dawns soon, I pray."

Nerissa had been squeezing Rittener's hands, not letting go. Just as Breonia finished, another cargo canister was flung off the Moon at a terrifying speed, announcing a new, now pressing foreshadow of the impending trial at hand. The noise scared Nerissa, enough to cause her to pull Rittener close and whisper against his cheek.

"Don't die," she said with her eyes wet and half-closed. And then in a voice louder, for everyone to hear, still embracing him tightly, she told him what he had first told her.

"Good flying, Clinton," she said bravely, but really, half-heartedly.

Rittener brushed her hair to the side, barely daring to touch, and promised.

"When I come back it won't be anything like the way I'm leaving."

Then he moved closer to perhaps kiss just her cheek, to seal those words, but she clasped him with both hands and kissed him on the lips. It was a first kiss, in front of her uncle and godmother, with a dozen soldiers and workmen looking on silently and sheepishly. But it was a real kiss and one that he'd waited his whole life for, in case it was the last one.

No one knew but him that this was what he'd wished for under Kepler's Arch.

CHAPTER THIRTEEN

RECKONING

TERRA SAW TO IT that Borealis would never be a problem again
and without even disrupting for a beat the never-ending shipments of helium-3 that headed to all parts. Terra never meant
to destroy her prideful rival; that would have been to devalue
their very prize. Instead, Borealis was just decapitated and
rendered at a stroke the most precious jewel in the Terran
Ring's crown.

The Terran attack fleet had scanned oddly from the start.
It was comprised of relatively few warships and an unrea-
soned number of freighters—*empty* cargo ships. The anomaly
was explained by the 12,657 names listed on the warrants
served. Every public official, engineer, doctor, scientist, and
business executive on Borealis was under arrest and sooner
or later shuttled to waiting transports in lunar orbit. Terran
colonists, selected in advance from an index of the most able
applicants, awaited their opportunity to flood in to take their
places. With stunning rapidity, Borealis was changed overnight
almost, with an unrelenting and quick-stepped military preci-
sion. Even the age-old proverbs from ancient Earth knew that
in times of war the law is helpless and mute, and nothing had

changed. There was only silence now about lunar partition, helium-3 rights, and war or peace in the Asteroid Belt, and anywhere else.

THERE HAD NEVER BEEN a set piece battle between large fleets in space—until the recent unexplained encounter, which was no battle at all, only a massacre. Strategists who had prepared to see their tactics validated now realized the game had changed so quickly. Their visions for how victory was to be wrested between fleets of indestructible warships would never be tested. It was as if they had drawn up plans for warfare between dirigibles when suddenly a biplane appeared on the horizon.

Tacticians had imagined dozens of warships engaged in hundreds of overlapping dogfights within an enormous three-dimensional battlefield. The goal would be to force an opposing warship into the destructive radius of an exploding tactical nuke, while keeping one's own vessels outside these danger zones. Many factors would affect the outcome of this type of war of attrition: speed and angle of attack, numbers and disposition of forces in the Field, and of course, the quantity of nuclear firepower stored on board in magazines. Just as important would be the morale and toughness of the combatants; war games showed that a grinding slug fest was the likely scenario. Repeated blasts from nuclear explosions would eventually and inevitably melt and crack the molyserilium coating on wounded vessels and those vulnerable spots would show up on enemy scanners, drawing laser fire from any opponent with a clear line of sight. Unprotected sections of stricken ships would have to be jettisoned, and quickly. The new molyserilium exteriors, laid bare by the loss of the destroyed compartments, would now be an integral part of damaged vessels' laser reflector—hopefully.

THE PILOTS OF BOREALIS

A warship could go on fighting, theoretically, for as long as its crew could stand being pummeled with non-stop g forces, while slowly losing parts of itself and squads of its crew, until a vital section were lost and every crewman on board was killed. The greatest advantage a manned warship had was due to the old-fashioned, hard-to-beat human capacity for patching and fixing on the fly. Fire ships and unmanned decoys were also part of the fleet, adding a further layer of complexity to the grueling match. Military scientists on both sides imagined a fight like that in store for the Terran and Borelian fleets closing on each other.

The great contest ended with even less than a whimper though, because it never took place at all. Borealis had other matters with which to contend now, and laying claim to the Object fell from the highest order of the most crucial undertaking of the state, to below worth mentioning directly as the order to disperse was issued. There was no base to which the prize might be brought home. Borealis, within hours, was to be converted into a puppet-state of the Terran Ring, a Vichy, only providing helium-3 to the conquerors instead of wine.

Standing and fighting now had very much the look of cavalry charging tanks. It had been done in history supposedly, but not too well, not lately. The Borelian fleet followed the last order of the Council, abandoning the Object to the victorious Terrans, fleeing toward the Outer, their morale matching their situation.

ONE OF THE FEW of the 12,657 indicted by Terra yet not in custody on the Ring was Clinton Rittener. There *are* those who say that the canister he rode off the Moon only escaped being instantly vaporized by the circling Terran fleet because they had orders not to fire. This hard-bitten, pessimistic scenario has Rittener far from a reformed mercenary trying to make amends for his life with a lasting peace, and rather as an agent of Terra after all, superbly ensconced now within whatever remained of the Borelian resistance. In their suspicious, world-weary view, Terra permitted him to be sent straight into the bosom of the last remaining cadre of armed resistance—the Borelian fleet. The truth was quite a bit different from this spine-tingling, clandestine double-agency. Like many truths compared to the speculation though, the simple facts didn't need to be adorned.

No one had ever taken a suicidal ride off the Moon inside a helium-3 canister. Strapped in, cushioned with foam, and injected with a concoction of pharmacons that played danger-ous games with internal organs and blood vessels, Rittener, even as the sedatives took effect just before launch, didn't hold much hope himself.

"This doesn't have a chance of actually working, does it?" Rittener groggily asked the chief engineer before the hatch was slid shut and locked.

"Just lay back and keep your fingers crossed," the chief answered, stowing the barest of essential supplies and tugging on the belts and straps. He added with a false bravado, "We've got a few tricks up our sleeves to get EMMA to go a little eas-ier on you." Since it had never been attempted it was certainly true, "We've never lost anyone yet."

The cartridge would have scanned something like a nor-mal helium-3 canister, being mostly gas; and there was no weaponry, machinery, or complicated circuitry within. It was headed away from the fleet, in the direction of Mars. And, unbeknownst to conspiracy theorists, there *was* an order to refrain from firing on outgoing helium-3 canisters. The Terran Ring was eager to show the entire Solar System that there was nothing terrible transpiring in this little fuss between them-selves and Borealis. All was going to be well, better even, with Terra now firmly at the helm. Helium-3 was on its way, like it always was. So thanks to Terran politics, and the fog of combat, by hook or by crook, Clinton Rittener made it off the Moon, eclipsing escape velocity, and coasting toward the emptiness of black space.

Aside from the few refugees on the few warships of a state that existed no more, everyone with any sense in the Solar System was cowed by this tremendous upturn in the fortunes of the Terran Ring. The people of Earth, Mars, the Asteroid Belt, and the Jovian moons, and as far out as Titan, had all only just been stunned with the news of the Object's existence. Now they found that Borealis had been extinguished over it, by the use of weapons beyond the ken of current military technology, perhaps it quite realistically and frighteningly seemed now, developed by the use of super advanced extra-terrestrial sources to which Terra had access.

If everything was moving too fast, it wasn't moving too quickly for diplomats everywhere to quickly adopt the same position: the surrender was immediate and total. No one lifted a finger or said a word in Borealis' defense, each state outdoing the other in its slavish pronouncements of allegiance to Terra. A truly new age had dawned and anyone could see that it was to be the Terran Ring that would be the protagonist in the chronicle to be written.

It was an Asian Alliance ship, *Kasuga*, under Captain Kanda Minoru, who picked him up. It was safer for fleeing Borelian warships to keep their distance, so the last gambit of having an allied vessel link up with Rittener seemed more prudent. Minoru, who knew Rittener personally, having served with him in Asia, probably would have been faithful to his erstwhile comrade, as would have been the Asian Alliance. Like most bellicose states on Earth, not knowing when to quit, and always keeping the dream alive of somehow, some way getting a blow in on Terra, their real policy hadn't changed—even now. The proof of that is that Minoru didn't deliver the body to Terran authorities, or even apprise them of his demise. Instead he consigned the body to burial in space, with full military honors, befitting a fallen commander in the Borelian Service.

Rittener, like so many of his generation, like so many children of groaning Earth in his age—starved, beaten, dispossessed, impoverished—didn't leave a scrap of physical evidence behind of his having even existed. There is one thing though that he accomplished that will last for an eternity. In a way, he'd placed into perpetuity a very poignant monument to Earth, one that should remain circling Sol long, long after the Terran Ring itself ceased to be. He carried with him into his final orbit, forever circling the Sun in the dead, somber space between Earth and Mars, a token of a turn mankind should have made at the beginning of the killing centuries before it was too late. His far-removed ancestor and some unknown British Tommie had known that, and here was the proof on his dead finger, floating tens of millions of miles above the senseless battlefields of the Western Front—a red salmon, leaping happily over three blue waves—the insignia of the Second Corps, but really the symbol of mankind's age-old, unrequited dream of . . . peace.

COSMOLOGISTS KNOW THAT HUMANITY and Earth have both ridden quite an amazing lucky streak. A bit closer or further away from the Sun and the blue paradise planet would be frozen or broiled. But for her weighty satellite, Moon, to steady her axis, and Earth's roiling, turbid, molten core to generate her radiation blocking magnetic shield, the planet would have remained a barren and lonely place. At every step of a billions-year-long saga, whenever the die were cast, with survival or death in the balance, Earth's life force overcame all no matter how long the odds. No lucky streak lasts forever though.

It was bad luck, indeed, that the Object detonated precisely when it did, when Earth's eastern hemisphere had wheeled under the section of the Terran Ring to which it had been orbitally nudged and quarantined. The last time an explosion this violent and strong occurred, in these environs of the Solar System, was four billion years ago when the proto-Earth collided with Mars-sized Theia to create the Moon. The blast instantly vaporized half of Terra, the entire semicircular section of the Ring, ninety degrees in both directions from the epicenter of the detonation. The force of the explosion tore through the Terran Ring like a sledgehammer through a cloud, and reached down to the surface of the planet to boil off the top layers of the oceans below, and to sterilize Europe, Africa, and Asia. The Old World disappeared—just like that.

On the other side of the Ring, the sections above Earth's western hemisphere, death came just a few heartbeats later. For the Terran Ring was no longer a "ring"; half of it had been erased. What remained was a shattered, fracturing, boomerang-shaped reservoir of potential energy that was now going horrifically, unbelievably, wildly—kinetic. It wobbled awkwardly, surreally, spinning once around the globe, playing out its inertia, before plunging to Earth in a ghastly dive, a fall so terrifying and unthinkable that the sound alone shattered the eardrums of most of the people still alive on Earth.

The sky—actually—*was* falling.

It was falling, and coming down on South America. Country-sized pieces of the Ring crashed to the ground at what had once been Ecuador, Peru, Venezuela, Colombia and Brazil. These places, along with almost all of Amazonia, which burned for months, disappeared as identifiable locales, their former identities pounded beyond recognition as trillions of tons of steel slammed into them with enough kinetic energy to alter the rotation of Earth.

The rest of what remained of the Ring splashed into the Pacific and Atlantic oceans, pieces many hundreds of miles long, some thousands of miles in length, raising tsunamis of unfathomable height, extent, and power. Coastlines around the planet were drowned. Central America was overtopped; all the land from Panama to Mexico completely submerged as immeasurable quantities of water sloshed out of the oceanic basins and then receded again.

Humanity had taken a savage punch, meant to be a killing blow. It didn't exterminate the human race, however, but it did send Earth stumbling backward several centuries. And, of course, the Terran Ring, with its five billion inhabitants, was just—gone. When those survivors still alive on Earth, mostly in the heartland of North America which had been spared, summoned the temerity to cautiously leave their homes and gaze up, a dumbfounded look was written across their faces. That same expression could be seen for many, many years whenever people looked up toward the equatorial skies, still not really sure that such an eternal feature in the heavens was actually, in fact—just gone.

The Terran Ring *was* gone, and with it went its age. Everything changed.

Borealis survived, actually was saved by the "Event," as it was called. Yes, at first there was a period of unrestrained rioting and disorder, as mobs hunted down and exterminated any of the unfortunate Terran overlords who had barely arrived to administer the newly acquired province. These ill-fated taskmasters now couldn't care less about helium-3 or any of the other great questions that had animated them yesterday. Their only concern now was how to manage to go on breathing hour by hour. When the bloodlust abated and cooler heads prevailed, Borealis was forced to appreciate how important these former conquerors were. The pool of scientists, engineers, doctors, administrators, and others necessary to efficiently run a society had been dangerously thinned, with billions of them just recently having been evaporated. Borealis' entire intelligentsia, sadly, had been among them, incarcerated on the Ring—Nerissa, too. They also realized that the Terran Ring's own storm trooper tactics, which had wrested the Object from Borealis' grasp, was ironically the very means by which the city had been saved, while the Ring destroyed. A marriage of convenience was hastily arranged and the last several thousand Terrans alive were assimilated into Borelian society.

That society was irrevocably sent down a different path. The price of helium-3 plummeted as fast as the Ring had fallen. Simply put, Borealis' customers were all dead. There was still a demand for it in the Outer and piddling amounts were sent to clients on Earth. The consignments for Earth, though, in a morbid yet telling way, were designated "American." Mother Earth, laid so low, having been downgraded from a world to just a continent, now almost lost her very name, the Borelians giving that catch-all moniker to anyone living on the planet below, including the few Australians, Argentines, and Chileans left with whom they also did business. But business was bad, and getting worse all the time.

The Event produced the profoundest effects in the Outer though, its aftermath forging the path of the course history was to follow. No matter the dreadful result, Mars, Titan, the Jovian colonies, and all the rest had seen everything unfold with their own eyes. The Object *did* move at just a fraction below light speed, must have somehow combined astounding amounts of anti-matter with matter—measured in the equivalent firepower of *millions of tons*—to effect such an explosion, and gave tantalizing clues as it streaked toward Earth that it certainly *wasn't* propelled by helium-3 but by quite a different energy source. Harnessing the power of vacuum fluctuations had been a dream with roots stretching as far back as the 20th century. It now became a real goal. The bizarre irony of the Event was that, in destroying Earth, it was the single greatest impetus transforming humanity into the anchorless, space-faring people that they became. If it had been the purpose of the Object to exterminate mankind, the result of the attack not only failed to snuff out completely the cradle of human civilization, but strengthened its reign tenfold, a hundred fold, by sending its tentative shoots out in every direction toward the stars. Titan was the first to construct an actual, working quantum ramjet. The colonies on the Jovian System followed up this astonishing achievement by mining anti-matter, and appreciable quantities of it, from . . . well, from nothing. The void itself—endless, ubiquitous, eternal—became the new larder to satisfy man's hunger for energy. This pantry could never run out.

Borealis in time became nothing more than a curiosity, with visitors taking in the place for the history, but wondering what people actually *did* here. The city was more museum than anything else. The great mansions were still there, but like grand saloons in ghost towns, even children could tell something was missing that used to be here. Parents explained things by taking their youngsters on excursions outside the city. The Field was one of the most visited tourist attractions in the Solar System so at least the Moon was left looking handsome and well-groomed. The harvesters had raked the lunar surface neatly—great, continental-sized sections of the Moon—squeezing Luna dry of helium-3, and in their wake leaving the greatest Japanese rock garden in the universe.

"What was helium-3? Did they burn it?" the young would ask. It was easy for children to confuse it with the one before. "No, it was petroleum they burned," came the corrections.

The greatest lessons however for the children of Earth were suavely combed into these cornrow lines scratched into the surface of her satellite, clues to the question that had been posed by every ten-year-old who ever heard the old, old epic tale. If the first Trojan horse caused a city to be razed, the second had eviscerated an entire planet.

"Who built the Object? Who built it, and why did they do that?"

"No one knows who built it," parents told their sons and daughters. "Nor how old it was, nor even if it was meant specifically for humanity. It may simply have been patrolling space to wipe out in advance any up-and-coming civilization that might be a potential adversary to them, whoever they were—or are." Some of the more lunatic ideas said it might have been constructed on Earth, by humans, but from a very, very distant past age. "No one knows though."

Parents scrutinized adolescent faces for acknowledgement of understanding. It wasn't just a story about heroes like Clinton Rittener, or guarding against dangers such as the unspeakably evil alien beings who'd brutalized Earth in ages past.

"Do you understand how Borealis' and Terra's and Earth's rivalry left them vulnerable to the greatest danger?"

As for Earth, well, for the first time in centuries it had peace. Cynics explained the phenomenon by pointing out that there were too few able-bodied men left on Earth to field an army. The Event, as mind-numbingly awful as it was, still was but the last and most brutal in a series of seemingly unending blows of death and destruction that had rained on Earth. It was, though, the tipping point. Whether mankind's cradle was to take this new opportunity to begin again properly, by disavowing violence finally and forever, by husbanding its resources suitably, by becoming astute stewards finally of the planet to which they'd fallen heir—all of this slowly, strangely, inexorably lost its power to interest even. Humanity, as if finally falling out of love with a dysfunctional paramour, was starting to look the other way: outward.

It didn't happen in a great rush, like so many for gold, oil, and land. It was more like spores on a soft but steady breeze rustling through a meadow on a fine day. From Titan the Sun was nothing more than the brightest star. The other billions in the Milky Way at long last had grabbed hold of mankind's undivided attention. The center of gravity of civilization had moved away from the Sun, its warmth and power ultimately, after so many eons, having lost the allure to hold its children spellbound any longer. And those on the far edges, slowly, inevitably, cautiously, simply let go.

If in past epochs even sages had pondered without answer what the meaning of existence was, that great enigma had been solved for the fortunate generation alive now, and those to come. Mother Earth, a single blue-green speck in the dead, silent void, had produced a progeny of demigods with the power and animus to convert the amorphous chaos of the galaxy into a vibrant, death-defying reflection of themselves—and their mother. To fill the Milky Way with life was the task at hand.

This is the race that made for the stars.